# Embracing Dove

Ashlynn Carter

Copyright © 2024 by Ashlynn Carter

All rights reserved.

No part of this publication may be reproduced, distributed, or transmitted in any form or by any means, including photocopying, recording, or other electronic or mechanical methods, without the prior written permission of the publisher, except as permitted by U.S. copyright law. For permission requests, contact Ashlynn Carter at ashlynn.carter@proton.me.

The story, all names, characters, and incidents portrayed in this production are fictitious. No identification with actual persons (living or deceased), places, buildings, and products is intended or should be inferred.

Book Cover by Ashlynn Carter

First edition 2024

# Prologue

Harper Anderson squinted her eyes as she peered through the windshield. They had been driving for three days and she was exhausted. The kids had been troopers the whole time, but she knew they were tired of being in the car. Alexis had been watching a movie on the tablet, but as Harper glanced in the rearview mirror, she noticed that the four-year-old had fallen asleep.

Harper returned her attention back to the winding mountain road they were on. They were nearly to the summit. After they dropped into the next valley, she vowed to find a motel for the three of them to stay in for the night. She also needed to feed Colton. Poor Colt had spent three out of the four days of his life strapped into his infant car seat.

The night was dark, and Harper desperately wished she could see beyond her headlights. The road had so many curves. With her sleep deprived brain, Harper was struggling to keep her eyes open. A bad feeling settled over her as the road began to slope down. Her grip on the steering wheel tightened as they started their descent.

She kept her foot on the brake to stay at a slow speed as she tried to spot any potential wildlife that might dart in front of the car. The car began to pick up speed as they approached the second switchback. She pressed the brake in an attempt to slow down for the unfamiliar curve. Nothing happened.

Harper's heart began to race as she slammed her foot on the brake again and again, with the same result. Her knuckles were white on the steering wheel as she managed to take the curve without sailing over the edge. She continued to pray and pump her brakes, but the car's speed continued to increase. Her headlights illuminated a sign informing her that another curve was coming up. She was already going 50 mph, picking up more and more speed, and the sign suggested 25mph. Tears of helplessness stung her eyes, but she blinked them back. Crying wouldn't help anyone right now.

Harper tried to make the turn but before she knew it, the car went careening off the road. Harper's head connected hard with the window as the car slammed back down to the ground and rolled. She blinked several times before her vision cleared. She didn't know how, but the car was back on all four tires and racing down the side of the mountain. She started yanking the steering wheel from side to side as she did her best to avoid trees and rocks. Alexis was screaming as they bounced on the rough terrain.

After what felt like an eternity, the sharp decline finally tapered off and they were on flat ground. Harper's sense of relief was short-lived. Her brakes still didn't work, and she caught sight of a wooden fence just before they crashed into it.

Wood exploded in all directions. The car didn't seem to slow much as they continued to race through a field. Both Colton and Alexis were screaming and crying in the back seat as the car once again nosedived. This time, Harper saw a solid wall of dirt in front of them, right before they crashed. The sound of glass shattering and her kids screaming were the last things she heard before everything went black.

# Chapter 1

Carter Michaels drove down the dirt road on the ranch. He had finished checking on the cattle in the south field. The sun had fully set by the time he was done. That had been a good forty-five minutes ago. He took some extra time to sit in the quiet and gather his thoughts. But now he could not wait to get home so that he could get something to eat, take a hot shower and fall into his bed.

He glanced to his left. He slowed his truck when his eyes landed on a gaping hole in the fence that marked the property line. He pulled the truck off the road, aimed his headlights at the fence, and threw his truck into park so he could get a better look.

He checked the gun on his hip and stepped out of the vehicle. He pulled on his plaid button-down, long-sleeved shirt over his t-shirt to ward off the evening chill. Reaching back in, Carter grabbed the flashlight that was in the middle console before cautiously walking towards the fence. The hole was wide enough for a vehicle to drive through.

He examined the ground, and sure enough there were tire marks in the soft dirt. Carter let out a heavy sigh. This was just what they needed, teenagers causing damage around the ranch. He would have to tell the guys about this, and they would need to expand their security system around the whole ranch. They had a top-of-the-line system at the main house and barns, thanks to Jeff, but not on the outer perimeter.

Carter looked from the broken fence back to the truck. He could go back home and come check the damage tomorrow when he could bring one of the guys with him, but something compelled him to follow the tracks. He didn't travel very far when the wind kicked up and a muffled cry reached his ears. He paused and listened more closely. The crying sounded like it was a young child and was coming from the dry riverbed. A second voice joined it. This one sounded like a baby's cry.

Carter increased his speed as he jogged in the direction of the crying. He skidded to a stop at the top of the wash, and his eyes widened. A car was down there. The front end of the vehicle was smoking and smashed into the opposite side of the wash. The crying was definitely coming from the vehicle.

He slid down into the wash and raced for the car. He pulled open the back driver's door. An infant car seat with a screaming baby was there. He quickly pulled the car seat from the back and moved it several feet from the vehicle. He did a quick exam of the baby, and he seemed to be fine. There were no cuts or any bruising that Carter could see. A child screaming for her mother pulled his attention back to the vehicle. He ran to the other side of the car and opened the door.

A little girl was strapped into a booster seat. She had some small scrapes on her face along with her tears. "Are you okay?" Carter asked the little girl. He kept his voice soft and calm to try to calm the child down.

The little girl turned to look at him. The terror and fear in her eyes tore at his heart. He reached for her buckle, but the little girl shoved his hands away as she started to scream again. "Shh. You're okay. I just want to get you out of the car and over to your baby brother. Are you hurt?" He tried again, but she wasn't having it.

Ignoring her protests, Carter unbuckled the child and lifted her from the car. She hit and kicked him as he walked her over to where he had set the baby, all the while she screamed for her mommy to help her.

He crouched as he set her down on the ground but held her firmly in place. "I need you to stay with your brother so that I can go help your mommy, okay?" He gave her a stern look. "Stay here so that when your mommy comes to get you, she will know where you are." He held her gaze until he saw the girl nod.

Carter gave her a nod in return and rushed back to the vehicle. He slowly pulled open the driver's door. A woman was slumped forward on the airbag. Her light brown hair was covering her face and he reached out to brush it back so that he could get a better look. Blood covered her forehead and cheek. He quickly pulled his cell phone from his pocket as he searched for her pulse. He let out a tense breath when he finally found it. He glanced at the phone and hit Devon's name.

"Hey, Carter." Devon's voice came through the line after two rings. "Everything okay? Thought you'd be back by now."

"Devon, grab your med kit and follow the road to the south pasture until you see my truck. Take an immediate left to the wash. We have a problem." Carter said in a low voice. He didn't want the little girl overhearing him.

Devon's voice immediately became serious. "What's going on, Carter?" He paused for a second. "Is that a baby?"

"Car Accident. A woman and two children. One is a baby." Carter said and Devon hung up the line with the promise to get there as quickly as possible.

Carter glanced back at the little girl and screaming baby. To his relief, the girl was still there. He returned his attention back to the woman. He managed to release her seat belt and pull her from the car. As he was laying her on the ground, her eyes fluttered open. She had startling blue eyes that held him captive. They reminded him of a girl he used to know from his childhood. She blinked slowly several times before she tried to sit up. Carter gently held her down. "Stay still. You were in a car accident. A medic is on the way."

"My babies?" she asked in a soft but frantic voice.

"Both kids appear to be fine. I will have the medic double check when he gets here, just to be on the safe side." Carter tried to soothe the young mother. At his words, she closed her eyes and let out a sigh. "No hospitals. Please, no hospitals." The woman begged as she fell back into unconsciousness.

Carter brushed the woman's hair out of her face so he could get a better look at the wound that continued to bleed. He felt someone move up beside him. He glanced down to see the little girl. The baby was still wailing, and Carter was at a loss as to what to do. He needed to assist the woman, try to keep the little girl calm, and he should check on the baby. His special forces training didn't cover taking care of children when providing medical aid to a car accident victim. Ignoring the little girl for a moment, Carter removed his button up shirt and pressed it to the woman's head to stop the bleeding. He was glad he had put it on over his T-shirt before finding the wreck.

"Is my mommy dead?" The little girl asked.

"No, sweetheart. Your mommy is just hurt right now." Carter glanced over at the girl who was holding her mom's hand. "I have a friend coming. He will help get your mom feeling better. Are you hurt?"

The girl was quiet for several seconds. "I thought mommy was dead." The girl started to cry again.

Carter put an arm around the little girl to try to comfort her, but she pulled away from him. She eyed him warily like he was going to reach out and hurt her, as she wiped at her eyes. The girl crawled to her mother's other side and continued to watch him carefully.

Carter periodically checked on the baby before going back to applying pressure to the woman's head wound. The roar of an engine finally reached Carter's ears after twenty long minutes. The baby had finally stopped crying not long ago.

Headlights shone near the edge of the wash and seconds later, Devon slid down the side of the wash and ran over to him. The little girl whimpered as she shifted closer to her mother. Devon dropped his bag in the dirt and immediately started pulling items from it. "What happened?" He asked, all business as he dug in his bag.

"I found a section of our fence broken and followed the vehicle tracks here to find this. Both children appear to have only minor scratches, but I found the woman unconscious. When I pulled her from the car, she spoke a few words before losing consciousness again. Her pulse is strong and steady." Carter reported. Old habits falling back into place with his friend's arrival. They had served for six years together on the special forces team with Carter's best friend Henry.

"I got the woman. You check the vehicle for any items that she and the kids might want." Devon removed Carter's shirt from the woman's head and examined the wound. "I can clean it here and stitch it closed, but she should probably be taken to a hospital."

Carter stopped several feet from the car, turning to look at Devon. "She asked not to be taken to a hospital. She was very adamant about it." Devon glanced at him before turning his attention back to his patient. Carter continued and started to rummage through the vehicle but didn't see a purse anywhere. "Hey, sweetheart?" Carter looked over at the girl who was anxiously watching Devon. At the sound of his voice, she looked over at him. "Can you help me find your mommy's purse and your brother's diaper bag?"

"Mommy doesn't have a purse. Only Colt's bag." The little girl said but didn't make a move to join him.

"Do you want anything from the car?" he asked, opening the back door again.

The little girl slowly stood and moved in his direction. She climbed back into the back seat and started packing a backpack with her tablet and a few toys. Carter saw a second bag on the floor and picked it up. Next, he moved to the trunk and removed three duffle bags. He asked the girl to stay by her mommy before carrying the duffle bags and the little girl's bag up the side of the wash to Devon's truck. He quickly returned and checked on the baby. The little guy seemed to be sleeping soundly, so he carefully picked up the carrier and moved it closer to Devon.

"Check the diaper bag for an I.D. or something that we can use to identify her." Devon said softly. He had already started stitching her head.

Carter dug through the bag and quickly found the woman's wallet. He gave a triumphant smile as he pulled it out and opened it, but his smile fell when he saw the woman's name. His heart skipped a beat at the same time his stomach clenched. It couldn't be possible.

He looked back at the woman. Now that Devon had cleaned most of the blood off and he was able to study her features, Carter could see her familiar characteristics. She was no longer the young girl he remembered, but it was her.

"Did you find out who she is?" Devon glanced over at him with a questioning look.

"Harper Anderson. Henry's little sister." Carter said as he continued to stare at the woman.

Devon's shocked expression would have been funny if the woman Carter had been in love with since he was ten, wasn't lying unconscious in the dirt. The little girl continued to watch them silently. Her wariness had Carter questioning if she was naturally shy of strangers, or if something had happened to the little girl to make her not trust easily. Either way, Carter needed to get her and the baby buckled into the truck so that he could help Devon get Harper out of the wash.

"What's the plan, Carter?" Devon finally asked. "I think she is stable enough to get her back to the ranch house."

"You stay with Harper while I get the kids strapped into your truck. I'll lock the work truck up and then we can get Harper out of here." Carter reached for the baby's car seat.

"I'm not going with you." The little girl said defiantly when Carter offered her his hand. "I'm staying with my mom."

"Listen, sweetheart." Carter once again dropped to her level. "Your mommy is hurt, and we need to get her back to the house where we can make sure she will be okay. I need your help with your baby brother. I am going to put him in the truck so that I can help Devon get your mom to the truck. Can you sit with him for me?" Carter waited for her response with an extended hand. Grudgingly, she put her hand in Carter's outstretched one and he stood.

It took him a few minutes to get both the baby and little girl back to the top of the wash. He had no idea how to strap the car seat in, and the baby had woken back up. He was screaming his little heart out. The little girl informed Carter that the baby was hungry and needed their mom.

Deciding to have Devon drive carefully, Carter gave up on buckling in the kids' car seats and closed the door. He ran back to his truck and locked it before racing back to Devon. Together they managed to get Harper up the steep side of the wash and to the truck without hurting her further. He told Devon to take it slow because the kids were not strapped in, as they climbed into the front seats. Carter held Harper in his lap as they drove back to the ranch.

Devon parked and took the kids inside first. He took them to Carter's room for the time being. While Devon was gone, Carter studied Harper. She had some bruising on her face but the light from the porch was dim and with no moon, seeing details was impossible.

The front door opened, and Devon jumped off the porch as he raced to Carter's side of the truck. He opened the door and Carter carefully slid out. He carried Harper into the house with Devon opening the doors and leading the way to Carter's room. The baby was still wailing when they got there. He laid Harper gently on the bed and Devon immediately started to give her a more thorough examination.

Carter grabbed the diaper bag, slinging it over his shoulder, and picked up the baby carrier. The little girl sat on the bed holding her mother's hand while she watched Devon like a hawk. Deciding to let the girl stay with her mother for the time being, Carter headed back downstairs to the kitchen. He set the baby carrier on the table and took every item out of the bag, hoping to find something to feed the baby with.

To his great relief, he found a premade bottle of newborn formula. He read the label and shook the bottle before putting the nipple on it. He unbuckled the baby and carefully lifted the little thing out of the carrier. The baby eagerly started eating once Carter offered him the bottle. Carter had never seen such a small baby. The little guy couldn't have weighed more than five pounds.

Carter walked into the living room and sat in the rocking chair. How had Harper Anderson ended up in the wash on his property? Last he had heard; she was living with her husband in Colorado. He looked down at the content baby in his arms and furrowed his brows as he tried to make sense of what was happening.

Two months before they were to head home permanently, Carter had asked Henry for permission to reach out to Harper. He had finally come clean to his best friend that he had been in love with his little sister since childhood, and Carter wanted to see if those feelings were still there.

Harper and Henry's parents divorced when she was eleven and he was fourteen. Henry stayed in their small town with their father while Harper went to live with her mother several states away. Carter had been crushed when Harper left. He knew he loved her ever since she bloodied his nose two years previous to her leaving. They had been kids at the time, but Carter still knew that he wanted to marry her when they grew up.

He had been disappointed when Henry had informed him that Harper was married with a little girl. Henry had said if Harper had been single, he would whole heartily approve of the match. Unfortunately, Carter was too late.

Not only was he dealing with the heartbreak of losing his chance with his first and only love, but Henry died a few weeks later in a raid. That had been nine months ago. He had looked forward to at least seeing Harper at the funeral, but she never came. Their mother had said something about Harper's husband not being able to get it off work.

Devon's footsteps on the stairs pulled Carter out of his memories. "How is she?" he asked quietly, seeing that the baby had fallen back asleep.

"She's lucky, Carter. The only thing I could see were bruises on her face, throat, and abdomen, the cut on her forehead, and a slight concussion. I didn't examine her too much though. The little girl freaked out when I tried and refused to let me look at her. I think Harper needs to see an actual doctor. They all should." Devon moved closer as he glanced back at the stairs. "The bruising looks like it is at least several days old."

"What do you mean?" Carter sat up straighter. How could Harper have bruises on her stomach that were several days old? The stomach is a very odd place to have bruising.

"The bruising is already in the healing phases and discoloring. She is still unconscious, so I couldn't ask her about them. The little girl has minor cuts on her face from the broken windshield, but she wouldn't let me touch her and she has refused to give me her name."

Carter nodded. "She doesn't seem to trust easily." He commented. "Jr. here just finished his bottle. Did you want to take a look at him too?" Devon lifted the baby from Carter's arms and laid him on the couch. "He seems really little."

"He can't be more than a few weeks old." Devon commented. "My sister's newborns were bigger than this, though."

The baby appeared to be just fine, not a scratch on him. Carter and Devon marveled at the miracle; none of the Anderson's were seriously injured, as far as they could tell. After changing a very wet diaper, Carter carried the baby to his room. The little girl was asleep next to Harper in his bed. He carefully laid the baby next to his mother and took a seat in the chair in the corner. He and Devon had talked about it. Carter would stay in the room with them to make sure that nothing happened in the middle of the night, and Devon would call his sister first thing in the morning to come check the Andersons.

# Chapter 2

Harper woke to her head pounding. She slowly cracked her eyes open to see Colton sleeping next to her and Lexi's head of thick brown hair poking out of the blankets. When had she made it to a motel? She didn't remember anything past reaching the summit of the mountain road they had been driving on.

She closed her eyes as she tried to recall the evening before. Snatches of memory flashed into her mind. The brakes not working. The car picking up speed. The feel of the car sailing over the guardrail. Swerving to avoid crashing into trees and rocks. Desperately praying for safety. Then there was a fence and a solid wall of dirt.

Her eyes flew open as she took in her surroundings more carefully. She was in a bedroom with a dresser by the window. Behind her was a door and closet. This wasn't a motel room, but somebody's bedroom. Harper looked back at her sleeping babies. Whose room was this? Where were they?

The creak of the door had her freezing. They were recently in a car accident. If she was in some kind of hospital, the person entering the room was probably a nurse coming to check on them. She was mostly covered by the blanket and the person entering probably would not be able to see her. If the person wasn't a nurse, then who would it be? What if Luther had found them?

Harper's heart rate picked up at the thought. She couldn't allow him to find them. Someone large jumped on her, pinning her to the mattress. "You're coming with me." A man's deep voice growled in her ear. She screamed, which caused her attacker to jerk back. Harper threw her elbow, connecting with something hard. The man let out a cry of pain as he fell off the edge of the bed.

Harper scooped up Colton and Alexis as she climbed off the other side of the bed. She glanced over at their attacker to see him still sitting on the ground with a startled expression as he looked down at his bloody hand and then back to her. She must have hit his nose because blood was coming from it. Needing to put the kids in a safe place, Harper yanked on the dresser and pulled it away from the wall, creating enough space for her to shove Alexis behind it. Lexi knew from experience that she needed to not resist climbing into her hiding place and that she needed to stay quiet.

As soon as Alexis was seated, Harper placed Colton in her arms. "Hold your brother." She whispered before standing back up and facing the man.

He was getting back to his feet. Harper frantically looked around for anything she could use as a weapon. A knife was sitting on the dresser, and she grabbed it. She had learned how to use a knife in a fight when she spent a few months in juvie. Memories from those lessons came back to her, giving her a small amount of confidence in her ability to protect her kids.

Two more men rushed into the room but stopped just inside the door. The first of the two newcomers had a somewhat familiar look to him. He assessed the situation.

The man that attacked her looked between the newcomers and her with a confused expression. "What the heck, man! Who is this and why is she in your bed?" The man snapped. Harper swallowed hard as she watched them.

"She stayed the night." The first newcomer said softly.

"I gathered that when I accidently jumped on her instead of you."

Harper's nervousness grew as she listened. All three men were at least six feet tall, had broad shoulders, and muscles that would put the Avengers to shame. The somewhat familiar man took a step towards her. Harper tightened her hand on the knife and widened her stance. She wasn't going to allow any of these men to come near her kids.

The man raised his hands in a show of peace, but she didn't buy it. "Easy Harper. We aren't going to hurt you." The man said in a soothing voice. That voice. She knew that voice. It was deeper than it had been before, but she knew it. She just couldn't remember who it belonged to.

Did they work with Luther? Had Luther sent them to kidnap her? She repositioned her grip on the knife in her hand. She had the blade pointing out from her as she raised her fists, ready for a fight. The man's eyes flicked to the knife before returning to her face. There was something about his eyes that drew her in. She blinked hard. Now was not the time to evaluate how she might know this man. She needed to focus on protecting her kids.

The man took a tentative step towards her again, and she stiffened. "Not another step." She warned.

"Harper, put the knife down. No one here is going to hurt you." The man said again. When she didn't lower her guard, he gave her a small smile. "Don't you recognize me?"

Harper's head was pounding and thinking wasn't going to be easy at the moment. "As fun as it would be to play the guessing game, I'm not in the mood." She glared at the man. "So, if you are wanting to do introductions, just do them so that we can get out of here."

"It's me, Dove. Carter Michaels." The man said with a crooked grin as he took a small step forward.

Dove? Carter Michaels? Henry's best friend? Carter had given her the nickname 'Dove' when she was nine or ten. He was the only one to call her that. She studied his face more carefully. He had been fourteen when she saw him last. He had definitely grown up and was no longer the gangly teenager she had known, but his brown eyes were the same.

"Carter?" Harper breathed out as all the fight left her.

She began to sink to the ground, but strong arms wrapped around her. Safe. That's what she felt as she started to cry. She really was safe for the time being. Carter wouldn't hurt her. She felt his hand move over hers. She willingly released the knife as he pulled it from her grasp. Harper wrapped her arms around Carter's waist as she continued to sob.

Carter held Harper tighter as she cried. He had taken the knife from her and put it in the top drawer of his dresser. The moment she had recognized him, a switch had been flipped. She went from scared and ready for a fight to relieved and exhausted. Carter rubbed her back in a soothing motion, but her sobs only increased, and her arms tightened around him. An overwhelming surge of protectiveness filled him. Someone had hurt her or her kids or both, and he would do everything in his power to prevent whoever it was from hurting them again.

"Momma?" A small, scared voice whispered.

Harper pulled back from him. With shaking hands, she wiped the tears from her face and took a deep breath. She gave Carter a watery smile as she turned back to the dresser. She reached behind it and lifted Colton from Lexi's arms. The little girl crawled out from behind the dresser and moved to her mother's side. Harper was aware that the three men in the room were studying her and the kids as she knelt on the ground and faced her daughter.

"It's okay, baby. They are not with him." Harper whispered to Alexis before pressing a kiss to her forehead.

Alexis looked over at Carter with a wary expression. It broke Harper's heart to know that her daughter had witnessed so much of Luther's abuse, that she didn't trust men. Alexis's eyes narrowed as she glanced at the other two men before returning her attention to Harper.

"Did he hurt you, momma?" Alexis asked while still looking at Carter out of the corner of her eye.

"Carter would never hurt me, Lexi. It's okay. We're okay." Harper tried to pull Lexi into a hug, but the girl pushed away and put her little hands on her hips as she faced Carter.

"You helped mommy out of the car." Alexis said, and Carter nodded. "Are you like him?" She asked.

"Lexi!" Harper scolded.

Carter crouched so that he was eye level with the little girl. "I don't know who 'he' is, but I can promise you that I would never hurt your mother." At the little girl's skeptical look, Carter gave her a reassuring smile. "I knew your mom when she was about your age. Her brother was my best friend. Devon worked with me and your uncle. That man there, his name is Jeff. He was also on our team." Carter pointed to each of the men in turn.

Alexis gave him a dubious look before looking back at her mom. "Mommy, I'm hungry." She whispered.

Harper looked up at Carter as he stood. "Why doesn't Jeff clean up while Devon starts on breakfast, and we can set the table." Carter smiled at the girl.

Devon and Jeff didn't need to be told twice, and they left the room wordlessly. Carter extended his hand for Lexi to take, but she shrank back. He reached out for Harper, and she put her hand in his. She winced as she stood. Her whole body ached. The car accident did not help her recovery after giving birth, nor did her most recent encounter with Luther. Carter didn't release her hand as he led the way slowly out into a hall and down the stairs. Harper paused in the living room and looked at the couches. A nice soft place to sit sounded amazing.

"Would you like to sit on the couch or at the table?" Carter asked.

"The couch, please." Harper said quietly.

Harper was relieved when Carter sat next to her. His presence made her feel safe and she hadn't felt that way in nearly five years. She repositioned Colton as she settled back into the couch with a sigh. "Lexi, if you have your tablet you can play on it until breakfast is ready." Harper smiled at her daughter.

"The bag is over there, next to the rocking chair." Carter pointed and Lexi crossed the room to retrieve her tablet. Harper watched her daughter settle on the ground behind the rocking chair and put her headphones on. Hiding behind furniture had been a necessity while living with Luther. He hated the little girl, and Harper had taken the brunt of his disdain and hatred to save their daughter from coming to harm.

Pans banged in the kitchen and Harper jumped. Her heartrate kicked into high gear until her brain registered that Luther wasn't there. "Can I ask you something?" Carter asked quietly.

"You can ask, but I can't guarantee I will answer." Harper turned her head to look at Carter.

Carter studied her face for several minutes. She could tell he had more than one question he wanted to ask. "Why weren't you at the funeral?" he finally asked.

She hadn't expected that question and tears filled her eyes. They came so suddenly that she didn't have time to try to blink them away before they coursed down her cheeks. She had told Luther that her brother was killed in action and that his funeral would be two weeks later. Luther had acknowledged what she had said, but when she tried to leave with Alexis to go to the funeral, he had gotten angry. He had grabbed her by the throat and slammed her up against the wall. He had hit her until she had lost consciousness. Harper blinked several times to clear the memories and noticed Carter watching her closely with a furrowed brow.

"My husband, well ex-husband now, couldn't get the time off for us to go." Harper whispered.

"Just because he couldn't make it doesn't mean you couldn't have." Carter stated and Harper closed her eyes. She had desperately wanted to be there. Henry had not only been her brother, but he had also been her best friend and her lifeline over the last few years.

"You don't understand, Carter." Harper lowered her voice as she glanced over at Lexi. "I wanted to be there. It killed me not to be there, but..." Harper turned her gaze back to Carter's. "He wouldn't let me."

"What do you mean he wouldn't let you?" Carter's eyes sharpened as he took in every detail of her face. She was sure he saw some of the bruises that were still fading. More tears fell from her eyes, and she shook her head as she tried to find the words.

"Food's done." Devon called from the kitchen doorway.

Harper wiped the tears from her face as she turned to Lexi. "Lexi, why don't you plug in the tablet and go sit at the table. I need to speak with Carter for a few more minutes and then I will join you."

"No." Lexi said as she glared at Carter. Carter was taken aback by the little girl's firm and instant dislike of him.

"Alexis Danielle, you will plug in your tablet and park your little butt at the end of that table." Harper said sternly and Carter had the urge to laugh but held it down. Softening her voice, Harper continued. "From the end you can see me, and I can see you. Everything will be just fine, and I will be there in a few minutes." Lexi's shoulders sagged, but she did as her mother said.

Once she was sure that Lexi was settled and eating, Harper looked back at Carter. She felt like she needed to tell him everything. She wanted to tell him everything. He had been her friend once, maybe he could be again.

"Luther didn't like it when I left without him. He made sure I wasn't able to go." Harper whispered as she closed her eyes and looked away. Tears were coursing down her cheeks as she remembered that day. Even though it was a terrible time for both her and Lexi, in a way it was also a blessing. It had led her to Bethany and a way to escape Luther.

"Harper," Carter kept his voice soft. "Did Luther hurt you and your daughter?" he asked carefully.

Harper swallowed hard as she fought the urge to cry. She didn't trust herself to speak so she nodded slowly. Carter put his arm around her and pulled her close. She rested her head against his shoulder as she fought for control. She didn't want Lexi to see her crying. The little girl was sensitive and often blamed herself for the things Luther did to Harper. When she saw Harper's tears, it often sent her into a panic, thinking she did something wrong.

"How old is Colton?" Carter asked as he ran his hand up and down her arm. He could sense that Harper was struggling with something, and he wanted to change the conversation to something a little lighter. He hated to see her upset. "He seems quite tiny."

"He is five days old." Harper pressed a kiss to the baby's head.

Harper sat there for a long time with Carter's comforting presence next to her. She was so emotionally exhausted. The past five days had been draining; the beating, having just given birth, losing a child, and driving. Not to mention the car accident and her pounding head. She leaned more heavily against Carter as her eyelids started to close. She could hear Lexi in the kitchen answering Jeff and Devon's questions. The knowledge that she and the kids were safe gave her the peace she needed, and she fell asleep.

# Chapter 3

Carter closed his eyes as Harper settled against him. Her breathing grew heavy, and he knew she had fallen asleep. His heart broke at what she had experienced over the last five years. Henry had made it seem like she was happily settled. Had Harper not told her brother what really went on in her marriage? The two had been beyond close, why did she not tell him?

He tightened his arms around her as he rested his head against hers. He closed his eyes and took a deep breath. If he ever crossed paths with Luther, he would let him know just how he felt about someone hurting Harper. A noise from the kitchen drew his attention. Jeff, Devon and Alexis were walking into the living room.

"Is my mommy, okay?" Lexi asked with narrowed eyes.

"She is just taking a little nap. Do you want to play on your tablet again?" Carter asked her with a smile.

"My mom is the only one who can say if I can play on my tablet or not." The little girl rolled her eyes at Carter, and Jeff laughed.

"A little spit fire, isn't she?" Jeff chuckled.

"She is just like her mother." Carter smiled at Lexi. "Your mom sure gave me and your uncle a run for our money when she was little. She was always putting us in our place."

Lexi continued to glare at Carter for another moment before she gently climbed up onto her mother's lap. In order for Lexi to be comfortable, she had to lean up against Carter like her mom was. She sat rigid for several minutes before she too grew heavy and fell asleep.

"Well Carter, I think it's safe to say that Harper is comfortable with you." Devon chuckled as he took a seat in the rocking chair. "But I'm a little confused. Is this the Harper you were asking Henry about? The one that was already married?"

"Yes. This is Henry's sister. However, she just told me that she got divorced last week." Carter looked back down at Harper.

Jeff let out a low whistle. "She is moving on pretty fast."

"It's not like that." Carter sent his friend a glare. "From what I was able to gather, her ex-husband was abusive. She said the baby is only five days old. It wouldn't surprise me if she has been running since he was born."

"Seeing her dad abusing her mom would explain the little girl's wariness of men." Devon said thoughtfully. "Is Harper worried that her ex will try to find her?"

"I'm not sure." Carter looked over at Jeff. "Just in case, we should take some precautions to keep the three of them safe. Jeff, find Tank and Casper. Check out Harper's car. Remove all items that can be traced to her and then have it towed out as if we found it empty. Devon, we need to get her a new phone and transfer all her pictures and personal data onto it. We should leave the old phone in the car."

Both Jeff and Devon agreed and left to fulfill their assignments. Soon the house was quiet, and Carter looked back down at the woman in his arms. Even asleep, Harper held her children protectively. He couldn't imagine living in a life where you feared for not only your own safety, but also your children's. And the man that was supposed to provide and protect them was the very monster they feared.

The baby began to fuss, and Harper jerked awake, immediately alert. She looked around the room before realizing that the baby in her arms was what had woken her. She glanced up at Carter and her cheeks flushed with embarrassment. How long had she been lying against him? She tried to sit up, but realized Lexi had, at some point, crawled onto her lap.

After the trauma of giving birth, Luther's most recent attack, and the car accident, Harper didn't have the strength to sit up from the angle she was at with Lexi on her. Carter carefully lifted Lexi from Harper and settled her against him. Harper sat up and gave him a sheepish smile. "Sorry I fell asleep." she said quietly as she pulled the blanket off the back of the couch. She threw the blanket over her shoulder so she could feed Colt.

"Don't apologize, Harper. You went through quite a bit of trauma over the last week, if not years, by the sounds of it. You deserve a little rest." Carter's deep voice sent a wave of security through her.

Just like when she was with Henry, Carter made her feel safe and comfortable. Unlike with her brother though, Harper wanted Carter's arms back around her. She gave herself a mental shake. She had just got out of an abusive relationship, and she had two children. No man would want someone with so much baggage. Even someone as good as Carter.

Carter had always been there throughout her early childhood. Henry and Carter had been inseparable, and Harper followed them around like they were her heroes. Because to her, they were. She found herself in trouble more than she cared to admit, and they were always there to save her. Henry was overprotective and hovered over her as they grew. When she started noticing boys, Henry had kicked his overprotective brother attitude into overdrive. Carter had been calm and steady, always there to comfort and support her. He also talked his way out of the tough situations she frequently found herself.

When they found out that their parents were splitting up, Henry had taken off. Harper had run from the house as well, but she didn't stop until she could no longer run. She collapsed to the ground and sobbed. She was there for hours before she felt arms pull her into a hug. She looked up expecting to see Henry, but it was Carter. He didn't say anything and didn't expect her to, as she continued to cry.

The door bursting open pulled her from her memories and caused her to jump. Lexi jolted awake and whimpered. Seeing she was no longer sitting with her mom, she let out a scream. Colt finished eating a little while ago, and Harper quickly tugged her shirt back down. She settled the baby against her shoulder as she reached for her daughter. She held her kids close as she whispered soothing words.

"Sorry I startled you." Devon said with an apology heavy in his voice. "I finished with the phones. I need to head into town, but I figured I would see if Harper and the kids needed anything while I was out."

"Oh no. I couldn't ask you to do that. I need to leave soon anyway." Harper's anxiety increased as she thought of herself sitting in one place for too long. Luther was no doubt looking for her.

"Harper, I think you should stay here. Between the four of us, you and the kids will be well protected." Carter said as he turned to face Harper. "You just had a baby, and you were in an accident. Don't you think you should take a few days to at least rest a little? Not to mention your car is totaled."

Harper bit her lip as she thought through her options. Luther was most likely hunting her. He made it clear the night of their divorce that he wasn't just going to let her go. He said he would put things back to how they were before the 'demon children' came into their lives. That threat still sent chills down her spine. She feared Luther would try to harm the kids.

"But Luther is dangerous. I cannot ask you to put yourselves in harm's way for us." Harper looked between Carter and Devon.

Both men chuckled. "You aren't asking, we are offering. And you do realize that all four of us were on a special forces team for years before we retired. Tank has a canine, Casper, that also served with us for a time." Carter touched her arm gently. "Please, Harper. Trust me when I tell you that you will be safest here."

"Carter, I don't know what to say." Harper tightened her arms around her kids. Would they really be safe here?

"Say you will stay." Carter held her gaze and she felt herself soften.

She nodded and Devon's smile grew. "Perfect. Now, what can I pick up for you and the kids?" Devon rubbed his hands together. "I know that you will need a crib, bassinet, clothes, diapers, blankets, and wipes."

"Sounds like you have done this before." Harper smiled at Devon.

"My sister dragged me along when she was preparing for her baby a couple of years ago." Devon shrugged as he handed Harper a pad of paper and pencil. She scribbled down a list of foods Lexi liked, and necessities for the baby and her before handing it back to him. "Thanks. I'll be back in a few hours."

Carter watched as Devon left. Once the door was closed, he turned back to Harper. She looked uncertain. Lexi had turned so that she sat on her mother's leg while leaning back on her chest. Harper was whispering in her ear and the little girl's brows were knit in concentration. When Harper pulled back and looked at her daughter's face, Lexi glanced in his direction.

"He won't hurt you?" Lexi asked in a loud whisper that Carter pretended not to hear.

"No, baby. He won't hurt me." Harper smiled at the little girl as she whispered back.

Lexi continued to size Carter up. "Okay mommy." Harper let out a sigh and kissed the girl's cheek. "Can I play on my tablet, now?"

Harper nodded and Alexis hopped off her lap with a smile. Colton started to fuss. Harper patted his little back as she watched Lexi settle down behind the rocking chair. Maybe someday, she and Lexi would be able to live without the constant fear of Luther's wrath. Living in fear is not really living, it's surviving. And surviving was exhausting. Harper was only twenty-four, but she already felt ancient.

Carter stood and Harper wanted to protest him leaving her, but she bit it back. She wouldn't get away from one man only to attach herself to another. Not that she wasn't already attached. She had always had feelings for Carter. He, on the other hand, never showed any interest in her. Harper needed to stand on her own two feet now and figure out where she and the kids would go after this.

"I need to make a few calls and check in on the ranch hands. I'll be back soon." Carter gave her a reassuring smile. "Make yourself at home and if you need anything, I'll be in the barn." Harper gave him a nod and he left.

Unlike the welcomed silence that followed Luther leaving, Harper felt alone and vulnerable. She looked over at Lexi to see her watching the closed front door with a worried look. She pulled her headphones off before running to Harper. "Mommy, why did that man leave?"

"His name is Carter and he had things he needed to do." Harper tucked some of Lexi's tangled hair behind her ear.

"I don't want him to leave." Lexi whined.

Harper shared her daughter's sentiment but forced a smile. "He will be back when he is done. Why don't we go back upstairs."

Lexi nodded and grabbed her things. When they finally made it back into the room, Harper closed and locked the door behind them, feeling a little safer. She had the uneasy feeling that danger wasn't far away. If danger was close, she needed to be prepared.

She laid Colton down on the bed and changed his diaper. Next, she went through each of their bags and mentally cataloged everything they had. She found her handgun that Henry had bought her for her birthday at the bottom of her bag. She checked the chamber, magazine and safety before tucking it into the back waistband of her pants, pulling her shirt down over it. She pulled a sweatshirt on to help conceal the gun and repacked her clothes.

Several hours passed, and no one had come back to the house yet. Harper sat on the chair near the window burping Colt after his latest feeding and kept an eye on the front of the house. Lexi played an educational game on her tablet as she sat on the bed. The little girl asked frequently where Carter was, but Harper had no answers.

Harper smiled as her daughter laughed at something on the screen. Lexi was so much happier now, even with complaining about her arm hurting, than she ever was when they lived in Luther's house.

The little girl's pain worried Harper and she debated trying to find Carter so he could take them to the doctor's office. Even with Tylenol, the pain was still there. Just when she made up her mind to find Carter, a large red truck pulled up to the front of the house.

Harper kept out of sight as she watched a man in a baseball cap step from the vehicle. He looked familiar from this distance, which put her on high alert. The only man around here that was familiar was Carter. And this man was not as big as Carter was.

"Stay here and watch your brother." Harper instructed Lexi as she laid the baby on the bed next to her. "I will be right back." Lexi's eyes were wide with fear, but she didn't protest as Harper slipped from the room and closed the door behind her.

As quietly as possible, Harper moved down the stairs and stopped at the bottom. The man was standing in the living room, looking around as if searching for something. When he caught sight of her, he smiled, and Harper's blood froze. Luther.

# Chapter 4

Carter wiped the sweat off his brow. He finished making his calls to Jeff and the sheriff right before word came in that several of their horses were out. He and two of their ranch hands saddled up and rode out to round them up.

Looking down at his watch, Carter realized he had been away from Harper much longer than he had intended. His phone buzzed, and he grabbed it off the clip on his belt. An alert came in saying that a truck had entered through the front gate. It was probably Devon, but he wanted to make sure Harper and the kids were okay. He had a nagging feeling he needed to get to them.

"I need to get back to the main house." He called over to the two men with him. "Put them in the west pasture for now." When they nodded their understanding, Carter spurred his horse into a run.

When he got to the house ten minutes later, an unfamiliar red truck was parked out front. He dismounted and ran for the door. The scene that met him when he opened the front door caused his blood to boil. A man had Harper pinned against the wall with her hands over her head as he kissed her. She had tears on her cheeks and looked to be struggling against his hold. Carter sized up the man quickly. He was close to six feet tall and toned. He easily overpowered Harper as if she were a child.

"Am I interrupting?" Carter asked as he slammed the door with a bang.

The man pulled away from Harper but kept a firm grip on her wrist. Carter saw her wince in pain, but she refused to look over at him. Instead, her gaze was fixed on the floor.

"As a matter of fact, you are." The man laughed, but his smile looked forced. "I'm just showing my wife how happy I am to see her after hearing her car was totaled in an accident." The man he now figured was Luther, pulled Harper roughly towards him and she let out a whimper.

"I'm not your wife." Her voice shook, but she lifted her gaze and glared at her tormentor.

Harper's heart stopped as she watched Luther slowly turn his head to face her. The look of anger in his eyes caused her to shiver in fear. Carter took a step closer to them, but he wasn't fast enough to prevent Luther from shoving her up against the wall again. Luther grabbed her jaw to force her to look at him. "You are mine." He growled out.

Before she or Luther could do anything, Carter was there pulling Luther off her, sending him stumbling backwards. Carter stood protectively in front of her as he faced Luther. "This is my house and my land. Nothing in or on it is yours. I will only tell you this nicely once, leave." Harper had never heard Carter sound so angry.

"She is my wife. You can't keep me from her. She belongs to me." Luther took a threatening step towards Carter as the front door opened.

"Whose truck is…oh." Devon's voice morphed from curious to hard as he took in the occupants in the living room. "I see."

Luther's smile turned smug. "Good, a witness. This man here is trying to keep me from my wife." Luther glared at Carter.

"From where I'm standing, she doesn't want to go with you." Devon looked angry, and Harper tried not to move and draw attention to herself. Having Luther angry with her was enough, she didn't need to add two more angry men to the mix.

"How dare you." Luther fumed. "She is mine and she is coming with me."

"No. She is not anyone's. A person doesn't belong to another person." Carter ground out through clenched teeth. "I'm guessing that is where you went wrong."

Luther swung his fist at Carter and Harper screamed. She covered her mouth in an attempt to stop the sound, but failed. The men were in a fist fight and Devon just stood near the door, watching them. Why wasn't he stopping them?

"Mommy?" Lexi's voice sounded from the stairs.

Harper saw the moment Luther and Carter heard Lexi. Both stopped for a second. Luther recovered first. He punched Carter in the jaw, causing him to stumble back a step, falling back over the coffee table and hitting the ground. Luther's zeroed in on Lexi and he moved in her direction. Harper ran for her daughter and shoved her behind her as she whirled around to face Luther. She pulled the gun from her waistband and pointed it at him, causing him to stop advancing towards her. He was only five feet away. The room became deathly quiet, and no one moved.

"You take one more step towards my daughter and I won't hesitate to pull this trigger." Harper warned.

"Babe, don't be like this." Luther said in his most soothing voice. It only made her angrier.

"I told you to leave, Luther." Harper said in a calm but firm voice. "We are no longer married, and I will not be going with you."

"That little brat ruined everything between us. Leave her here and…" Luther started to say, but stopped as she flipped the safety off.

"We have nothing more to do with you, Luther. Now leave." She ground out.

This time Devon stepped forward and grabbed Luther's arm. He yanked her ex from the house and slammed the door. As soon as the door was closed, Harper turned around and hugged her daughter. A movement behind her had Harper spinning around, gun at the ready.

Carter stood there with his hands raised. Harper let out a relieved breath as she lowered her gun. He wrapped both Harper and Lexi in his arms and held them for a few minutes. "Did he hurt you? Either of you?" He asked as he leaned back to get a better look at them. He immediately saw blood at the corner of Harper's lip and her cheek was red.

"Me? What about you?" Harper asked with tears brimming her eyes. "He had a knife."

Carter lifted Harper's chin when he saw more blood running down her throat. Besides a small cut, her throat was red as if someone had grabbed her there.

"Mommy, you're bleeding." Lexi started to cry as she leaned into Harper.

"Jeff and Tank are escorting that lowlife off the property and local authorities have been called." Devon said as he slammed the front door. "He tried to stab me."

Devon stopped when he saw Lexi crying against Harper and Carter holding both of them.

"Harper, what happened?" Carter asked as he slowly released her and led them to the couch. She was starting to shake from the fear and adrenaline that had coursed through her body. "Where is Colt?"

"He's up on the bed." Harper glanced over at the stairs. Devon jogged up them before she could say anything more and returned seconds later with the sleeping baby. He handed Colt over to her.

"What happened?" Carter asked again.

"We were upstairs in the room when I saw a truck pull up. I told Lexi to watch Colt and I came down here to see who it was. Luther was standing in the living room. He told me to get in the truck, and when I refused, he hit me then shoved me against the wall. He threatened me with a knife." She gestured to her throat and Devon moved to get a better look.

"Carter." Devon said as he went into the kitchen and returned with a first-aid kit. Carter lifted Colt from her arms and pulled Lexi into his lap. "We need to up the security at the gate." Devon tilted her chin up and began cleaning her neck. "What happened next? How long was he here?"

"He didn't like that I refused to go with him. Then he tried to convince me to go with him, which was worse than the threats. That's when Carter came in." Harper hissed as Devon put something on that stung.

"Sorry." Devon apologized as he put a bandage on her throat.

"I'm so sorry he was here. You both could have been hurt." Harper said softly, looking down at her hands.

"You don't need to apologize, Dove. I'm sorry for not being here when you needed me. We knew he was a threat but had assumed it would take him a few days to track you down. We will not make that mistake again. I promise." Carter said firmly.

Harper took a deep breath and let it out slowly. The moment she saw Luther standing in her safe haven, she nearly panicked. But a calm had come over her. She knew Carter would come. However, that knowledge hadn't stopped the fear she felt when the knife pressed against her neck, or how disgusted she had felt when his lips had pressed to hers. She had never liked Luther's touch. A month into their marriage and she still couldn't bring herself to even kiss him. She had even asked for an annulment. A shiver ran down her spine. He repulsed her.

The front door burst open, and Jeff stomped in. "That was your ex?" He yelled.

Harper shrank back as she nodded. "My roommate used to tease me about having a type." Thinking back, Luther had totally fit with all of the other men she had dated. Tall, brown hair, brown eyes, kind, selfless, supportive. Unfortunately for her, that hadn't lasted long.

"You dated other men like that?" Carter asked through clenched teeth. Harper looked over at him to see a muscle working in his jaw.

"No. In fact, I had a very high standard. Very few men actually met it. Henry told me I would die alone if I wasn't willing to give on some things. Then I met Luther, and he met all my requirements, until he found out I was expecting."

"Requirements?" Jeff asked.

"Yes, requirements." Harper rolled her eyes. She had a list, and in order for her to agree to a date, a man had to meet each one. "Taller than me, good with kids, served others, respectful, a member of the church, kind, and didn't give up easily on what they wanted." She blushed as she remembered why she had the list.

Carter had been her brother's best friend, and she had liked him since she was nine. He was the first boy she had a crush on, and she had dreamed about marrying him. The last item on the list was added when he never came for her. She had thought he would, once she graduated high school, but only Henry had come to her graduation. She had been heartbroken. Truth be told, she still was. She hadn't recognized the depth of her feelings for Carter until she realized she most likely would never see him again. So, she created the list to help her find someone like him.

"How did that man pass your list?" Jeff scoffed as he came around the couch and sat in the rocking chair.

"According to Henry, Luther worked at several charities and was a really cool guy." Carter grudgingly supplied.

"Yeah, he fooled us all, until it was too late." Harper said bitterly. She looked back over at Lexi, and Colt in Carter's arms as tears filled her eyes. She reached for her crying daughter who went willingly into her arms. She sat Lexi so they were facing each other and wiped the little girl's tears.

"I'm sorry, Mommy. It's all my fault." Lexi cried.

Harper knew all too well how much guilt Lexi felt. Luther had yelled about a lot of things being because of Lexi over the years. The little girl had had many breakdowns crying about it being her fault that Luther would hurt Harper. Harper did her best to comfort the child and to tell her none of Luther's behavior was because of her , but it didn't seem to be enough.

"You know I would do everything all over again just to have you and Colt, don't you?" Harper whispered, but Lexi shook her head. "Can I tell you a secret?" she asked quietly hugging her daughter close.

"Can Carter and Devon and Jeff know the secret too?" Harper blinked before glancing around the room. She had forgotten about the men there. She wiped her cheeks, returning her attention back to Lexi.

"Sure, my love." Harper pressed a kiss to Lexi's cheek. "I know that you think a lot of what has happened is your fault, which it isn't. But did you know, you were saving me this whole time?" Lexi's eyes widened in surprise as she shook her head. "It's true. Without you, I wouldn't have made it through the last five years. You were my reason to live. You gave me hope when I had none. If I didn't have you, I don't think I would have survived." Harper paused and blinked back tears. It was true. If her kids didn't need her, she wouldn't be alive today. "You and Colt are my world. Do you understand?"

"I love you, mommy." Lexi wrapped her arms around Harper's neck and the two of them held each other for several minutes.

"I love you too, baby girl." Harper whispered.

"He hit Carter in the face." Lexi pouted as she glanced over at Carter, who was watching them with a look Harper couldn't read. "I think he needs a magic band aid."

"Carter is a big boy. I think he will be just fine." Harper felt a blush trying to heat her cheeks, but she refused to let it. How had her heart to heart with Lexi turned to this?

"What is a magic band aid?" Devon asked with a smile. "I'm sure Carter could really use it if you have one." Harper sent him a glare.

"It's when Mommy kisses it and makes it all better." Lexi explained.

"Lexi, why don't you give Carter a magic band aid?" Harper suggested desperately. She made the mistake of looking over at Carter. His eyes that were normally a light chocolate brown, were slightly darker and he was smiling. He was enjoying this, was he? "Better yet, why doesn't Devon do it? After all, he is a medic." Harper smiled sweetly, even as she sent him a glare. "I'm sure his magic band aids work much better than ours."

"That's right, he is a doctor. Devon, you give Carter the magic band aid." Lexi's eager demand was met with a protest from both Devon and Carter.

To Harper's surprise, after Lexi insisted several times, Devon placed a quick kiss on Carter's cheek with a look of disgust. Harper laughed. It had only taken her four-year-old less than five minutes to convince two men to do magic band aids. It was endearing that they were willing to endure that, just to make her daughter happy. Jeff roared with laughter as he stood. Devon sent him a glare, and then excused himself to get his groceries from his truck.

"For being so good to Carter, if your mom agrees, would you like to go look at the horses in the barn with me, Lexi?" Jeff asked, Lexi looked at Harper for an answer.

"Oh yes, please, Mommy." Lexi looked up at Harper with large pleading eyes.

Harper glanced over at Carter who gave her a slight nod before she looked back at Jeff. Her recent encounter with Luther was still fresh in her mind and she wanted her daughter close. The hatred and anger in his eyes as he moved toward Lexi had unsettled Harper. But Jeff would be with Lexi, and she would be safe with him for a little while. Not trusting herself to speak, she gave Jeff a nod and watched as Lexi held Jeff's hand as they left the house. Panic tried to grab hold of her with her daughter's absence, but she fought against it.

"Jeff will watch her." Carter said beside her. Harper pulled her eyes from the closed door and looked at him.

"I know. It's just…it's just I have never left her side before. I couldn't." Harper's eyes returned to the door. "I feel like a part of me was taken away."

Carter's large hand grabbed hers and gave it a squeeze. "You aren't alone anymore, Harper. Jeff will protect her, and they will be back soon. Everything will be okay."

She nodded and leaned her head against Carter's shoulder. Harper was selfish. She knew she shouldn't rely so much on Carter, but at the moment she needed reassurance and he had always been her greatest source of comfort. He, no doubt, only thought of her as a little sister, while her heart still yearned to be close to him.

The front door opened, and she was grateful for the distraction. Devon walked past them and deposited several bags in the kitchen. Before he left for a second load, Colt woke up crying. Carter passed him over to her. Devon suggested she use the spare room to feed the baby. That way he and Carter could set up the crib and she wouldn't be left downstairs alone.

Harper willingly went upstairs. She found the room easily. It was right next to hers. She took in the room as she stood in the doorway. There was a twin bed in the corner and a small dresser on the opposite wall. That was it. Just the two pieces of furniture. A hand touched her lower back, and she glanced over her shoulder to see Carter standing there. She turned to face him, and he gently put his arms around her, giving her a hug. Harper fought the tears that burned her eyes.

When he finally pulled back, he cupped her face and used his thumb to brush away a tear that had escaped. "Devon and I will be in the next room if you need us." He said quietly. His eyes dropped to her lips and her stomach did a flip. His gaze returned to hers and held her captive. He took a half step closer just as Colt let out a cry, breaking the spell surrounding them.

Harper blinked quickly several times as she pulled her eyes from Carter's to look down at her baby. "I should feed him." Her voice came out airy.

Carter nodded before heading back down the stairs. What had he been thinking? He almost kissed Harper. Under normal circumstances, kissing her would be a dream come true, but she had just experienced something traumatic. He couldn't allow himself to confuse her need for comfort with her real feelings. She was in a vulnerable state at present. He couldn't give in to his attraction to her right now if he wanted any hope of having a chance with her in the future, after all this craziness settled.

Devon was waiting next to the truck when Carter walked outside. He took a deep breath of the clean, fresh air and let it out slowly. Devon raised a brow as Carter approached. "How is she?" Devon asked, glancing at the house before settling back on Carter. "How are you?"

Carter glanced up at the window he knew was the spare room. "I almost kissed her."

Devon laughed as he started pulling things from the cab of his truck. "I'm guessing your feelings from childhood haven't changed then." Devon paused before walking back to the house, waiting for Carter. "What stopped you from kissing her?"

Carter ran his hand through his short military style haircut. "Colt started to cry, but she was just attacked by her ex. I felt like I would be taking advantage of her if I had kissed her." He shook his head as he grabbed a couple bags. "I'm just her older brother's best friend, and she probably sees me as a brother. A kiss would destroy our friendship."

"Or it could change it for the better. That woman has been through more abuse than she has told us. She was willing to fight three men who are easily twice her size to protect her kids, but as soon as she knew it was you, she immediately collapsed in relief." Devon lowered his voice as they walked into the house. "If I were her, I don't know if I could trust any man for a long time. But she cuddled up to you and slept. She let her guard down in a strange place with several unknown men because you were there, that has to mean something."

"We knew each other as kids." Carter argued.

"You haven't seen each other in over ten years, Carter. You are practically strangers." Devon retorted. "Let's take the crib up next." Carter wordlessly followed his friend to the bed of the truck. As they carried in the crib box, Devon continued. "Think about what I said, Carter."

Carter nodded. They changed the conversation to rearranging the bedroom and setting up the crib. It had taken just over an hour, but the crib was next to the bed and the rocking chair from downstairs was now by the window. His chair had been moved downstairs where the rocking chair had been. Carter looked around his room. His king-sized bed took up a good portion of the area, but the baby furniture didn't make the space feel crowded. It somehow felt right being there. Devon went down to put groceries away, leaving Carter standing alone.

He was covered in dirt and sweat from the last two days, so he gathered clean clothes and stepped into his bathroom. After he was showered and shaved, Carter went to check on Harper. She was sitting on the floor next to the twin bed where the baby lay sleeping. She was softly stroking the baby's head with silent tears rolling down her cheeks.

"Harper?" He kept his voice soft so as to not startle her.

She didn't look in his direction as she continued to watch her son. He slowly moved closer but stopped a few feet from her when she started to speak. "Over the years, I have asked myself why me and Lexi had to go through what we had. But this feels different, Carter." She turned to face him. "Why did Bo have to be taken from me? Why, Carter? He was just an innocent baby." Her eyes pleaded with him.

Carter scooped her into his arms and sat on the edge of the bed. Harper's arms went around his neck, and she held him tight. "I don't know, Harper." Carter felt her body shake with her quiet sobs. Who was Bo? "Unfortunately, God can't always save the innocent, but those people who do them harm will be held accountable for their crimes before God." He tightened his hold on her when hers tightened on him.

Devon peeked into the room and raised both eyebrows in question. "Harper, can Devon take Colt for a little bit?" She nodded, but a sob caused the amusement in Devon's expression to turn to worry. He didn't say anything as he carefully lifted the sleeping infant and left the room, closing the door behind him.

"I'm sorry." Harper whispered into his shoulder.

"If you need a good cry, a gallon of nacho cheese sauce and salsa, then so be it. You need to allow yourself to mourn, Harper. And I'm betting you need to grieve for the loss of your brother as well." Carter rubbed circles on her back as she continued to cry.

A long while later, Harper's death grip on Carter loosened and she shifted so her head lay against his shoulder. "Carter?" she asked softly. She was just realizing that she was sitting in his lap.

"Hmm?" He was equally as quiet. He continued to hold her and rub soothing circles on her back.

She relaxed against him. "My head hurts."

"I bet, Dove." Carter chuckled. She thought she felt him kiss her head, but that would have been ridiculous. Carter didn't feel that way towards her. "You hit your head pretty hard in the accident and crying tends to leave you with a headache. I bet you have a whopper of one." A small smile turned up the corners of her lips. How did Carter remember that she got headaches after having a good cry?

A knock sounded at the door as it opened. Lexi ran in, followed by Jeff and Devon. Lexi was covered in dirt from head to toe with straw in her hair.

"Mommy, I got to see horses and puppies." Lexi squealed in delight.

Harper sat up straight, but Carter kept his arms around her, preventing her from moving off his lap. Instead of feeling afraid like she knew she should, she felt safe and protected. "How did looking at horses turn into such a dirty task?" Harper smiled at Lexi.

"Well, it didn't start out that way." Jeff rubbed the back of his neck. "Tank came into the barn and before I could blink, she disappeared. It took us an hour to find her."

"The doggy found me." Lexi held her knuckles out for Harper to fist bump. Harper had taught her daughter to hide whenever a man entered the room. It was a preemptive defense against Luther's anger.

"That's my girl." Harper laughed and fist bumped Lexi.

"You do realize that without Casper, we wouldn't have found her." Jeff crossed his arms clearly annoyed that Harper was encouraging Lexi.

"I'm sorry she scared you, Jeff, but you do realize who we have been living with for the past several years. Lexi's ability to hide was a matter of life and death." That comment sobered the room. "Lexi sweetheart, can you go into the next room and find some clean clothes please?" Harper asked and Lexi immediately agreed. As soon as she was gone, Harper looked at Jeff. "When she was a year old, I made the mistake of not barricading the bathroom door when I was giving her a bath. Luther picked the lock and came in. He was angry about something, and he attacked us.

"He tried to drown Lexi in the tub, breaking her arm in the process. Since you all have met him, you know I am no match physically for him. I got desperate and ran to get a pan from the kitchen. I hit him twice over the head until he was knocked unconscious. I immediately pulled Lexi from the water." Harper swallowed past the lump in her throat and Carter's arms tightened around her. "I nearly lost her. I had to do CPR and she coughed up so much water. We spent four days in the hospital."

"How did the police not get involved?" Devon asked angrily.

"I tried, but Luther said it was a pool accident. He had called the cops before the hospital did to explain things." Harper wiped a tear. "He threatened to finish what he started if I tried to go against him. I was barely twenty and terrified. I didn't know what to do or who to call. So, I taught her to hide." Harper raised her shoulder with a sad smile. "Out of sight, out of mind."

"How did we let that piece of scum just walk away?" Jeff growled.

Harper sagged back against Carter. She closed her eyes trying to rid her mind of emergency responders trying to save Lexi's life. The fear she had felt when Luther had threatened Lexi, had been enough to keep her quiet. It didn't take long for Harper to find multiple hiding spots in each room of the house for Lexi. Harper came back to the conversation flowing around her when she heard her name.

"Harper mentioned her head hurts. Do you have anything she can take?" Carter asked Devon.

"I'll call my sister to see what a nursing mother can have." Devon said as he pulled his phone from his pocket and left the room.

"I just need Tylenol." Harper said with an exhausted sigh.

"Let Devon call his sister to see if we can get you something stronger, Dove. While he is making the call, why don't you and Lexi jump in the shower. I will watch Colt for you." Carter whispered in her ear. His hands moved to her hips and propelled her to her feet. He stood and moved a hand to her back as he guided her to the next room where Lexi had pulled all of her clothes out of her bag.

Harper gasped as she took in all the changes to the room. She took in the crib and changing table combo, rocking chair and basket of toys. "Carter, what is all this?" Her voice was barely above a whisper.

"Don't ask me, Devon was the one that went shopping." His deep chuckle filled her with warmth, but she also felt like she couldn't breathe. "You needed a crib for Colt and a comfortable place to feed him. Devon couldn't resist getting the toys after he noticed the kids didn't have many."

"Mommy, look at my new shirt! It's got a horse on it. I love horses." Lexi was jumping up and down as she showed off the shirt in her hands.

"You can't live on a ranch and not love horses." Devon's voice sounded from behind them. "Clara said she is on her way. She wants to examine you herself and get you a prescription if needed."

Harper felt so overwhelmed. What was happening? Was she moving in? She watched her daughter's excitement over several new outfits and a baby doll. Harper couldn't tell them no and take away Lexi's joy at having her first doll. Blinking back her tears, Harper turned to Carter. "Thanks for the offer to watch Colt, but I need to give him a bath too. He hasn't had one yet."

Carter slowly nodded as if he wanted to protest but said nothing as Devon handed the baby over to her. She closed the door in their faces and locked it. She had promised Lexi that as soon as they got away from Luther, it would be just them and the baby. They would rely on each other, and not take chances on letting anyone else in for a long time. But here they were, staying with four retired military men and Harper didn't know how she felt about it.

Harper warred with herself as she got the kids bathed and dressed in clean pajamas. Should they stay here, or should they leave and try to outrun Luther? Harper fed Colt and tucked him into his crib before setting Lexi on the bed with her tablet to watch a movie.

She left the door open while she took her first shower in nearly a week. The hot water was cathartic and after getting clean, the tears started up again. She sat on the floor and allowed herself to cry, to feel the regret and the sorrow of losing Bowman. Losing her brother. Her regret at not being at Henry's funeral. The tears she wasn't able to shed for five years living with an abusive man.

# Chapter 5

Harper ran a brush through Lexi's hair as they sat on the bed. Once all the tangles were brushed out, Harper pulled it into a French braid. Lexi smiled back at her when Harper finished the last twist of the rubber band.

"Lexi, do you remember what we talked about when we were planning to leave Luther?" Harper asked slowly. She couldn't make this decision herself. After all, it involved both of them.

"You said you weren't going to allow another man into our lives that would hurt us. You said we were a team and that no one would have power over us." Lexi nodded as she played with the baby doll.

"What do you think about staying here for a little while? Or do you think we should go?" Harper handed the baby bottle to Lexi so she could feed the doll. Lexi looked up at her with brows knit in confusion.

"I like it here. Devon said I could call him uncle because he and my real uncle were brothers in arms. Jeff is funny and makes me laugh. Tank was scary at first, but he has the cutest doggies. He said I could have one if you say I can. I like my new toys and I like seeing you smile." Lexi moved to sit in Harper's lap.

"Would I be breaking my promise to you, to not allow anyone in our lives that would hurt us?" Harper studied her daughter. She knew very well that if they stayed, the chances of Carter breaking her heart again was a very real possibility. Even if he didn't know it or mean to.

Lexi eyed Harper with a thoughtful expression. "If we stay here, would you marry one of them?" Harper was surprised at the sudden direction the conversation took. "You told me that God didn't like it when men and women live together without being married. Are we breaking one of God's commandments?" Worry filled Lexi's voice.

"We are just visiting, Lexi. They want to help keep us safe from Luther. As soon as we know we are safe, we will leave. Mommy is doing her best to follow God's commandments, honey. And soon we will be able to go to church." Harper's response seemed to appease the little girl, because she went back to playing.

Harper let Lexi enjoy her new toys while Colt continued to sleep. She needed to figure out her car situation and decide how long they would be here before moving on. She saw a book on the nightstand and picked it up. When she saw it was a worn Book of Mormon, she reverently opened the cover. The once familiar words were a balm to her battered spirit. The calmness that overcame her as she read was what she had needed.

A month after they were married, Luther had started planning at-home dates during church time. As newlyweds, Harper didn't see the harm in missing a few weeks of church. Looking back, she could easily see that Luther was alienating her from everyone.

Then he had burned her scriptures as punishment when she got pregnant with Lexi. He refused to allow her to go to church or have any sort of religious items in the house. That hadn't stopped her from praying or teaching Lexi about God and Jesus. They prayed every day together and Harper did her best to instill in Lexi the teachings of Jesus, well as much as she could remember.

Harper had read several chapters when a knock sounded at the door. She returned the book to the nightstand and crossed the room. She wasn't ready yet to face Carter and the guys. She still felt overwhelmed by their attention and kindness. "Look I just need..." She pulled the door open, fully expecting to see Carter, but stopped mid-sentence when she saw a woman standing there instead.

"Space?" The woman finished for her. She was several inches shorter than Harper. The woman looked a lot like Devon with her blonde hair and hazel eyes.

"I'm sorry, I thought you were someone else." Harper's cheeks heated with embarrassment as she apologized.

"Don't worry about it. I totally get it. They can be a bit much sometimes." The woman gave a friendly smile. "I'm Clara McCall, Devon's sister. Can I come in for a few minutes?" Harper stepped back and opened the door wider so Clara could enter. Harper closed and locked the door after her. "I'm a family physician, but I also do OBGYN. Devon tells me you recently had a baby, and that you were in a car accident."

"Yes. My baby is five days old." Harper smiled at Clara. She liked the fact that Clara cut right to the chase. There was something about her that Harper instantly liked and trusted. "My daughter has been complaining about her arm hurting. I have been giving her Tylenol for it, but it still bothers her."

Clara nodded and started talking with Lexi. She asked about the baby doll and once Lexi began to feel more comfortable with her, shifted her questions to the girl's arm. Clara examined it carefully before moving back to Harper's side. "Good news is, I don't think it is broken. There is some bruising, but no swelling or pain when moving the arm. I think she just hit it pretty good in the accident." Harper let out a relieved sigh. "How is the baby doing?" Clara asked as she looked over at the crib.

On cue, Colt woke up crying. Harper lifted him and he immediately settled down. She handed him over to Clara who looked over him carefully. "He appears to be in perfect health." Clara smiled at the baby. "Now, how is mom doing?"

Harper hesitated. How was she doing? She was a complete mess. Clara probably only wanted to know about the accident. Seeing her hesitation, Clara informed Harper that she was under the doctor-patient confidentiality agreement and that whatever Harper wanted to say, she was welcome to.

Harper helped Lexi get her earphones on and a movie going before sitting on the bed to feed Colt. Clara was patient and waited for Harper to get the kids settled before sitting next to her.

Harper told Clara everything. Her marrying Luther against her better judgement and wanting an annulment after the first month. Luther's abuse, his hatred of Lexi, feeling alone and helpless, the funeral and attack. When she got to the birth of Colton, she fought back tears.

"I had twin boys. Bowman was given less than a five percent chance to live. Colton and I were released from the hospital after twenty-four hours. I was left with a choice. Do I stay in town and wait for Bo to finally pass away and run the risk of Luther finding us again, or do I take Lexi and Colt and run?" Harper felt ashamed of her actions. "I contacted my lawyer and put her as the emergency contact for the hospital. She has permission to act on my behalf. I told her where I wanted Bo buried and set up all the arrangements for when he passed. I'm a terrible mother. Who leaves their dying baby?" Tears were rolling freely down her cheeks.

"You were given an impossible situation, Harper. You did what was best for you and your two children that were alive and healthy. No one can fault you for that." Clara put an arm around Harper's shoulders. "Now that Colt is done eating, would you allow me to examine you to make sure you are okay and healing properly?"

Harper put Colt back in the crib and lay on the bed. As Clara did her exam, they continued to talk. "I lost my phone in the accident and don't even know if Bo is still alive or if he passed away. I could have missed his burial." Harper confessed.

"If you know your lawyer's number, you can borrow my phone if you want." Clara offered. At Harper's eager nod, Clara fished her phone out of her pocket and handed it to her.

"Thank you." Harper said excitedly as she sat up and punched in the number she needed. It rang several times before it was answered.

"This is Bethany Black." Harper's lawyer gave her usual greeting.

"Beth, it's me." Harper breathed out, suddenly feeling nervous. Clara continued her examination by taking several vials of blood.

"Harper? Thank goodness. Where have you been? I've been trying to reach you for two days." Bethany's voice came out in a rush.

"I had bad service and then I lost my phone." Harper started to explain, but Bethany cut her off.

"I have good news and bad news. What do you want to hear first?" Bethany asked, and Harper told her to start with the bad. "The doctors documented evidence of both yours and Bo's injuries and your neighbor gave a description of your attacker. Everything together is enough to bring Luther in for questioning, but the police haven't been able to find him. They checked his house and his work with no luck."

"He was here earlier today. He tried to get me to go with him, but he was stopped by a couple of good guys that were looking out for me." Harper pinched the bridge of her nose. How did Luther always avoid her attempts to get him out of her life?

"Harper, where are you? I will let the police know that he was last seen at your location." Harper heard Bethany typing on her computer as she spoke.

Harper opened her mouth to speak, but realized she had no idea where she was. Clara saw the uncertainty on Harper's face and smiled. "We are at the Henry River Ranch in Pinedale, Wyoming."

Harper repeated what Clara said. "Can the police even do anything? We are no longer in Colorado."

"Luther is wanted for breaking and entering, assault, and attempted murder. If authorities catch him, they will transport him back here for his trial." Bethany's voice was reassuring, but something she had said caused Harper to freeze.

"Attempted murder?" She barely managed to ask. Clara looked up at her quickly.

"That brings me to the good news." Bethany's typing stopped and Harper held her breath. "Bo is still alive, Harper." Bethany's voice had softened. "According to the doctors, after those men from your church visited him, Bo has slowly been improving. They don't know what to make of it. He still isn't out of the woods yet." Bethany warned as Harper started to cry. "The hospital isn't allowing anyone in to see him because of a nasty sickness hitting the area, but they sent me a few pictures of him."

"I should come back. I should be there with him." Harper managed to say through her tears.

"No, you stay right where you are. You sound like you and the kids are safe, and you wouldn't be able to see him anyway. I will give you updates on him as I get them. Is this a good number to reach you?" Bethany said firmly.

"No. This is a friend's phone. I will get a new phone tomorrow and give you a call, so you have it." Harper sent up a prayer of gratitude. Bo was improving. "Is Bo really getting better?" She couldn't help but ask. It seemed too good to be true.

"Dr. Honey gave me an update just this morning. Instead of a five percent chance of survival, Bo has a forty-five percent chance." Bethany's words were an answer to Harper's prayers. She thanked Bethany and promised to call her tomorrow.

Once the line went dead, Harper stared at the phone in her hands. Bo might live. Before she was discharged from the hospital, Harper had met a nurse whose brother was a priesthood holder and worked at the hospital too. She had asked if the nurse could have her brother give Bo a blessing. The nurse eagerly agreed, and it looked like they had been able to do it.

A hand on her shoulder brought her out of her thoughts. Clara sat next to her with a look of concern. "Are you okay?" she asked softly.

"It's a miracle. Bo is still alive and has a forty-five percent chance of living now. He's going to be okay." More tears gathered in her eyes.

"That's great!" Clara smiled. "When can you see him?"

"He is in Denver. They are not allowing anyone up into the NICU. And Luther is being hunted by the police now." Harper wiped the tears from her eyes. She could smell food cooking downstairs and her stomach growled.

"I hope they find Luther quickly." Clara pulled her phone from Harper's hands. "I haven't even met him, and I hate him. And I hope Bo gets better soon. Just say the word and we will go get him." Harper nodded as Clara's phone chimed twice really quickly. Clara unlocked the screen and looked at her messages. "Dev says dinner is ready whenever we are." Clara paused for a moment before her mouth fell open and she handed the phone back to Harper.

On the screen was a baby with tubes all over. The name tag read 'Bowman Carter Anderson'. Just below that was another sign. 'Even though mommy can't be with me right now, she sent angels to watch over me'. Harper's precarious lid on her emotions burst open again. Clara held her until she could pull herself back together. She would have either Clara or Bethany send her that picture once she had her new phone.

"Well, on that note," Clara wiped her own eyes. "You are healing well from giving birth. You are going to be sore and a bit achy from the accident, but other than that, you are healthy. No strenuous exercise, riding horses, or heavy lifting for another five weeks when we do a follow up appointment. I do want you to rest for the next couple of days though, and let your body recover from the blood loss and trauma." Clara took a deep breath and let it out in a huff. "Should we go down for dinner?"

"Before we go, the guys don't know about Bo." Harper felt sick at the thought. She didn't want them to know about him yet. She was terrified they would judge her for leaving him behind. She didn't need any more guilt over it than what she was already heaping on herself. "Please, don't say anything."

"Mums the word. Now let's get some food and fluids in you, doctor's orders." Clara smiled and gave Harper another quick hug.

Clara walked down with Lexi while Harper followed with Colt. She needed to hold at least one of her baby boys close for a few minutes.

All four men were sitting at a large wooden table when the women walked in. There was a bassinet near an empty chair and Harper gladly took it before laying Colt down carefully. The room was uncomfortably quiet as everyone waited for someone else to speak. Harper kept her eyes on her empty plate, too afraid to look up. Her emotions were everywhere, and she was close to exploding again. Not to mention her head was still pounding.

Carter finally broke the silence and asked Tank to say the prayer. After the prayer, two white pills were placed on her plate. Startled, Harper looked up to find Clara sitting next to her. She pointedly looked at the pills and gave Harper a stern look. Mechanically, she took them with a large glass of water. To her surprise, Clara even dished up her plate for her. Harper gave her new friend a thankful look before picking up her fork. Even though her stomach growled, she couldn't bring herself to eat much.

"Harper mentioned losing her phone, maybe tomorrow one of you could pick her up one?" Clara commented as she took a large bite of potatoes.

"No need." Carter said from Harper's other side, and she looked up to find him watching her with worry in his eyes. "We were concerned about Luther tracking you with your phone, so we transferred all your personal data, pictures and contacts over to a new phone." He pulled a phone from his pocket and handed it over to her. Harper took it slowly, but Clara grabbed it quickly from her. "The number is different from your last one, so he can't contact you."

"Thank you." Harper whispered as she blinked back tears. This wasn't good. She wasn't in an emotional state to have a family dinner or deal with Carter and the way he made her feel. Clara put the phone back into her hands and it buzzed immediately. Harper looked down at it.

**Clara:** You need to eat. Doctor's orders!
**Harper:** I'm trying.
**Clara:** Try harder! Lexi, Colt, and B need you to keep up your strength.

Harper took several bites of her food when her phone buzzed again. She took a sip of water before checking the phone.

**Clara:** How are you holding up?
**Harper:** I think I'm okay. Just…processing.
**Carter:** Is everything okay?
**Devon:** If Carter did something to upset you, I can smack him for you.
**Jeff:** Say the word and I'll take you to see the horses and puppies. I have been told by a little girl that it makes everything better.

Harper looked up at the occupants sitting at the table. All eyes were on her. She ignored the adults and gave her attention to her daughter. Lexi was happily munching on her chicken nuggets as she talked with an even larger man than Carter. At his side sat a German Shepherd. He must be Tank. The phone buzzed again, and Harper glanced at it.

**Clara:** I think everyone is worried about you. I haven't seen these men look so glum since they got here.

Harper felt a tear slide down her cheek. She hadn't meant to cause anyone to worry about her. No one had worried about her for a very long time, except Lexi. And Lexi was blissfully unaware of Harper's swirling emotions. Harper tried to blink the tears back, but it only caused more to spill out on her cheeks. Harper sent an S.O.S. text to Clara and waited with her head bowed so hopefully no one would see the tears fall.

"Oh, before I forget, I have a few things for you in my truck, Harper. Why don't we grab them really quick?" Clara said as she stood. "You boys can handle the kids for a few minutes, can't you?" Clara didn't wait for a response before she grabbed Harper's arm and pulled her from the house. Once they were on the far side of the truck, out of view of the house, Clara pulled Harper into a hug.

Carter watched Harper fight back tears until she sent Clara a text and Clara pulled her from the house. What just happened?

"Was I the only one who saw Clara and Harper having a private conversation before they left?" Tank drawled.

"Nope." Devon sat back in his chair.

"Mommy was crying a lot upstairs. She said she didn't want you to know yet and asked the doctor lady not to say anything." Lexi shrugged as she took her last bite of her chicken nuggets.

"Why was your mommy crying?" Jeff asked.

"I don't know. I was watching a movie." Lexi climbed off her chair and started petting Casper. "But she made a phone call and talked about him and my brother."

Carter digested what Lexi said. Harper made a phone call and talked about Luther, now she was upset and keeping secrets. He didn't like the thought of Harper not trusting him. She had been pretty open with him from the start. What would she feel the need to keep from him?

Clara walked back in and took her seat, but Harper didn't appear. "Where's Harper?" Carter asked as he looked over at the kitchen door, half expecting Harper to be walking in.

"She is in her room. She needed a few minutes to herself." Clara said calmly.

"What is wrong with her?" Devon asked.

"She experienced a bit of a shock and is needing some time to process." Clara said to her brother.

"Lexi said she was on the phone." Jeff probed.

Clara sat back in her chair and eyed each of them in turn. "I am Harper's doctor and can't discuss a patient's health with anyone."

"Really? Doctor-patient confidentiality?" Devon glared at his sister.

"That and as her friend, I won't be breaking her confidence. You will just have to wait until she is ready to share her news with you." Clara glared right back. Silence fell around the table again.

"Is she pregnant?" Tank asked, causing Carter's stomach to clench uncomfortably.

Clara blinked several times before her brows drew together. "I can't confirm nor deny that. I told you; I can't discuss my patient's health."

Did that mean yes? Somehow that didn't sound right to Carter. He scooted his chair back from the table and rose. He cleared his dishes, but instead of going to the front room, he made a peanut butter and jelly sandwich. Without a word to the others, he climbed the stairs and knocked on Harper's bedroom door. To his relief the door cracked open. But Harper's tear-streaked face had him tongue tied.

"Was there something you needed, Carter?" Her voice sounded so tired.

"You didn't eat much at dinner, I figured you might want a sandwich." Harper's gaze dropped to the plate in his hands.

Several heartbeats later, she uncrossed her arms and accepted the offering. "Thank you." She whispered as her phone dinged. She hurried back to the bed, setting the plate down on the nightstand and picked up her phone with shaky hands.

She had left the door open, but Carter couldn't bring himself to step into the room without her inviting him. He stood there and watched her slowly sit on the edge of the bed with one hand covering her mouth, eyes glued to the phone.

"Harper?" he asked softly. He was desperate to comfort her, but he would respect it if she wanted space.

Her eyes met his and he saw her vulnerability and hesitation before she gave a small nod. He moved to the bed and sat down next to her. As soon as his arm was around her shoulders, she leaned into him. She didn't say anything as she took slow deep breaths. She clutched the phone tightly as she struggled for control.

Harper was a mess. And for some reason, Carter's presence made her feel more in control. She needed him and that thought terrified her, but she wasn't strong enough to push him away at the moment. Bethany had sent her three pictures of Bo and each one tore at her. She wanted to be there with him, but both Bethany and Clara were right, she couldn't. The hospital was in lockdown due to sickness. All she could do was sit and wait to see if her son would live for another day. She prayed he would.

"Carter?" Harper finally broke the silence.

"Yes?"

"Are you still an active member of the church?" She desperately needed the Lord's help right now.

"I am." Carter looked down at her.

Nervousness and doubt caused her to pause. She had skipped church for a while before Luther had fully forbidden it. Would God even care about her since she had pulled away from Him first? She chewed her bottom lip as she considered what to do next. It wouldn't hurt to try. If He was too busy for her, that would be okay. At least she knew He was helping Bo.

"Can I get a blessing?" Harper asked. Carter was quiet for a few seconds.

"What kind of blessing are you wanting?" He quietly asked.

"Comfort and counsel."

"Who would you like to perform the blessing? All of us are able to." His question made her think.

Who did she want to give her a blessing? She looked up at him and their eyes met. "Will you give me the blessing?" Carter nodded and stood. He asked for her full name. "Harper Nicole Anderson." She supplied. At his raised brow she explained. "Luther didn't want me to take his name. He said there was no need to." Carter nodded and stepped close to her.

Peace. That was what Harper would describe the feeling that washed over her as Carter placed his hands on her head. The blessing was everything she needed. The blessing told her that as she rebuilt her faith, her family would be made whole again. She was told that He was mindful of her situation and if she continued to listen to the promptings of the spirit, she would remain safe. She was counseled to allow those around her to help her during this difficult time. And she was reminded she wasn't alone and the He and many others loved her. When the blessing closed, both Harper and Carter remained still for a moment.

Carter slowly removed his hands from her head and sat back down beside her. She immediately leaned her head against his shoulder and closed her eyes. "Thank you, Carter."

"Anytime, Dove." He whispered as he slipped his arm around her waist.

A noise at the door caused Harper to open her eyes. Clara stood there with Colt in her arms. "How are you feeling?" she asked as she walked over to Harper.

"Better." She sighed as she reached for Colt.

"His diaper is full, and he was beginning to fuss as he rooted." Clara explained. Harper started to stand, but Carter stopped her.

"Why don't I change him while you lay down. You look exhausted, Harper." Carter said as he stood and then held out his hands for the baby.

"But I'm just going to have to feed him when his diaper is changed." She protested.

"And I will bring him right back to you when I am done changing his diaper." Harper relented and Carter carried the baby over to the changing table.

"Jeff and Tank are watching Frozen with Lexi. When the movie is over, they will bring her up to bed. I need to head out, my hubby and kids are wondering where I am." Clara gave Harper a reassuring smile. "If you need anything, call or text. I'll check on you in the morning, regardless."

"I will and thank you, Clara." Harper said as she laid down. "For everything."

After Clara left, Harper closed her eyes. Exhaustion pulled at her, but she fought it. She needed to feed Colt before she could allow herself to sleep. A warm hand on her cheek had her opening her eyes. Carter stood over her with an apologetic smile. She shifted into a sitting position and Carter passed the baby over to her.

"Would you like me to stay or go?" he asked as he tucked his hands in the front pockets of his jeans.

"If you hand me the blanket from the crib, you can stay." Carter handed her the blanket and she covered herself with it before she started to nurse Colt.

"You look exhausted. What can I do to help?" Carter asked as he took a seat in the rocking chair. He was now sitting slightly behind her, and it made her smile. He was giving her space without leaving her alone.

"I'm not sure there is anything anyone can do." Harper yawned.

They fell into a comfortable silence while Colt finished eating. He ate for a good thirty minutes, and Harper could hardly keep her eyes open. After pulling her shirt back down and placing the blanket off to the side, Harper raised Colt to her shoulder to burp him. Carter rose from the chair and came to stand next to her again.

"Let me burp him while you lay back down." Carter offered. Harper looked up into his eyes with uncertainty. "I am actually really good with babies, despite how I acted in my younger years." He smiled at her. "When he is done, I'll put him in his bed. Lexi will be up here soon."

"But what about..." Harper started to object but he cut her off.

"I will be in the next room over and two of the guys are down the hall. Devon is patrolling the outside of the house with a couple ranch hands tonight." Carter said as he lifted Colt from her arms and settled the baby against his shoulder. "You need rest."

Harper nodded and laid back down. She faced the rocking chair and watched as Carter settled himself into it. He patted Colt's tiny back with his large hand as he gently rocked. Harper closed her eyes. She hadn't thought Carter could look any more handsome, but he definitely raised the bar sitting there with a baby in his arms. He still had his thick dark brown hair and his chocolate brown eyes that she loved. He was taller and his youthful appearance had morphed into a man with a chiseled jaw, muscles and facial hair that gave him a rugged look. She couldn't help liking what she saw. Harper fell asleep chastising herself for not having more control over her heart.

Carter finished burping Colt and changed his diaper again before laying him in the crib. He grabbed his scriptures off the nightstand and sat back in the rocking chair. He would stay with Harper until Lexi came to bed. He opened the book and immediately saw a scrap of paper as a bookmark. He glanced over at Harper and wondered if she had placed it there. He flipped forward until he got to the place he had left off and began to read.

The door creaked open, and Lexi came in with Tank right behind her. Carter gave Tank a nod and he left Carter to tuck Lexi in. When she saw her mother already asleep, she frowned. The little girl turned to Carter with pouty lips, and he tried his best not to smile. "Mommy always helps me pray before bed."

"If you want, I can help you." Carter kept his voice down, so they didn't wake Harper.

After a moment to think about it, Lexi nodded. Carter knelt next to the bed and listened as the four-year-old thanked God for keeping them safe and finding new friends. She asked that they could continue to be protected and that her mommy could be happy. When she closed her prayer, she climbed into the bed. Carter tucked the blanket around her and started to stand.

"What about goodnight kisses?" Lexi protested. "Mommy always kisses me good night and says she loves me."

Carter leaned down and pressed a kiss to Lexi's head. "Goodnight, Lexi." Seeing she was about to protest again, he winked at her. "I love you, kiddo." The smile that spread on her face was radiant and he found that he meant every word. He had known her for only twenty-four hours, but he loved Lexi and Colt. He was almost to the door when Lexi called out to him.

"What about Mommy?" She asked.

"Your mommy is asleep. And you should try to sleep as well, Lexi." Carter looked back over at the bed.

Lexi was sitting up and staring at him. "But she needs goodnight kisses, too." The girl had a determined look in her eyes. He knew that look.

Harper had given him that look many times while they were growing up, and there was no getting away from it.

He crossed back to the bed and leaned down. Just before his lips touched Harper's forehead, he looked back over at Lexi who was smiling. She saw his hesitation and offered him an encouraging nod. When he kissed Harper's forehead, he lingered a little longer than he had with Lexi. "Goodnight, Dove." He whispered. In his mind he added, "I love you, Harper."

Lexi did not push him to say the last part out loud, which he was grateful for. He knew he loved her but didn't want to say it out loud just yet. As he left the room, Carter flipped the light off and closed the door. He entered his new room and sat on the bed. The bed was a normal twin, but too small for his large size. He had slept in worse while overseas. What he really wanted was to be in his bed with Harper.

He let out a groan. He needed to get his head on straight. Harper wasn't in a position to start a relationship, and he knew it. He understood. She had been abused for five years. No way would she want to start something new right now. He needed to keep his distance from her until he could control himself better.

# Chapter 6

Harper woke to the sound of Lexi playing peekaboo with Colt. She smiled as she watched her kids play. Colt had woken up every two hours during the night, but she felt like she had actually gotten some sleep.

"Good morning." She pulled Lexi into a hug and kissed her cheek. "Shall we get dressed and go down for breakfast?"

Lexi clapped and quickly got changed into her new horse shirt. Harper fed, changed, and dressed Colt before looking through her duffle bag. She had no clean shirts. Every last one, including the one she was wearing, had spit up all over them. She grabbed her phone and sent a text to Carter.

**Harper:** Can I do some laundry today?

**Carter:** Of course, Dove.

**Carter:** Jeff is at the house today. Just let him know and he can show you where everything is.

**Harper**: Okay. Thank you.

Harper chewed on her lip. What was she going to do in the meantime? The three shirts she brought had spit up all over them, and they smelled horrible.

**Harper:** Can I borrow something?

**Carter:** Go ahead, Dove. Whatever you need.

**Harper:** Thank you.

Harper tossed the phone on the bed and walked to the dresser. She started pulling open drawers looking for a T-shirt but found none. Next, she moved to the closet. T-shirts hung on the left side and were arranged by color. The center had his coats. On the right side hung several button-down shirts. She never would have pictured Carter to be so organized. As a kid, his room was always messy. He called it organized chaos.

"Watch doing, mommy?" Lexi asked, coming to her side.

"Colt got all mommy's shirts dirty, so I need to borrow one of Carter's until I can wash mine." Harper explained as she looked through the T-shirts. She pulled one off its hanger and held it up to her. "What do you think?"

"No, I like this one." Lexi tugged on a blue plaid button-down shirt.

Harper rehung the plain black T-shirt and grabbed the shirt Lexi liked. It didn't make a difference to her. Carter was a lot bigger than her own five-foot four-inch petite figure. No matter what she wore, she was going to drown in it. She pulled on her last pair of maternity jeans and Carter's shirt before putting her hair in a messy bun. She rolled the sleeves up to her elbows before she picked up Colt and they headed downstairs.

The house was quiet as they entered the kitchen. Harper set Colt down in the bassinet before rummaging through the cabinets. "What should we make for breakfast?" She asked Lexi.

"Pancakes." Lexi pushed a chair up to the counter. "Can I help make them?"

"Of course you can, baby girl." Harper pulled out everything they would need for pancakes. "Music or no music?"

Lexi brightened at the mention of music, so Harper downloaded an app on her phone and turned on some country music. The two of them got to work making breakfast. Lexi insisted on pouring the ingredients in the bowl which resulted in flour everywhere. Because of Lexi's excitement, the amount of batter ended up being much more than Harper had intended. With the number of pancakes they were making, they could feed an army.

They were laughing and singing when a throat cleared. "Something smells good." Jeff said from the doorway. When he saw the state of the kitchen and Lexi covered in flour, he laughed. "Well, little chef, you sure know how to get into your work."

"We made pancakes." Lexi said proudly.

"I see that. Are we feeding the horses the pancakes, too?" Jeff asked with a straight face.

"Horses don't eat pancakes." Lexi giggled.

Harper listened to the playful banter as she flipped the pancakes on the stove. While she waited for them to finish cooking, Harper found a pad of paper and a pen in a drawer. She started writing a list of things she needed, starting with burp rags and clothing for herself.

"How can I help?" Jeff asked beside her. "Need to go into town?" He gestured towards her list.

"If we can go to town today, that would be great. I only have three shirts and Colt is the spit up king. Speaking of which, I need to do laundry today. I texted Carter and he said you could show me where everything is." Harper jotted down a few things she needed for some meals she planned to make.

"That explains you wearing Carter's shirt." Jeff smiled at her, and her cheeks flushed. "I used the last of the laundry soap yesterday, so we will need to pick some up. I can finish up here if you want to run out to the barn to see if Tank and the others want any food."

Harper nodded and headed for the door. As she stepped out onto the porch, a light breeze blew, and she took a deep breath. She loved the fresh air the countryside provided. Harper enjoyed the feel of the grass on her bare feet as she walked towards the barn. She entered the large structure and a smile spread on her face. Stalls lined both walls and almost all had a horse in them. A large black horse stuck his head over the stall door as she made her way down the aisle. She stopped to greet him.

A metal nameplate was on the door and her breath caught. Mozart. The horse was named Mozart? That was the name she had always wanted to name her horse, whenever she could get one. She ran her hand down the solid black head of her dream horse as he sniffed her other hand. She rested her forehead against his for a moment, before shifting slightly to the side so she could run her hand over his sleek neck. Friesians were gorgeous creatures and Mozart was no exception.

"He doesn't like most people." A deep voice sounded from right behind her.

Harper whirled around to see Tank and Casper. "He is a beauty. I had always dreamed of owning a Friesian when I was younger." Harper turned back to Mozart with longing.

"I'm surprised he even let you touch him. Henry was the only one to be able to ride him. Carter has only been able to lead Mozart out to the pasture." Tank gave her a small smile. "I'm glad you are out here; I want to show you something."

Harper gave Mozart one more pat before following Tank to the back of the barn. She blinked in surprise. There were at least twenty kennels with a dog in each one. The breeds ranged from German Shepherds to Collies to beagles.

"I thought you only had Casper?" Harper said as she walked up to a fence and a Border Collie licked her fingers.

"No, I train dogs for all sorts of things. Casper is retired military and we served together for a few years." Tank explained. "I want to assign a dog to both you and Lexi. They are trained in personal protection. I want Bella to be Lexi's guardian." He pointed at a Pitbull a few cages down. "Whenever Lexi leaves the house, Bella will be by her side, if you are okay with it."

Harper moved down the cages to get a better look at Bella. Tank opened the gate and Bella came to her with her tail wagging. The dog certainly has a great temperament. After her blessing, Harper knew she could trust the men she was staying with, and she trusted Tank's knowledge. "That would definitely put my mind at ease." Harper smiled as she rubbed Bella's head.

"For you, I was thinking Raider would do nicely." Tank moved to the end and opened another gate.

A large Doberman exited the cage and approached her. Harper raised her brows. "I thought Bella was for both me and Lexi?" she asked as she crouched down to Raider's level. He had his ears and tail docked, which gave him an intimidating appearance, but his tail was wagging as he licked her face.

"Bella has a mothering instinct, which makes her ideal for kids. She will stay on the porch so if Lexi leaves the house, Bella is there. When Devon's nephew was here a month ago, she kept him away from the lake and other dangerous areas, but she hates being inside." Harper nodded her understanding. "Raider will be with you all the time. If anyone tries to touch you, he will step in. He will also protect Lexi and Colt."

Tears stung her eyes as she looked back at Tank. "Thank you, Tank." He nodded and she gave him a smile. She turned her attention back to Raider and Bella as her phone buzzed. She pulled it out of her pocket and read the message.

**Jeff:** If I don't hear back from you in two minutes I'm sending out for the cavalry.

**Harper:** Got distracted by Mozart. I'm with Tank and the dogs. Heading back to the house in a minute.

"So, I originally came out here to see if you wanted pancakes." Harper said as she tucked her phone back into her pocket.

"Sounds good to me." Tank gestured for her to lead the way.

As she walked, Raider walked next to her while Bella trotted behind her. Just like Tank said, Bella laid on the porch while Raider walked inside with her. Tank gave a low whistled when he saw the massive tower of pancakes. Lexi was excited to see Raider and it took several minutes to get her to settle back down at the table to eat.

\*    \*    \*

Carter was rounding up some of the cattle in the south pasture when his phone buzzed. Harper was asking to do laundry and to borrow some things. He ignored the way his heart sped up just seeing her name on the screen and sent back quick replies so he could get back to his chores. He had been up for hours, and the sun was warm. Sweat rolled down his back as he rode through the field. Less than an hour later his phone buzzed again. He pulled back on the reins, slowing his horse, Ranger, to a walk as he pulled his phone from the belt clip. A text from Jeff.

He opened it and blinked. Harper was wearing one of Carter's button-down shirts with the sleeves rolled up to her elbows. Her hair was pulled up in a messy updo and all her attention was on Lexi, who sat on the counter next to her. They were looking at each other with flour on their cheeks and laughing.

Carter's heart skipped a beat at the sight. She was absolutely beautiful. If Carter had any doubt that his heart belonged to Harper, this image solidified it. He was truly in love with Harper Anderson. A shout from one of the ranch hands pulled his attention back to the task at hand, and he quickly put his phone away.

He caught up to the herd and was barely getting that image of Harper and Lexi out of his mind when his phone buzzed again. This time it was a text from Tank. Opening it, Carter was met with another image of Harper. This one was in the barn. She was still in his shirt as she stood before Mozart with her forehead on his. She had one knee bent slightly and he noticed she was barefoot. Another message came in.

**Tank:** Thought you might enjoy the view from the barn this morning.

Carter wished his friends didn't know that he had feelings for Harper. It would make keeping his distance easier. He doubted they would have sent those pictures if they didn't know that he liked her. He took a moment to save both images to his phone before putting it away. He volunteered to move the cattle today in order to put distance between him and Harper. He needed to focus on what he was doing, not on the woman he loved but who was out of his reach.

The morning and afternoon dragged on as the images of Harper wearing his shirt kept resurfacing. Seeing her like that had caused him to feel a little possessive. He had to keep telling himself that she was not his. He grew irritable as the day continued to tick by at a snail's pace. When they finally got the cattle settled in the west field and made it back to the barn, the sun was setting.

He was tired and dirty as he entered the house. Voices came from the kitchen, but instead of joining them, Carter headed up to shower. He entered his room and closed the door behind him. A startled squeak had his head snapping up. Harper stood there in a pair of jeans and a bra. He blinked in surprise before his brain registered what he was seeing. He spun around so his back was facing her. His cheeks heated with embarrassment.

"I am so sorry, Harper. I wasn't thinking." He apologized quickly. He heard her moving around behind him.

"You can look now." Harper said softly.

Slowly Carter turned back around. She had put back on the shirt she had been wearing in the pictures. His mouth felt a little dry as he looked at her. She was even more beautiful in person. Her cheeks were flushed, and she dropped her gaze as soon as their eyes met.

"I'm so sorry, I should have remembered to knock before coming in." he said as he stuck his hands in the pockets of his jeans.

"No, it was my fault. I should have locked the door before changing." Harper shook her head and then started gathering up several items of clothing off the rocking chair.

"Were you able to get your laundry done?" He asked in an effort to change the subject.

Harper paused her gathering and looked at him. "No, Jeff used the last of the detergent yesterday. After breakfast we went to the store and picked up a few things so that I could do laundry tomorrow. And some more shirts so I wouldn't have to steal your clothes when my old ones are dirty."

"You went to the store?" That caught Carter's attention. They hadn't discussed security for Harper off the ranch.

"Don't worry, Tank and Jeff were with me and the kids. We also had Raider and Casper with us." Harper pointed to the floor at her feet and Carter saw the Doberman laying there for the first time.

The tension that had been building in his muscles relaxed as he realized she and the kids were well protected. He took a few steps forward, even though his brain told him to leave. He picked up one of the shirts from the rocking chair. "This is cute." He said as he looked at the shirt. No doubt the cut of the garment would flatter Harper's figure.

"That's what Jeff said, too. Well, to be fair, he said it about most of the shirts he picked out." Harper shrugged, unaware of the jealous feelings coursing through him. He was tempted to march downstairs and punch Jeff in the face for calling his Harper cute.

His Harper. There were his possessive thoughts again. Harper did not belong to him. "Is that okay?" Harper's question had him snapping back to the present. He had no idea what she was asking.

"I'm sorry, Harper. I missed what you said." He gave her a small smile as he ran a hand through his hair.

"I still need to wash my new clothes. Would it be okay if I borrowed another shirt or two until I'm able to do laundry?" Harper blushed, which only fueled his desire to pull her into his arms.

"That's fine." He managed to say. "You are welcome to use anything you need." He swallowed hard. He could easily wrap his arms around her and pull her close. His eyes dipped to her lips against his will, before moving back to her eyes again. He cleared his throat. "If it's okay, I'm going to jump in the shower before dinner."

Harper nodded and watched Carter walk into the bathroom. He closed the door and she let out a tense breath. Something was bothering Carter. He seemed distracted and tense when he came in. They both had been surprised to see each other, especially with her half-dressed. But Carter had been a gentleman and turned around. Maybe that was the problem, he was mad that he had to share his space with her and the kids.

Harper collected her new clothes and put them with her dirty ones, before walking out of the room. She made sure to close the door behind her as she walked downstairs. Before reaching the kitchen, her phone buzzed. She pulled it from her pocket to read the text.

**Bethany:** Just got an update on Luther. Call me.

This didn't sound good. Instead of going into the kitchen, she walked out to the barn for a little privacy. Raider was glued to her side the whole time and she loved the feeling of having him nearby. After checking to make sure she was alone, Harper entered Mozart's stall with a brush while Raider laid down just on the other side of the door.

She dialed Bethany and waited. "This is Bethany Black." Beth answered.

"Hey, Beth." Harper said as she ran the brush over Mozart's back.

"Harper, thank goodness. Are you still in a safe place? Are the kids okay?" Bethany sounded upset.

"We're fine. What's going on?" Harper's anxiety rose with Bethany's obvious worry. Beth was always so calm and collected.

"The Wyoming police are working with the Colorado authorities in looking for Luther. The men that helped you told the police that Luther tried to kidnap you, and then he tried to stab one of them. Those charges are being added to the list that Luther already has. Unfortunately, they were not able to find him after he was kicked off the ranch." Bethany informed Harper.

"I'm glad the police are working together. I hope he gets picked up soon." Harper continued to brush the horse's shoulder. "Your text made it sound like something urgent was discovered."

"The police looked at your car and found that the brakes were cut. They also found Luther's car five miles from the ranch. Inside was a note." Bethany paused.

"What kind of note?" Harper's stomach filled with dread as her brushing movements stilled.

"It was a murder-suicide letter signed by you." Beth said slowly.

"What?" Harper could hardly breathe.

"I don't know exactly what it said, but Officer Morgan said the letter outlined that you couldn't keep the kids anymore, that it was too much. The note apologized to Luther for putting him through so much over the last several years and that you were sorry. It was signed, 'I love you Luther, Forgive me'." Bethany explained.

"I would never." Harper said quickly.

"Oh, we know. Especially after all the domestic violence reports on file. The police think Luther was planning on killing all of you and leaving the note to explain what happened. Bethany paused again. "I have to be in court in a few minutes, but I felt you needed to know the extent Luther is willing to go."

"Thank you for telling me, Beth." Harper's voice was small as she tried to process everything.

"You're welcome, sweetie. Stay safe." Bethany said before hanging up.

Luther was planning to kill her? And her brakes were cut? Did Luther cut her brakes? Had he hoped she and the kids would die in a car accident? Harper sent up a prayer of gratitude for the Lord helping to keep them safe that night, and for leading her to Carter and the others. If she hadn't found them, Harper wasn't sure she would still be alive. Luther had gone off the deep end, and that scared her even more.

Harper heard her phone buzz several times, but she didn't look at it. She needed a few more minutes to herself. She started brushing Mozart again and the repetitive motion calmed her racing heart and mind.

A while later, Raider growled and Harper heard approaching footsteps. "Hey boy, where's our girl?" Tank said, but Raider continued to growl.

"I think you trained him too well, Tank." Carter commented quietly. "Harper?" He called a little louder.

Harper took a deep breath and opened the stall door. Raider positioned himself in between her and the two men. "Stand down, Raider." She said as she patted the dog's head, and he looked up at her. "What do you gentlemen need?"

"Is everything okay?" Carter asked. "You weren't answering our texts."

"I'm just peachy, Carter." Harper snapped. She knew none of this was his fault, but she was angry. Angry at Luther for everything he had done to her and the kids. Angry she couldn't be there for Bo. Angry, she missed her brother's funeral. And angry at herself because all of this was her fault.

"You don't sound 'peachy'." Tank furrowed his brows as he studied her.

Harper nearly laughed at Tank's inability to recognize her sarcasm, but Carter caught it. Her eyes burned as she turned her back on them so they wouldn't see her angry tears. Mozart stuck his head over the stall door, and she ran her hand down his face. She hated that she cried when she was angry.

"She's all yours." Tank whispered and she heard his retreating footsteps.

When the barn was once again quiet except for the occasional shifting of horses, Carter spoke. "Angry tears?" he asked softly.

A laugh escaped at the same time the dam on her tears broke. Harper squeezed her eyes shut in a vain attempt to stop them. A hand cupped her cheek, and she opened her eyes to see Carter standing in front of her. His chocolate brown eyes were filled with concern as he studied her face. He gently wiped her tears with his thumb.

"Please don't cry, Dove." His voice was soft and comforting. Harper leaned into his touch. Carter put his other hand on her hip and used it to pull her to him.

Harper rested her head on Carter's chest as he held her. As she stood there, her anger started to fade, and she relaxed against him. After taking several deep breaths, Harper leaned back so she could see Carter's face. He had been her rock when they were children, and he was her rock now. Without thinking, Harper raised up on her toes and pressed her lips to his. At first, he didn't respond, but then he cupped the back of her neck and kissed her back.

Warmth spread through her, and her heart thundered in her ears. The kiss was soft and sweet. He allowed her to have the lead. Slowly she drew back, ending the kiss. Carter watched her with an unreadable expression. That's when she realized what she had done. She just kissed her brother's best friend, her friend. She blinked several times as she took a step back. What had she done? She didn't even know why she did it. She had promised herself she was going to keep her distance. She had kissed him without thinking.

"I'm so sorry." She breathed out as she dropped her gaze to the ground. She didn't want to see Carter's reaction to her kiss. She was afraid she would see pity in his gorgeous brown eyes. "I don't…I shouldn't have…" Harper stammered out as she continued to back away.

Harper turned and ran. As she stepped out into the fading sunlight, she wrapped her arms around herself as she tried to make sense of what she had been thinking. She looked at the house, but couldn't bring herself to go in. Glancing back at the barn, she knew she couldn't go back in there. Looking around her, Harper spotted a path that led around the edge of the house.

Not wanting Carter to catch up to her, Harper took the path and followed it. On the other side of the house, the trail led her into the woods. Raider trotted alongside her with his head held high. The farther she walked, the more guilt she felt over the kiss.

She hadn't even thought about it. It felt so natural to be in his arms and to kiss him. Which was insane because she just got out of an abusive marriage, and she had not seen Carter in over ten years.

Luther had stopped trying to have any affectionate contact with her two months into their marriage. It was the moment he came back home after being gone for three days; which looking back, was a blessing.

The path came to an end at a cemetery and her steps faltered. There weren't many headstones, and she slowly walked through them, reading each one. She stopped when she read: Henry Robert Anderson. She dropped to her knees before her brother's grave and wept. She had no idea her brother was buried here.

Harper didn't know how much time had passed as she sat there. Her phone buzzed and she pulled it out of her pocket as she wiped her cheeks. She ignored the five texts from earlier and read the newest one.

**Tank:** Where are you?

**Harper:** Safe.

Harper repositioned herself on the grass, so she was sitting crossed legged. She thought of her brother and the man he had been. "I miss you." She whispered. "We were wrong, you know. Luther was more of a wolf in sheep's clothing instead of my knight in shining armor." Her phone buzzed again, and she looked at it.

**Devon:** Tank said he left you in the barn with Carter. Carter said you headed back to the house thirty minutes ago. Where are you?
**Harper:** I'm fine.
**Devon:** Not good enough. Location?
**Harper:** Pinedale, Wyoming.
**Devon:** More specific!
**Harper:** Henry River Ranch.

Harper set the phone down on the grass in front of her. Raider lay beside her with his tongue lolling out. She ran her hand over his side as she continued to talk with her brother. "I'm sorry I didn't keep in better contact with you. I should have found a way to send you a letter. The night you called shortly after Lexi was born, Luther was there, and I couldn't tell you what was going on. I should have been braver and reached out, but I was scared, Henry. I was so scared."

A breeze blew through the cemetery and Harper shivered. The days were getting colder. She scanned the trees before turning to look back at Henry's headstone. "I tried to be here. But by the time I woke up, it was too late." Raider licked her hand. "I think I did something stupid, Henry." She lowered her voice even more. "I kissed Carter. I don't know what I was thinking. Truth is I wasn't, and it just happened. And the worst part is, it was amazing." Her phone rang and she looked at the name. Carter. Of course it was Carter. She debated answering it, but decided to ignore it and sent him a text instead.

**Harper:** I'm busy!
**Carter:** From what Dev and Tank are saying, you are missing.
**Harper:** Exaggerations.
**Carter:** What's going on, Dove?

What was wrong? Harper took a deep breath and let it out slowly. They had just kissed. That is what was wrong. She knew she needed to tell them the latest about Luther, and she needed to face Carter. She could not hide from him forever.

**Carter:** Harper?
**Harper:** Give me an hour.
**Carter:** Where are you? I'll come get you.
**Harper:** Carter Michaels! What part of "give me an hour" did you not understand?
**Carter:** Colt is hungry.

Harper felt a stab of guilt. Her baby needed her. Both of her babies needed her. She just couldn't go back yet. She needed to find her equilibrium again.

**Harper:** Give him a bottle if he needs it.

**Harper:** Going silent.

**Carter:** Report every 15 minutes or these soldiers are going to suit up for a recovery mission.

**Harper:** Aye, aye Cap.

**Carter:** We aren't pirates, Dove.

Harper chuckled as she set a fifteen-minute timer on her phone. She couldn't help it. Carter could always coax a smile and laugh from her, even when she was furious with him. She leaned back on her hands and looked up to the sky. She was in so deep. Carter had been her first love and being with him again stirred up those old feelings.

"I don't know if you knew this, but I had the biggest crush on Carter when we were kids. I named my twin boys after the two men I loved most. Bowman Carter and Colton Henry." She looked back at her brother's grave. "Bo is still in the hospital. He wasn't expected to live because of the beating we took from Luther. I wish you could have met them, Henry. And Lexi. Carter has said multiple times how much she is like me, and we have only been here for a few days."

Harper sobered. "I know you probably don't want to hear about your little sister kissing your best friend, but I need someone to talk to, and you were always there for me before mom and dad's divorce. I need help sorting my thoughts. Kissing Luther never felt the way kissing Carter had. Luther's kisses were always demanding and possessive. With Carter it was soft and sweet. It always felt like Luther was taking from me. I had a hard time allowing him to kiss me. Looking back, I can see that I never really enjoyed his physical attention. Not even holding his hand. I think I was in love with the idea of having a good man in my life, and not actually in love with him." Harper's alarm went off and she picked up her phone.

**Harper:** Still alive

**Carter:** Telling the boys to put their guns away.

Harper reset the alarm. "I think I was still heartbroken over Carter not sharing my feelings that I latched onto the first decent man I could, even though I never felt comfortable with him. I was young and foolish, Henry. But I can't regret that I married him. If I hadn't, I wouldn't have Lexi, Bo, or Colt, and they mean everything to me." Raider yawned and Harper smiled. "I should probably get back to the house before the soldiers deploy." Harper got to her feet and looked down at Henry's grave. "I'll bring the kids by to see you soon. And Henry, keep an eye on Bo for me." She blew her brother a kiss before heading back to the path that led back to the house.

The sun had set, and the air was cool. She shivered as she quickened her steps. Harper hadn't realized how long it had taken her to reach the cemetery. She was just stepping out of the trees when her alarm went off again. She silenced it but didn't feel the need to send Carter a text to check in, since she was at the house.

She was just rounding the front of the house when the front door burst open, and four men stepped out onto the porch. They hadn't seen her yet since she was in the shadows.

Her brows rose in surprise when she saw they were in full tactical gear and armed. She could hear Tank's deep voice but couldn't make out the words as he spoke to Carter, Devon, and Jeff. Clara's truck was parked out front. Harper cautiously moved closer, not wanting to surprise them and get a bullet in her chest.

"I think you guys are being a bit ridiculous." Clara's voice came from the open front door.

"Carter warned her this would happen if she didn't check in." Jeff said matter-of-factly.

"She is going through a lot right now, not to mention coping with the abuse she has suffered for years. Give the girl a break, she probably needed some air." Clara shot back.

"It's dark and she doesn't know the land." Devon pointed out.

"She also has Raider to guide her home and protect her." Harper put in. Carter's head snapped in her direction and their eyes met.

"That's beside the point. Harper is family and we don't leave family to fend for themselves." Tank growled out.

"I agree with Harper, Raider is more than capable." Clara smiled.

Carter took a hesitant step towards her. Then another. When she didn't move away or stop him, he closed the distance between them and pulled her into his arms. "Where have you been?" He breathed out as he squeezed her.

"I went to see Henry." Harper responded, pulling away from him. She needed to keep her distance from him, even though she would have preferred staying in his embrace.

"What happened to you?" Devon asked, clearly frustrated with her. And her hackles rose. "You need to tell us where you are going."

She clenched her hands into fists as she tried to suppress her rising anger. She was not a child. She was a grown woman with children that depended on her. Sure, she was relying on them to keep her safe at the moment, but that didn't mean they could treat her like this. She wasn't fragile. She was a survivor.

Before she could say anything, Lexi burst through the door. "Mommy!" Harper crouched down and caught her daughter.

"Were you good while I was gone?" Harper asked, giving her daughter a smile.

"Uncle Jeff and Uncle Devon played Barbies with me." Lexi smiled at Harper. "Now that you are home, can we eat? I'm hungry."

"Of course, sweetheart." Harper stood back up and held Lexi's hand.

"What are you wearing, Carter?" Lexi asked as she looked him up and down.

"They wanted to play soldiers and dressed up." Harper explained while shooting them a glare. "Let's head inside, it's getting cold out here."

Harper gave Clara a hug in greeting as she walked in. She closed the door behind her, shutting the men out on the porch. The two of them walked into the kitchen where mac and cheese sat on the stove. Clara started to dish up a bowl for Lexi while Harper walked to the bassinet.

"And how was my handsome boy?" Harper cooed as she picked up Colt. She snuggled him close and pressed a kiss to his cheek.

"You had the men worried. First, you disappeared after Carter got home, and then you weren't here when he came back from the barn." Clara said quietly.

"I know. I got a call from Bethany and needed to work through some things." Harper whispered back.

Clara turned to face Harper with raised brows. She mouthed: Bo? Harper shook her head as the men came into the room and sat at the table. "I gave Colt a pacifier, which seemed to satisfy him while you were gone, so don't be surprised if he starts demanding food soon." Clara spoke in her normal voice.

Harper nodded as she continued to snuggle Colt. She couldn't wait to be able to hold Bo again. They will be a week-old tomorrow. While the others started to eat, Harper swayed and whispered in Colt's ear. She wasn't ready to face Carter and the others just yet. Her anger was still close to the surface and Lexi didn't need to see her yelling.

"Are you mad at my mom?" Lexi asked and Harper looked over at the table. Lexi was looking from one person to the next with furrowed brows.

"No, princess. We aren't mad at your mom." Tank said gently.

"Then why were you yelling about her?" Lexi looked confused. "He would always yell about her."

"We were worried about her, that's all. Sometimes when people worry, they are loud." Jeff said as he smiled at Lexi.

"Were you worried because Bethany called? Mommy usually is worried after talking with Beth." Harper's mouth dropped. Lexi picked up more than Harper thought she did. All eyes turned to her, and she quickly looked away.

"I'm going into the other room to feed Colt." She muttered as she walked from the room.

Harper settled on the couch in her usual place and used the throw blanket as a cover so she could feed Colt. He eagerly nursed, making all sorts of noises. Harper closed her eyes as her thoughts turned back to the phone call with Beth. How had she forgotten about that? Luther appeared desperate enough to want to kill her and the kids, but she had been worried about a kiss. The couch cushion shifted as someone sat beside her and she knew it was Carter.

"Want to talk about it?" he asked softly. Harper opened her eyes and turned her head to look at him. There was no hint of how he felt about the kiss. And why would he want to talk about the kiss in the living room where anyone could overhear them? "Is this Bethany the same person you talked to last night when you were upset?"

Of course, he was talking about the phone calls. He was probably trying to forget their kiss ever happened so that it wouldn't ruin their friendship. Well, if he could do that, so could she. The kiss never happened. "Not yet, Carter. Not until Lexi is asleep." She whispered and he nodded in understanding.

Not long after Carter sat down, the rest of the gang joined them. Since Harper was back, Clara left to go home. She had stopped by to check on Harper, and Devon asked her to stay to babysit until she came home. Harper was quieter than normal tonight. And Carter wondered if it was the phone call with Bethany or if it was the kiss that had caused her to pull away from them. She had only been with them for two days, but at the same time, it felt like she had always been there.

His mind strayed back to the barn as Tank put on Tangled for Lexi to watch. Harper had been ignoring their texts, so he and Tank went to the barn to see if she was there. They had spotted Raider next to Mozart's stall. As they approached, the dog had taken a defensive stance. Carter had been pleased and frustrated with the dog's protectiveness. But when Harper had stepped from the stall, he knew why the dog was acting so protectively. Something had Harper upset.

She had been angry. It was written all over her face and in her tone. Tank sensed it too, and bailed, leaving Carter to try to defuse the situation. When he had seen her eyes well up with tears just before she turned her back to him, he knew she was furious. As a kid, whenever Harper was angry, she would often cry. She hated it that she cried when she was angry, but Carter had always found it cute. Now, it broke his heart.

She leaned into him as he tried to comfort her. And then she kissed him. He had been surprised at first, but then he had allowed himself to enjoy it. He didn't want to push her, so he allowed her to lead. Warmth had spread through him, and he was even more lost to her. When she pulled back, he was still reeling from the sensation of her lips on his. She got a panicked look in her eyes as she backed away from him. It was like a bucket of ice water had been dumped on his head. By the time he came to his senses, Harper was gone.

He figured she had gone back to the house, so he texted Devon to meet him at the barn. He told Devon what had happened. Carter wished he could have done something to turn back time. Maybe he could have done something different so that Harper didn't feel so upset.

That kiss had been amazing, and Carter didn't regret it. He only regretted how Harper had felt about it, that she had run. Devon suggested acting as if it didn't happen, unless Harper brought it up. He said that maybe Harper was confused and scared after what happened with Luther. And Carter could understand that. He would be patient and he would be there for her whenever she needed him.

The movie ended and Lexi was asleep on the floor. "Would you like me to carry her upstairs for you?" Carter asked quietly.

"That would be great, thank you." Harper said as she stood. "Devon, could you hold Colt so I can tuck Lexi in?" Devon nodded and Harper followed Carter upstairs.

Carter laid Lexi carefully on the bed and took a step back to give Harper room. Harper sat on the edge of the bed and brushed the hair back from Lexi's face. "Lexi, baby." Harper whispered and Lexi's eyes fluttered open. "We need to say our prayers. Do you want to say it, or would you like me to?"

"I'll do it." Lexi yawned and sat up slowly before climbing into Harper's lap. Lexi's voice was soft as she prayed. "Please help mommy and

Carter to not be mad at each other anymore. And help my brother to be better." Carter's heart skipped at the little girl's words. She ended her prayer and Harper tucked her back into bed.

"Lexi, Carter and I aren't mad at each other." Harper whispered as she stroked Lexi's face.

"You don't hug anymore." Lexi complained and Carter knew his cheeks were probably as red as Harper's.

"Sweetheart, Carter only hugs me when I'm sad." Harper explained as the color in her cheeks deepened.

"So, him not hugging you means you are happy?" Lexi asked as her brows pinched together. "I don't like that."

"It's time for sleep." Harper leaned down and kissed Lexi's cheek. "I love you, baby girl."

"I love you too, mommy." Harper stood and started to walk to the door. Carter followed, but stopped when Lexi called after him. "Carter?"

He turned to face her. "Yes, Lexi?"

"Aren't you going to tuck me in, too?" Carter looked over at Harper who gave him a small shrug as she leaned against the wall by the door.

Carter knelt on the floor as he smiled at Lexi. "How am I supposed to tuck you in if your mom already did such a great job?" He whispered so only Lexi could hear him. Lexi pointed to her forehead, and he chuckled. He kissed her forehead. "Goodnight, Lexi. Love you, kiddo."

As he got to his feet, Lexi smiled at him. "Goodnight Carter. I love you too." Carter's heart stuttered as he watched Lexi roll over and close her eyes.

He swallowed hard as he watched her for a few more minutes. He finally looked over at the door to find Harper with tears in her eyes. He crossed over to her and she wiped her face. "I'm sorry." She whispered. "It's just, you are the first person, other than me and Colt, that she has said those words to." Harper wiped her eyes again and then walked from the room, leaving Carter to follow behind her.

By the time they reached the living room, Harper had pulled herself back together. She retook her seat and Carter sat next to her. He didn't know what to say about Harper's admission about Lexi, so he remained quiet. All eyes were on Harper, and she took a deep breath as if calming herself. He wanted to reach for her, but he promised himself that he would allow her to make the next move, not him.

"As Lexi said, I had a phone call with my lawyer, Bethany. Last night she told me the police were looking for Luther. He has multiple charges against him. Assault, breaking and entering, and attempted murder." She licked her lips before continuing. "Tonight, she gave me an update on things. Thanks to his appearance here, more charges have been added to him, and both police departments are working together to find him."

Harper looked over at Carter as she continued. "They found his car five miles from the ranch. Inside was a murder-suicide note."

"He's confessed to murdering someone?" Jeff sounded surprised.

"He's dead?" Tank asked at the same time.

"No, he's alive as far as we know." Harper turned to look at the others. "The note was made to look like I signed it." Silence. Harper took a deep breath. "According to the note, I hate my kids and felt such grief over ending things with Luther that I couldn't take it. I got rid of the 'problems' and begged for his forgiveness."

"That's a bunch of bull." Tank growled.

"Thankfully, the police think so too. I guess having over ten domestic violence charges in five years and a divorce made Luther look suspicious." Harper paused for a second before continuing. "And the police looked at my car."

"Your car? Why would the police look at your car again?" Carter asked.

"I'm not sure, but they found that the brakes were cut." Harper shrugged. "I don't understand. The brakes worked until a little after the summit coming down the mountain."

"Your brakes gave out on the mountain?" Jeff jumped to his feet. "I thought Carter found you in the wash?"

"I did." Carter stated.

Harper explained about her brakes not working and the car going through the guardrail. Carter grabbed her hand, unable to stop himself. He needed the contact to reassure himself that she was okay. "Honestly, I don't know how we didn't crash on the mountain. I think your fence and the field slowed us down enough that when we hit the wash, it wasn't as bad as it could have been."

"You could have been killed." Devon said angrily.

"I think that was the point." Carter muttered. "He had to have been following you from the start and cut the brakes at your last stop before heading up the mountain. If we can get footage of him doing it, that would be more evidence we can turn over to the police." Carter turned to look at Jeff.

"I'll see what I can find." Jeff nodded.

"I think we need to have an escort for you and the kids whenever you leave the house." Tank told Harper. "The dogs are nice, but Luther seems to be unstable and unstable people are hard to predict."

Harper nodded as she laid her head on Carter's shoulder. "Whatever you feel is necessary." she said quietly. "I can't risk him hurting the kids." With that, the men started splitting off to various tasks.

Jeff asked Harper about her route from Denver before leaving to see if he could find anything useful for the police. Carter let go of Harper's hand as Devon handed Colt to her before leaving to patrol the grounds. Tank went to the barn to feed the dogs and horses. Carter sat with Harper and Colt as he processed everything Harper had said. Luther was angry enough to kill Harper and the kids, but why?

"Harper, can you tell me about Luther?" Carter finally asked. He needed to know how the man's mind worked, so he could hopefully know what to expect when he tried again. Because Carter had no doubt that Luther would be back.

# Chapter 7

Harper looked over at Carter like he was crazy but did as he asked. "I met him within the first week of college. He asked me out, but I refused. I wasn't emotionally ready to date after…" She cleared her throat. Had someone broken her heart? He would ask her about it later. "I turned down several guys over the first several weeks, but my roommate finally convinced me to go out with a guy who had the courage to ask me out three times. He was nice, but not who I could see myself with. Luther tried again one Sunday at church. I had not seen him there before, but I wasn't very observant when it came to guys."

Carter again had to bite his tongue. Now was not the time to discuss her possible broken heart, he needed information on Luther. "I said yes. He took me to an animal shelter to volunteer to walk the dogs. At first, I was surprised because my first impression of Luther was that he was selfish and egotistical. The date went well. However, when he asked for a second date, I hesitated. I didn't want a relationship, but my roomie said to give him a shot, so I did. Whenever we were together, he was respectful and in tune with what I needed. He served at many charities, and we sat together at church. He was attentive and we had several deep gospel discussions." Harper shrugged.

"After four months, he asked me to marry him. My first reaction was a firm no, but he convinced me to think about it. Two days later, Henry came to visit. I introduced the two of them. Henry and I talked about the proposal. He said he knew something had happened to me to make me not want to fall in love, but Luther was a good man. He said he would support me either way. After Henry left, I went to return the ring. I felt like I was betraying someone if I accepted it. Long story short, Luther convinced me to give us a shot. During the three months of our engagement, Luther was extra attentive, and I began to believe that we could be happy together and I would eventually learn to love him like he loved me."

Harper ran her hand over Colt's head causing his small amount of hair to stand at crazy angles. "A few weeks after we were married, he accepted a job in Denver. I was so mad. He did not even talk with me about it. I told him I was in school, but he told me I could enroll in a school in Denver or online. So, we moved. A few weeks after that, I realized I couldn't do it anymore. I never felt comfortable with him. I wanted out. I asked for an annulment. He started planning more time together. I thought he was trying to convince me to give him more time. A month later, I found out I was pregnant. I was scared and alone in a city I didn't know. I needed someone to tell me everything was going to be okay. I went to Luther."

"What did he do when you told him?" Carter asked.

"He yelled and accused me of so many things, including cheating on him. He left the house and was gone for three days. During that time, I tried calling Henry, but the base said he was on a mission for the next several months." Harper took another deep breath. "I was beginning to realize that Luther wasn't the man I thought he was. When he returned, I was reading my scriptures. He took them from me, went to the fire pit in the backyard and set them on fire. I cried and he told me that he had proof I was cheating on him. He said that someone like me didn't need religion. Hell was the only place for a slut like me. He told me he knew that the child belonged to some military man. I guess he saw my calls to the base when I reached out to Henry."

"Didn't he know your brother was on base?" Carter asked.

"I don't think it mattered. After a few weeks of ignoring me, he started claiming that I purposely got pregnant and that I wasn't taking my birth control. He fluctuated between pretending I didn't exist and yelling at me. I did my best to keep my head down and not make him mad. He started bringing women home. He said he couldn't bear to touch me. Honestly, I was relieved he stopped trying. But sleeping with women while I was in the house, that was when I realized how wrong I was about him. I left, and stayed in a hotel until I could figure out what to do. He found me there and begged me to forgive him. He said the shock of the baby drove him to do things he normally wouldn't do. He asked if I was willing to go to counseling with him to save our family."

"So, you went back." Carter reached for her hand, and she squeezed his.

"I was scared at the prospect of being a mother, and the thought of being a single mother terrified me. I decided to give him a second chance. As soon as we got home, I started to notice little things. My cell phone went missing, and Luther replaced it with an old flip phone. I lost all my contacts, so I could not even call Henry. My laptop broke and I couldn't get it replaced.

My keys would go missing. I was so sick from the pregnancy that I didn't have the energy to go anywhere. I had to walk over to the neighbors when I went into labor because Luther didn't answer his phone. One of the nurses had to drop me and Lexi off at the house because I had no one to call."

"Luther never went to the hospital?" Carter asked and Harper shook her head.

"I had never seen him so angry as when I walked through the front door with Lexi. He asked why I didn't get rid of her and to take her back. When I refused…that was the first time he punched me. He threatened to take care of the 'thing' if I didn't keep it quiet. I locked myself in my room. I prayed that Lexi would be a quiet baby and that I would know how to be a mom. Lexi was such a quiet baby, and when she did cry, Luther was passed out or gone. Luther brought more women home. He became more…physical. The neighbors had made multiple calls to the police, but nothing changed. I was so ignorant of how the laws worked, and I didn't know I had options. I tried to leave a few times but stopped after he threatened to "sell" Lexi to some friends and make me watch." Carter squeezed her hand, and she squeezed back.

"I got the call about Henry. I hadn't talked with him since shortly after Lexi was born. Luther didn't seem to have an issue with me attending the funeral when I mentioned it. But when I tried to leave, he threw me against the wall and Lexi ran. When I woke up, I found Lexi in the closet, and we spent the next several days in my room. I started getting sick, and when Luther left for a meeting, I went to the nearest urgent care. I told them that my husband attacked me, and they documented it. A nurse gave me Bethany's number. After talking with her, we started gathering evidence. We were able to force a divorce and Luther was furious. The night the divorce was finalized, he broke into my apartment and attacked me. He kept saying that I was his and he would make me regret allowing another man to touch me."

"He thought your second pregnancy was because you cheated, too?" Carter asked in disbelief.

"Yes." Harper sighed as she leaned against the back of the couch. "Lexi screamed and a neighbor called the police. I was taken to the hospital. I went into labor in the ambulance."

They lapsed into silence for several minutes. When Carter was sure Harper was done talking, he stood and tugged her to her feet. "I'm sorry I had you relive all that, but I needed to know." He tucked some of her hair behind her ear. "Now that I know more about his character, we can know better how to anticipate his next move." Harper nodded, but she didn't raise her eyes to his. "Let's get you to bed. You have to be tired."

Carter held her hand all the way to her room. She gave him a tired smile before closing and locking the door. Carter let out a long breath as he pulled out his phone. He sent out a text to the guys telling them to meet in the living room in five minutes.

Carter paced the front room as the others took their seats. He didn't stop his movements as he began talking. "I talked to Harper about Luther. It seems that he may have targeted her before they met. She initially turned him down, but when he started exhibiting behavior she liked, she gave him a chance. It seems he might have manipulated their every encounter. Once married, he started isolating her. Moving to a different city and pulling her away from church. He accused her of cheating when she became pregnant. Pulling phone records as evidence."

"Was she cheating?" Tank asked dubiously.

"No, the number in question was to the base. It was all her phone calls to Henry." Carter explained. "He became controlling and possessive. She became pregnant again and forced a divorce. He attacked her and claimed she was his and no other man could have her."

"You're thinking we are dealing with a possessive stalker who lost his trophy." Jeff said thoughtfully.

"It's just a theory. She did say that her first impression was that Luther was selfish and egotistical." Carter turned to face the group.

"Seeing she wasn't giving him the time of day; he changed his behavior to match what she wanted." Devon shook his head. "As far as crazy stalkers go, he's smart. We can't underestimate him."

Over the next few hours, they discussed plans to keep Harper and the kids safe as well as finding Luther. The sooner he was behind bars, the sooner Harper could get on with a normal life.

# Chapter 8

Harper woke to an empty bed. She sat up and listened. She could hear Lexi's squeals and laughter coming through the open bedroom door. It had been five weeks since they had arrived on the ranch. After the first day when Luther came, there had been no other sign of him. Raider still stayed by her at all times, and whenever they went outside, Bella followed Lexi everywhere.

The household had fallen into a comfortable routine. Once a week, Harper and the kids visited Henry's grave. Carter had started teaching Lexi to ride on a pony. Harper received regular updates on Bo. She still hadn't told them about him, and she knew she would have to eventually, but she wasn't ready.

Yesterday, Clara had cleared her to ride again, and she planned on not wasting any time. As she got out of bed, she glanced at the crib. Colt was gone too. Harper dressed and was pulling on her shoes when her phone rang. She answered it when she saw Bethany's name.

"Hey, Beth." She said into the phone.

"Harper!" Bethany sniffled. Was the woman crying? Bo! Harper slowly sat in the rocking chair. Her gut clenched as she prepared herself for the worst news she could get.

Two weeks ago, the hospital lifted the no visitors ban. Only authorized visitors were allowed. At the moment, only Bethany and herself were allowed to see Bo. Beth had been visiting him every few days and sending her pictures and updates. Yesterday, they were waiting for the specialist to come and look at him to see if there was going to be lasting damage or if he would make a full recovery.

"He's…he's…he's going to make it. Dr. Honey ran tests and Bo is going to make it." Bethany broke down sobbing.

It took a few moments for Beth's words to sink in, and when they did, tears of relief and excitement coursed down Harper's cheeks. She couldn't say anything as she listened to the full report. If by tomorrow his levels continued to hold, Bo would be released from the hospital on Thanksgiving. Harper managed to say thank you before hanging up the phone.

After her tears were spent, Harper went into the bathroom to take Tylenol and tried to cover the evidence that she had been crying. Looking into the mirror, Harper realized it was a lost cause. Her eyes were still slightly puffy and bloodshot. Giving up, she made her way downstairs. Clara and her family were coming over today and Harper planned on asking for a few favors.

The kitchen was a lively place when she walked in. Tank was baby talking with Colt, causing him to give a big toothless grin while Carter tossed Lexi to Devon, and she squealed in delight. Harper could not help smiling.

"Mommy!" Lexi called and all activity ceased as Lexi was set down. She ran to Harper and threw her arms around her neck.

"Good morning to you too, baby girl." Harper hugged her daughter back and pressed a kiss to Lexi's cheek. "Did I miss breakfast?" Carter handed her a plate of scrambled eggs, bacon and toast with a smile. She accepted it and sat at the table.

Over the last five weeks, Harper's feelings for Carter only grew, making it harder and harder to keep her walls up. Lexi adored him and he seemed to adore the girl just as much. They had never talked about the kiss in the barn, even though it wasn't far from her mind. There were several times over the weeks that she thought he was going to kiss her, but he would pull away if she didn't first. She was walking a dangerous line with him. She knew that when Luther was arrested and it was time for them to leave, Harper and Lexi would be brokenhearted.

As she listened to the chatter around her, Harper noticed that Lexi called each of them uncle except for Carter. Harper had heard him tell Lexi she could, but she never did. A knock at the front door was followed by kids yelling and laughing. Clara and her family must have arrived.

Harper cleared her plate and joined the chaos in the front room. Clara had three kids. A son who just turned six, a daughter Lexi's age and a two-year-old little girl. Clara's older daughter, Hannah and Lexi were instant friends and were already playing in the corner. Clara walked over to Harper and gave her a hug.

"How are you?" Clara asked with a smile, but Harper could hear the deeper meaning in the question. Clara could tell she had been crying.

"I need to talk to you." Harper said quietly, so only Clara could hear her. A worried expression crossed her features before she masked it as Carter stepped up to them. "Carter, can you keep an eye on the kids for me, I need to talk with Clara really quick?" Harper asked with a smile.

Carter narrowed his eyes as he took in her face, and she could tell when he realized she had been crying. He hesitated but nodded before sending her a "we will talk later" look.

Harper grabbed Clara's hand and dragged her up the stairs to her room. She closed the door behind them and locked it. When she turned to face Clara, Clara's brows were lifted in surprise. "Okay, I'm listening." Clara sat on the edge of the bed.

Harper started crying again as she relayed everything Bethany had told her. Clara hugged Harper as she squealed. "That means you can pick up Bo in four days! That's great." Clara stepped back, wiping her own cheeks.

"There is so much I need to do." Harper said as she took a seat in the rocking chair. "Lexi knew she had a baby brother that was going to die. I need to tell her that he is alive. The guys still don't know about Bo. And Luther still hasn't been arrested. I also need to get more baby things."

"Slow down. One step at a time, Harper." Clara said with a smile. "I will start getting the baby stuff, and when you are ready for it, I can bring it by. As for Luther, it is just a matter of time before he is caught." The two of them discussed a plan to drive to Denver to pick up Bo in the next few days.

"I'm going for a ride on Mozart today. When I get back, I'm going to talk to Lexi." Harper blew out a long breath.

"Go for a ride. Relax. And we can finish planning our trip when you get back." Clara stood and at Harper's confused look, laughed. "Peter is a police officer. The guys can't object to you, Colt, Devon and Raider going on a trip to Denver with us. My in-laws can watch my kids so we will have plenty of room."

Harper didn't know what to say and Clara didn't give her any time anyway. She opened the door and was halfway down the stairs by the time Harper caught up. Carter caught her eye as soon as she stepped into the room.

"Who's up for an excursion?" Clara announced with enthusiasm.

"What Clara means is, I need an escort or two for the afternoon." Harper shook her head at her friend. The guys exchanged looks before Tank and Carter gave her a nod.

Harper fed Colt and said goodbye to Lexi before stepping outside with Carter and Tank. They didn't say anything as she crossed the grass to the barn. Her earlier excitement about riding returned with each step. She stopped in the tack room and grabbed Mozart's bridle.

"Uh, Harper?" Tank asked. "What are you doing?"

"I just got the green light to ride again from my doctor." Harper walked down the aisle to Mozart's stall. "Hey, boy. You ready?" She kissed the horse's muzzle before slipping the bridle on him. She spent time with Mozart every day over the last five weeks; brushing him, talking to him, leading him around the pasture.

"Aren't you going to stop her?" Tank asked Carter.

"Mozart is her horse. Henry bought him for her birthday before he was killed. Plus, she has that determined look in her eyes." Carter chuckled. Harper whirled around to face them with wide eyes and Carter just shrugged.

"My horse?" Harper asked in shock and excitement.

"Henry called Mozart a birthday present, but I called it a bribe. He was hoping you would come visit more if you had Mozart here waiting for you." Carter smiled at her.

Harper couldn't control her excitement. Bo was going to live, he was coming home soon, and Mozart was her horse! She jumped into Carter's arms and kissed his cheek. She immediately caught her mistake and threw her arms around Tank's neck next and kissed his cheek, too.

Carter smiled at her with a crooked grin as he leaned against the stall door next to Mozart's. "Henry said you would be excited."

"What are you waiting for?" Harper laughed. "I only have a couple of hours before Colt will need me. Let's go." Carter and Tank both laughed as Harper opened the stall door and led Mozart out.

Harper tied Mozart to a hitching post and saddled him with ease. She was sitting in the saddle waiting while the guys finished saddling their horses. "I didn't realize you knew anything about horses. Other than brushing them." Carter commented as they trotted from the main yard.

"You don't know everything about me, Carter." Harper laughed. "Mom tried to make it up to me after the divorce and put me in riding lessons until I was fifteen. When I turned sixteen, I started dating a guy who lived on a ranch. He took me riding all the time. We broke up when he realized I was more interested in the horses than him."

Tank laughed. "You dated a guy for his horses?"

"I don't even remember his name. He tried to kiss me, and I punched him. When he asked why, I told him the truth and we broke up. Two weeks later, he asked me why I dated him when I could have just applied for a job on the ranch." Harper laughed at the memory. "I worked there part-time during the summers until graduation." Tank chuckled and Carter smiled over at her.

They rode in silence for a while and Harper enjoyed every second of it. The feeling of being watched had her shifting uncomfortably in her saddle. She glanced to her left; Tank was looking out over the field. She glanced over at Carter, but he too was scanning the field on his side. Casper and Raider were trotting along beside them.

"Hey, Carter?" Harper said quietly. He turned to look at her. "I think I'm ready to head back."

"You sure? We have only been out for an hour." He asked, and Tank turned to her.

"I'm sure." Harper immediately turned Mozart around and kicked him into a run, knowing Carter and Tank would be right behind her. She pulled Mozart to a walk right before the barn and rode him inside before dismounting.

She was shaking, causing her to fumble with the reins as she tried to tie Mozart up so he could be untacked. Carter stepped to her side and took the reins from her. He tied up Mozart before turning to her. He grabbed her arms, worry evident in the way he studied her.

"Are you okay? Harper, talk to us." Tank asked as he stepped to her other side. "Man, you are pale."

"I'm fine." Harper shook her head trying to dispel the feeling of being watched. "I just...I felt..."

"What scared you, Dove?" Carter asked gently.

Harper stepped closer to Carter, and he put his arms around her. It had been weeks since she allowed Carter to hold her, but she was scared and needed his comfort. Tank put his hand on her shoulder as another shiver shook her.

"I don't know. I felt like I was being watched, and then I felt like we needed to get out of there." Harper whispered.

"Take Jeff with you and call the sheriff. Tell him we might have an intruder." Carter told Tank and Tank took off at a run. "Let's get you inside, Dove. I'll send Devon out to unsaddle the horses." Harper nodded and he kept his arm around her all the way back to the house.

To Harper's relief, everyone was in the kitchen, and no one noticed them entering the house. Carter led her to the couch and sat with her. He pulled his phone out and she watched him send Devon a text about the horses. Harper was still tucked against Carter's side with his arm tightly around her.

"Are you okay?" He whispered in her ear. She leaned her head against his forehead, needing his comfort. "It's going to be okay." Carter continued to hold her and whisper calming words until she was no longer shaking.

The front door opened, and Devon stepped in. He crouched down in front of Harper with a serious expression on his face. "Did you see anything?" he asked quietly. Harper shook her head. "Not even in the barn? Nothing out of the ordinary?" Harper shook her head again.

"Did you find something?" Carter asked.

Devon pulled out a small white envelope with her name on it. "This was in Mozart's stall when I put him back." Harper stiffened. She knew that handwriting.

"Did you read it?" Harper asked.

Devon shook his head. "I wasn't sure who left it."

Harper took the envelope with shaking hands. Devon and Carter watched her carefully as she pulled out a small piece of paper. 'You think you can live with them and not pay the price? You think I don't know about him? Well Babe, maybe you will actually make it to a funeral after all. Helps when it has already been planned.' Blood roared in Harper's ears. She didn't know she was crying until Carter pulled her onto his lap and crushed her to him.

Harper barely registered Devon taking the note from her hand. "He's been here." Harper gasped for air. "He's going to kill him." She sobbed. She felt herself being lifted and carried upstairs. She didn't even know which room Carter had taken her to, not that it mattered. Luther was still around, and he knew about Bo.

By the time she stopped crying, Jeff, Devon and Tank were sitting in Carter's room with them. "What does this note mean?" Tank asked. "Who is he referring to?"

"Luther knows about my son." Harper said quietly as she sat up. Carter kept an arm around her as she slid off his lap and onto the bed beside him.

"He's after Colt? What did it mean by a funeral being already planned?" Jeff asked.

Harper stood and moved several feet away from them. She wrapped her arms around herself as tears slid down her cheeks. "Luther's not talking about Colt, but Colt's twin, Bowman." Looks of surprise and confusion crossed all their faces. "When they were born, Bo suffered injuries from the beating I took from Luther. The injuries were so severe that he was given less than a five percent chance to live, if he even survived the night. Colt and I were released the next day. I was terrified for Lexi and Colt's safety. I didn't even return to the apartment. I met with Bethany, made arrangements for Bo's funeral and left."

"I'm confused." Devon said slowly.

Harper pulled out her phone as she explained. "I asked a nurse if she could find someone to give Bo a blessing, just before I left. According to Bethany, after the blessing, Bo's health began to improve. The hospital has been in a sort of lock down and only Bethany and I are allowed in to see Bo. It's been really rocky, but as of this morning, he is almost ready to be released." Harper handed the phone over to Devon with a picture of her holding both boys right after they were born. He flipped through several pictures before handing the phone to Carter.

"Why didn't you tell us about him?" Tank asked as he flipped through the pictures next.

"At first, I didn't know he would even live and then as he started to get better, I've been dealing with the guilt of leaving my son behind." Harper closed her eyes as she waited for their reaction.

Arms pulled her into a hug, and she choked down a sob. "Don't feel guilty, Harper. You did not abandon him. You had Bethany and others watching out for him. You did what you had to do in order to keep the four of you alive." Tank said as he hugged her.

Tank released her and Jeff gave her a hug. She laughed when Jeff let her go only for Devon to hug her. She never thought telling these guys about Bo would go so well. She had imagined them judging her and accusing her of abandoning her son. Not hugging her and providing much needed comfort.

Carter stood and smiled at her. "I'm so glad he lived, Harper. Now, we just need to bring him home." Harper bit back more tears. Home. Was this home? As he handed her back her phone, Carter put an arm around her waist, and she leaned against him.

"We need to get to him before Luther does. He is safe in the hospital, but as soon as he is released, he is vulnerable." Jeff crossed his arms. "Do we know when we can pick him up?"

"Beth said Thanksgiving." Harper said. "Clara and I planned on going down a day or two early just in case he gets released early."

"Did you now?" Carter murmured as he pulled her a little closer. "You thought I would allow you to drive to Denver without us?"

"Not exactly. Since Peter is an officer, it was going to be Peter, Clara, Devon, Raider, me and Colt." Harper shrugged.

"Why would Devon get to go?" Jeff pouted.

"Carter couldn't come, that was non-negotiable. And I needed you and Tank to protect my daughter." Harper explained.

"Why was I non-negotiable?" Carter asked, curiosity filling his voice.

"Lexi is going to be upset when I leave." Harper said. "She would have been inconsolable if you left too."

"She has a point. You are Lexi's favorite." Devon laughed.

"As plans go, it's not bad, but I think we need to come up with a new one." Carter said. "I'm not taking any chances when it comes to the lives of you or those kids."

# Chapter 9

Harper held tight to Lexi. Was she making the right decision? Carter placed a hand on her back, and she looked at him. He gave her a reassuring smile and Harper set Lexi down.

"I'll miss you, mommy." Lexi said as she kissed Harper's cheek. "But I can't wait to meet Bo." Lexi clapped excitedly.

"We'll see you soon, kiddo." Carter ruffled Lexi's hair before kissing her forehead. "Be good for Clara and Peter."

"I will." Lexi promised and Clara took her inside, followed by Bella.

Carter grabbed Harper's hand and led her to his truck, where Devon and Colt waited for them. Tank and Jeff were in a separate truck. He opened the back door and Harper climbed in beside Colt. Raider jumped over the seat and laid down.

"Looks like you're riding in back, Carter." Devon laughed and Carter climbed in beside Harper.

They were only driving for five minutes before Harper was peering through the back window. Carter grabbed her hand and she turned to look at him.

"She will be just fine. She has Peter, Bella, and half the police force." Carter reassured her.

"And if all goes well, we will be back in four days." Devon added.

Harper nodded, but her grip on Carter's hand tightened. "I wish I could have left Colt. I feel like I'm putting him in danger."

"You said the hospital will release Bo only to you, correct?" Carter asked and Harper nodded. "I wish we didn't have to bring him with us, too, but he needs you, Dove."

"I've been curious about something, but afraid if I asked, you'd find an excuse to leave without answering. Now that you are stuck…" Devon glanced in the rearview mirror and smiled. "Why do you call Harper 'Dove'?"

Carter laughed and Harper's cheeks flamed. "Henry and Carter caught me singing in the shower. Henry said I sounded like an angel, while Carter argued that I was a dove." Harper explained.

"That was when Henry started calling her Angel and I started calling her Dove." Carter smiled over at her.

"How old were you?" Devon asked as he chuckled.

"I was nine, almost ten." Harper couldn't stop the smile that spread on her lips. "I had no idea they snuck into the bathroom and were sitting on the counter, listening to me. I'm glad I grabbed the towel before opening the curtain."

"And then you gave me a bloody nose and Henry a black eye." Carter finished the story.

Devon laughed so hard he wiped tears from his eyes. "Now, the real question is, do you still sing?"

"I haven't really sung a lot since my parents' divorce." Harper turned to look at Colt who was watching her with his blue eyes. He smiled and her heart melted. "I've only sung at church and to the kids when they get scared or upset. It is one of the few things that seemed to calm Lexi as a baby."

"So, you do have the voice of an angel dove." Devon glanced at her again. "Will you sing for us?"

Harper laughed. "Not a chance, Dev."

"I'll turn on the radio and you can sing along if you'd like." he said with a chuckle as the radio came on. Harper shook her head and closed her eyes. Not a chance would she sing for them.

Before long, Harper's head slid down the back of the seat until it rested against Carter's shoulder. Her breathing had deepened, and he was pretty sure she had fallen asleep. He pressed a kiss to her head and relaxed. He was a little disappointed that she hadn't sung. He was curious to know what her voice sounded like now that she had grown.

"When are you going to tell her?" Devon asked several minutes later. "And don't tell me that you are giving her time after the divorce. She has been with us for a month, and you have only fallen for her more."

"I don't know. Maybe when the Luther situation is over." Carter sighed.

"You two are ridiculous. The moment you walk in the room, you scan it until you find her. You hold her hand every chance you get. She seeks you out for comfort." Devon shook his head. "You need to tell her how you feel, Carter."

"I know, Devon. I know." Carter closed his eyes and listened to the radio.

They had been driving for three hours when Colt started to fuss. Harper sat up and rubbed her eyes as she turned to the baby. She started talking to him while Devon took the next exit into a rest area. He pulled into an empty spot away from the other vehicles and got out.

"We are going to get out and take up positions around the truck while you feed him. I'll also take Raider out to go to the bathroom." Carter explained the plan to her. "Do you need to use the bathroom while we are here?"

"I'll feed Colt first. Then I'll get my vest on." Harper said as she unbuckled Colt and lifted him from his seat. Carter slipped out of the vehicle and opened the front door. Tank called to her dog, and she watched as he took both Raider and Casper into a grassy area. Jeff put down the tailgate and sat on it while Devon leaned against the driver's door. Carter stood next to her door and scanned the parking lot.

The longer they stayed there, the more anxious she was to be on the road, but Colt had other plans. He took his time eating. Tank had returned and stood near the front of the truck with both dogs. When Colt was done, Harper took her extra-large shirt off, leaving her in her tank top. She tapped on the window to get Carter's attention. He opened the door and climbed in.

"Everything okay?" He asked.

"I need help with the vest, Colt still needs to be burped, I need to use the bathroom and I'm anxious to be back on the road." Harper said in one breath.

Carter chuckled. "I'll help you with your vest and I'll burp Colt while Tank and the dogs take you up to the bathroom. Does that sound like a plan?"

Harper let out a tense breath and nodded. She set Colt back in his seat while Carter helped her put on the bulletproof vest. "Anyone with eyes will know that I have this on." Harper pointed out as she pulled her oversized T-shirt down over the vest. It still bulged.

"Here." Carter said as he pulled his hoodie off and tugged it down over her head. "Now, no one will know."

Harper gave him a smile and Carter climbed out of the truck so she could get out. Before Carter could climb back in, Raider was at her side. Walking quickly, Harper made a beeline for the women's bathroom. Her steps faltered as she got the uncomfortable feeling of being watched. As casually as she could she scanned her surroundings.

A dark blue sedan was parked at the far end of the parking lot. A man stood next to it. He had a beard and was wearing sunglasses with a familiar baseball cap. As she watched him, he blew her a kiss before he climbed into the car and drove away towards the on ramp.

Harper shivered at the man's actions but kept going. Something about the man nagged at her. Sure, his actions made him come across as a jerk, but there was something else about him that bothered her. She couldn't shake him from her thoughts as she and Raider entered the small two-stall room. She was washing her hands when she remembered where she had seen that hat before. Luther had been wearing it when he had come to the ranch. She had not recognized him at first, because of the beard. He had never been anything but clean shaven.

Harper ran from the building and straight towards the truck. Devon grabbed her as she tripped on the uneven ground. "Wow, girl. You look like you've seen a ghost."

"Luther." She panted. "Blue sedan. Baseball hat. Beard."

Devon tightened his grip on her and practically carried her to the truck. He opened the back door and shoved her inside. Carter caught her with a confused look, as the tailgate was slammed into place. Raider was loaded in through the driver's door, and within two minutes of her telling Devon she had seen Luther, they were peeling out of the parking lot and merging into traffic.

"What did I miss?" Carter asked as he buckled Colt. Harper was shaking and looking at the cars around them.

"I felt eyes on me again, and when I looked around, I saw a man standing next to a blue sedan. At first, I didn't recognize him, but then I remember seeing the same baseball hat on Luther when he came to the ranch." Harper shook her head. "Maybe I'm being paranoid."

Carter put his arm around her, and she leaned into him. "Maybe it was Luther, maybe it wasn't. It's better to be paranoid than dead."

"When he saw me watching him, he blew me a kiss as he got in the car and drove away." Harper whispered. She didn't miss the look Devon and Carter shared. Or Carter pulling out his phone and sending a text. "You think it was him, too." It wasn't a question. She could feel the tension coming off both men.

Carter pulled her closer and kissed her temple. "You are safe with us, Dove."

Harper blinked several times before looking up. Did Carter just kiss her? She met Devon's gaze in the rearview mirror, he winked and returned his attention to the road. What was going on? Her mind was swirling with the danger Luther posed to her and her kids. She couldn't think straight. If it hadn't been for Devon's wink, she would have convinced herself that it didn't happen. She glanced up at Carter, but he was scanning the vehicles on the road. Did he even realize he had kissed her?

He caught her staring and his brows rose. "What?" he asked, confused.

"Nothing." Harper said as she turned her attention back to the road in front of them. Devon made a coughing noise from the front, and Harper thought she saw him cover a smile with his hand as he wiped his face. She felt Carter shrug and Devon put the radio back on. The rest of the drive was uneventful. They made one more stop to get gas and to grab food.

Devon pulled into her parking spot at her old apartment and turned off the truck. Harper looked at the building and felt sick. She had been paying rent this whole time, and Bethany said she had stopped by several times to check on the place.

"I'll go with Tank and Casper to check out the apartment first." Devon said as he turned to look at her. "Jeff is going to stand nearby and help keep an eye on you."

Harper nodded her understanding as she handed Devon her keys. "It's apartment 4C on the third floor." she said softly. He gave her a reassuring smile and left the car.

Carter had kept his arm around her the whole second part of the drive and as they sat there, his thumb rubbed up and down her arm slowly. "We can get a hotel if you want." he said, breaking the silence.

"No, it's fine. I need to get our things anyway." Harper reached up and laced her fingers through his.

"It's going to be okay, Harper. You have four of the country's finest, plus two dogs trained in personal protection. One of which is also a veteran. You and Colt will be safe." Carter placed his other hand on her knee and gave it a squeeze.

They fell into silence as they waited for the 'all clear'. Harper was ready to jump out of her skin when Tank and Devon came back. She saw them nod to Jeff before Devon let Raider out. Next, he moved to her door, but she hesitated before stepping out. All four men could sense her unease and they stood close. Devon led the way and she followed with Carter and Raider at her side. Jeff held Colt in his carrier as he walked right behind them with Tank and Casper bringing up the rear.

They barely fit everyone in the elevator. Carter wrapped his arms around her stomach, pulling her back against him and holding her close. Harper had forgotten how slow the elevator in this building moved. It took several minutes for them to reach the third floor. When the doors opened, Devon once again led their party. Her apartment was on the opposite end of the hall from the elevator. Devon moved quickly and held the door open for them all to enter. He closed the door, and she heard the lock click into place.

Memories from that night flashed into her mind. Lexi was in the back bedroom getting her pajamas on while Harper had been sitting on the couch with a bowl of popcorn. It was their first night of freedom and they had planned on watching a movie. There was a weird sound at the door, but before she could get up to see what was going on, Luther burst in.

"Harper?" Carter's voice pulled her from her memory, and she blinked.

Harper looked around the small living room and kitchen area. The place was spotless. Bethany said she had cleaned it. Her eyes wandered over to the couch. It was missing. Not that she had any love for the thrift store couch, but she wondered where it had gone. The carpet looked new and there was fresh paint on the walls. Beth had mentioned the amount of damage and blood had required her to order repairs.

"Harper?" Carter called her name again. This time she turned to look at him. "Are you okay?" He asked.

She noticed that all four of them were looking at her with worried expressions. "Yeah. Just tired from the trip, I guess."

"Why don't we sit and chill while we wait for the pizza to arrive?" Jeff suggested. He turned towards the living room and paused when he saw no couch.

"There is a note from Bethany on the counter saying they had to remove the couch because it was beyond saving." Tank said. "Whatever that means."

Harper took a deep breath and walked down the short hall to the bedroom. The room was just how she left it. Their stuff was still in boxes, and there was a baby bassinet and a twin sized bed pushed up against the wall. Lexi's clothes were still on the floor, and she bent to clean them up. As she put them back in the box marked 'clothes,' she saw the only picture she had out. It was a picture of her sandwiched between Henry and Carter the day before she was sent away with her mom.

"That was a long time ago." Carter's voice sounded from behind her. She turned to face him. He was holding Colt as he smiled at the picture in her hands. "I think that was the last time I saw you."

"Why didn't you come to graduation?" Harper couldn't stop the question that had bothered her for so long from escaping.

Carter looked into her eyes. "I wanted to, Harper. But we were assigned a mission. Our commander gave Henry and I the choice: him or me. I took the mission so that Henry could be there for you."

Harper looked down at the picture again. She ran her finger over Henry's face. "I miss him, Carter."

"I know, Dove." He whispered. "I do too." Harper blinked back tears.

A knock sounded at the front door and Carter quickly closed the bedroom door before passing Colt over to her. He stood between them and the other part of the apartment with his hand on his gun. Harper barely breathed as they waited. The front door closed, and then a knock on the bedroom door came. Carter opened it and Jeff stood there.

"Pizza's here." Jeff announced with a smile.

"Thank you, but I'm not hungry." Harper said, sitting on the bed.

"But Carter made me order a chicken, bacon, and ranch pizza. He said it was your favorite, and no one else is going to eat that." Jeff complained.

"You think that is still my favorite pizza?" Harper asked.

Carter gave her a crooked grin. "Are you saying I'm wrong?"

Harper smiled as she shook her head in disbelief. How did he remember so much about her? "Fine, I'll eat the pizza, but I can't eat it out there."

Jeff gave Carter a look before he called out into the other room. "Pizza party in the bedroom!" The rest of the gang squeezed into the small space.

Carter sat next to her on the bed and took Colt from her, placing him in the bassinet. Jeff sat on her other side while Tank and Devon sat on the floor with the dogs. "I didn't mean you all had to come in here." Harper laughed. "I just said I couldn't go out there."

Tank finished the bite he was chewing. "The couch, is that where he..." He asked.

"Yup." Harper looked down at the plate of pizza in her lap. She lifted the slice to her mouth, but hesitated.

"We asked for no onions." Carter smiled.

"How do you remember so much about my pizza preferences?" Harper asked as she took a bite.

"I'm sure it's not just your pizza preferences he remembers about you." Jeff laughed.

Out of the corner of her eye, Harper saw Carter's face turn red as he looked away. Interesting. Devon started laughing, too, but he cleared his throat after Harper saw Carter send him a glare. Carter changed the subject. "What are the plans for tomorrow?"

"I'm going to the hospital. I got permission to bring in one guest, my service dog, and baby." Harper said before taking another bite. When only stunned silence filled the room, she continued. "I've waited six weeks to hold my son, I'm not going another day without him."

"Fair enough." Tank said. "I will call the local authorities and inform them of our location. I will also be outside with Casper. Devon and Jeff can wait in the waiting room for you."

"Why does Carter get to go in with Harper?" Devon asked, a teasing note in his voice.

"Because he knows her pizza preferences." Tank laughed.

Harper half listened to the rest of their plans and teasing as she nibbled on her pizza. Carter ended up changing Colt's blown out diaper before passing him to her to feed. She could tell that all four men were watching her closely as the night wore on. Sleeping arrangements were made. Tank and Devon left to sleep in the front room. Jeff grabbed Lexi's unicorn stuffed animal and used it as a pillow as he laid on the floor near the door. Carter settled on the ground near the bed.

It was an hour after the lights went out when Harper's phone rang. She answered it immediately when she saw Clara's name. "Hello?" She said as she put the phone to her ear. She kept her voice quiet so she didn't wake anyone up.

"Hi, mommy." Lexi's cheerful voice came through the line. "Clara said it's time for me to go to bed, but I miss you."

Harper sat up and brought her knees to her chest. "I miss you too, baby girl. But it is getting late, and you need to sleep."

"But I can't sleep without you." Lexi whined.

"Did you say your prayers?" Harper asked.

"Yes. I asked God to keep everyone safe." Lexi yawned.

"Lexi, that's great. We appreciate your prayers, but it is time for bed, honey. I know it's hard, but we will be home soon, okay?" Harper closed her eyes as she pictured her daughter's face.

"Will you sing me a song?" Lexi asked.

"Which one?" Harper smiled.

"The one with the angels." Angel Lullaby, Lexi's favorite.

Harper took a deep breath as she began singing. When she finished, there was silence on the other end of the line for several seconds before Clara's voice whispered. "She's asleep. I'll call you in the morning." And then Clara hung up.

"Wow." Jeff breathed out.

"You weren't exaggerating, Carter." Devon commented from the door.

Harper's eyes flew open. "When did you all come in here?" Harper was mortified. "And why aren't you asleep?"

"When you started to sing, I thought you turned on some music or something for Colt, but Devon bet it was you." Tank said. It was dark in the apartment, and she could only make out faint outlines of those in the doorway. They left and Harper fought her embarrassment at being overheard.

Carter moved to sit by her. "Your voice has only gotten better since the last time I heard you sing." He smiled at her, and she buried her face in her knees. She had forgotten she wasn't alone with Lexi.

Carter's hand touched her back, but she refused to give into the urge to lean into him. "Harper, your voice is amazing, it always has been. It is nothing to be embarrassed about." Carter whispered close to her ear so only she could hear him.

Harper turned to face him, and their noses touched. She used that as a guide in the darkness as she brushed her cheek against his until her lips found his ear. She could hear his breath catch. "Goodnight, Carter." She whispered and she felt his cheek move as he smiled.

He turned and pressed his lips to her cheek in a gentle kiss. "Goodnight, Dove." He whispered back. Slowly he got off the bed and she heard him settle back on the floor.

How in the heck was she supposed to sleep now? Was that kiss a brotherly kiss? A friend kind of kiss? Or did he like her? Harper's mind whirled. Raider crawled up on the bed until he could lick her fingers. Harper pulled out her phone and looked through the pictures of Bo until her eyes grew heavy and she finally fell asleep.

Men's voices sounded from the front room and Harper slowly blinked her eyes open. Sunlight was streaming through the window filling the room with early morning light. Jeff sat up against the wall looking tired. He had his phone in his hand, playing a game.

"I didn't realize babies were up so much at night." Jeff said quietly before looking up at her. "How do you function?"

Harper smiled as she sat up. "Where is he now?" She asked.

"About an hour after you fed him, he woke up again. Carter took him in the other room so you could sleep." Jeff smiled as he moved closer to her. He glanced at the open door before looking back at her. "Bo's middle name." He said so quietly she almost didn't hear him.

Harper's cheeks flushed, but she patted the bed beside her, so he didn't need to stay on the floor. Over the past several weeks, Jeff had become like a brother to her. He reminded her so much of Henry. She knew she could trust him to keep her secret. She gave a smile and a shrug as she explained the best she could. "Both Bo and Colt were named after the only two boys I ever loved." Admitting it out loud sounded silly, but Jeff didn't laugh.

He studied her face more closely. "You still love him, don't you?"

Harper glanced at the door. "I tried not to. I tried to move on." She gave a small laugh. "I'm so mad at him for not allowing me to move on."

Jeff laughed too. "Your list sounded an awful lot like Carter."

"What can I say, he set the bar pretty high. I knew he didn't feel the same way I did, but I wanted someone who was like him." Harper laid her head on Jeff's shoulder and yawned. "A friend in high school and my roomie in college asked why I only dated boys with brown eyes. I didn't realize why until I crashed on your ranch."

"If you ask me, you and Carter are good for one another." Jeff put an arm around her shoulders and gave her a squeeze. "You should tell him how you feel."

Colt's cry from the other room drew a sigh from Harper. Carter appeared in the doorway a few seconds later. When he saw them, his expression hardened. "I think Colt's hungry again." He finally said.

"Thanks for the chat, little sis." Jeff stood and walked towards the door where Carter still stood. Carter didn't take his eyes from hers as Jeff squeezed by him.

Colt let out another cry and Carter blinked, pulling him from his jealous thoughts. He handed Colt over to Harper before sitting next to her. He kept his eyes on the door as she put a blanket over her shoulder. Colt's crying quickly changed to the little sounds he made when he ate.

He sat quietly as he tried to rein in his emotions. The image of Harper leaning against Jeff with his arm around her while she wore *his* hoodie, sent his possessiveness into overdrive.

Maybe Devon was right, and he needed to tell her how he felt. If she returned his feelings, they could talk about their future. If she didn't, then he would at least know and could start moving on.

"It's nice having a brother figure in my life again." Harper said as she shifted to get more comfortable. Carter's stomach clenched. Was she talking about him? He did not want to be her surrogate brother. "Jeff, Tank, and Devon don't come close to Henry, but they make okay substitutes." Carter let out a tense breath.

He was pleased she didn't add his name to her list. Carter finally looked over at her, and the rest of the tension slipped from him when he saw her looking at the picture of the three of them on her nightstand. "Thank you for taking Colt for a little bit." She turned her mesmerizing blue eyes on him.

"Any time, Dove." Carter whispered. Their faces were so close, all he could think about was kissing her. His eyes dropped to her lips, and he slowly leaned closer, giving her plenty of time to stop him.

Their lips were just a breath apart when Carter's phone rang, causing Harper to jump. Carter bit back a groan of frustration as he pulled it from his pocket and answered it. "Michaels." He said while keeping his eyes on Harper. Her cheeks were a pretty shade of pink, and she looked everywhere but at him.

"Carter?" Lexi's voice came through the line. Harper must have heard her daughter because her head snapped in his direction.

"Good morning, kiddo. Did you sleep well?" He softened his voice when he realized it was Lexi. "You were up so late; I was sure you would have slept in."

"I slept okay. I want to go home." He didn't need to see her to know that Lexi's lower lip was sticking out in a pout.

"Did something happen?" he asked, trying not to let his worry show for both Lexi and Harper's sakes.

"No, but I miss you. Did both you and mommy have to go?" she asked, her little voice pulling at his heartstrings.

"I wish you could have come with us, Sweetheart. But we talked about this, remember?" When there was only silence on the other end of the line, he continued. "Your mommy needed to come get your brother and she needed help. We are getting all of the stuff you left behind and bringing it back with us."

"I don't need my stuff; I just want you and mommy and my brothers." Lexi argued.

"Not even a purple unicorn? Jeff said he wants it if you don't." There was a pause before he heard Lexi giggle.

"Jeff can't have Popcorn." Lexi said matter-of-factly. "Clara says it's time to eat."

Carter chuckled. "Go eat, Lexi. We are getting ready to go see your brother in the hospital. We will send pictures to Clara's phone so you can see him."

"Okay." Lexi said happily. "I love you, Carter."

"Love you too, Sweetheart." Carter hung up the phone and looked over at Harper. She was watching him with a raised brow. "What?" He asked.

"I told you she would have a hard time with both of us gone." Harper pointed out. "Maybe you should have stayed with her."

"There is no way I would send you and Colt into a dangerous situation alone. Luther knows you are here, and he knows about Bo. I am not risking you or the boys. Lexi is safe and well protected." Carter gave her a stern look. "I'm not leaving your side until that man is behind bars."

Harper's eyes went wide at the fierceness of Carter's statement. She knew he cared about her and the kids, but the way he was looking at her now had butterflies taking flight in her stomach.

"Are you two done yet? I'm starving." Devon called from the other room.

"You will just have to wait until Colt is done eating, Devon." Harper called back as she pulled her eyes from Carter's. This man was dangerous. She honestly didn't know how her heart would survive once they went their separate ways. "Plus, I need a shower and to change. The hospital won't let us in for another two hours anyway."

"I'll go grab something from the store on the corner." Tank said. "Harper, what are you in the mood for?"

Was a kiss from Carter on the menu? Or better yet, a shot of steel to protect herself against him. "I would be fine with a granola bar." She called back.

She thought she heard him mutter something along the lines of, "Yeah, that's not happening." But she couldn't be sure. The front door closed and a minute later Carter's phone buzzed. He glanced over at her with a thoughtful expression before he replied to the text. She would put money on that text being from Tank, asking Carter what she liked.

Carter took Colt after he was done eating so Harper could get her shower. She dug through a few boxes until she found an outfit that she was happy with. Most of her clothes were new. She had bought them shortly before the divorce so she would have something to wear after the baby was born. Bethany had done the shopping and had impeccable taste.

She was in such a good mood, she started to sing as she shampooed and conditioned her hair. Nothing could dampen the joy she felt with the knowledge that she would be holding Bo in just a few short hours. She continued to sing as she dried her hair and applied a little makeup. Before leaving the bathroom, Harper gave her appearance a final look.

The top she wore was a blue plaid button up shirt that hugged her in all the right places. She rolled the sleeves to mid forearm. The color made her eyes pop. She wore skinny jeans and cowgirl boots. Harper also tucked her firearm into her ankle holster, making sure her pant leg and boot covered it. The final touch was the Mother's Day necklace Bethany and Lexi had picked out for her. It was a heart with a mother holding her child inside it.

She opened the door, feeling more like her old self than ever, and walked into the main rooms. She refused to look over at the living room, and instead stood at the counter with her back turned to it to block the bad memories. She dug through the brown bag and pulled out the last breakfast burrito. She felt eyes on her as she took a bite. Slowly she turned around to see the stunned faces of the guys. Devon was holding Colt as he looked her up and down.

"Wow, Harper. You look amazing." Devon smiled. "What's the occasion?"

"Occasion?" Harper furrowed her brow and looked down at her clothes. Understanding dawned. "Oh. I guess you would think that after seeing me in only large T-shirts and baggy jeans for six weeks." Harper laughed. "No, this is my normal get-up. T-shirts and loose-fitting jeans were just more comfortable after having a baby." She took another bite of the burrito. "And thank you Tank for following Carter's suggestion on my food, it tastes great."

Tank laughed. "How'd you know I asked him?"

"No offense, but you guys aren't exactly subtle. Plus, Carter's eyes squint and his brows knit together. Then he purses his lips causing the dimple at the corner of his mouth to appear. It's his classic thinking face." Harper shrugged her shoulder and took another bite.

Jeff and Devon laughed. "It's true. Henry would point out Carter's thinking face on missions." Jeff smacked Carter on the back.

"You must have been a deep thinker for both Andersons to pick up on your thinking face." Devon chuckled.

"Not really." Harper laughed. "He mainly got the look when he and Henry had to bail me out of trouble. Carter would get his thinking face and Henry got his 'I'm going to kill you' face."

"You've mentioned a few times that they had to bail you out of trouble, what did you do?" Tank asked eagerly.

Harper saw the smile on Carter's face grow. "Carter, don't." She warned.

"Don't tell them that you caused a stampede of wild mustangs to race down Main Street, and that you were riding on the lead stallion?" Carter quirked an eyebrow.

"I was six. And they were scared being locked up in the horse trailer." Harper defended herself.

"Or about the time you hustled over $300 from high schoolers?" Carter laughed.

"I still can't believe you and Henry made me give it back. I had plans for that money." Harper crossed her arms over her chest as she glared at Carter, which only made him smile bigger.

Tank roared with laughter. "How old were you?"

"Eight." Harper and Carter said at the same time, which made everyone laugh.

"What did you plan on doing with the money?" Devon asked.

"I was saving for my dream horse." Harper's smile became reminiscent. "It took several weeks and multiple bribes for Henry to get me to tell him why I was gambling with five sketchy and armed sixteen-year-olds."

"How did you stay out of trouble after you left with your mom?" Jeff asked.

Harper smirked at him. "I didn't. Riding lessons were her way of shoving me off on someone else for a few hours each day. I was kicked out of three schools, spent a couple months in juvie, and had to finish up my schooling online. Mom stopped taking me to church as soon as the divorce was finalized. I became wild, well wilder. When I was thirteen, I forged my mom's signature and got a tattoo. When it was finished, I cried. I think I had hoped Henry would swoop in and stop me. That was the day I realized I was truly on my own. Mom thought I was sneaking around with boys on the weekend, but I found a ward close by and started going to church by myself." Harper threw her wrapper away and took a drink of orange juice.

"I didn't know you had a tattoo." Devon said, surprised. "After the accident, I made sure you and the kids were unharmed, but I didn't see one."

Harper's face flushed. At least she knew he didn't examine all of her. "Now I have to know what it is and where it is." Jeff sat forward eagerly.

Why did she bring up the tattoo? At least she had had the forethought to put it where not many people would see it. Harper turned her back on the guys and began cleaning up the trash from breakfast. "I chose a symbol that stood for courage, strength, loyalty and perseverance. Everything I wished to be."

"A wolf." Carter said. "You always loved wolves and what they stood for."

Harper glanced over at him as she put the leftover orange juice in the fridge. "I may not have been smart enough to avoid getting it, but I at least had it put where not many would see it." When she turned back to the room, Jeff was still watching her with eager anticipation. "You're not going to drop this, are you?"

"Nope." Jeff smiled at her. Harper raised her right arm and pointed to her ribcage where her bra strap sat. "How big is it?" Jeff pressed.

"Bigger than a penny and smaller than a grapefruit." Harper smirked. At least each of the three figures were.

"I thought for sure she was going to say a tramp stamp." Tank sat back in his chair with a teasing smile.

"I almost got a tramp stamp of…you know what, never mind." Harper crossed the room and lifted Colt from Devon's arms. "My tattoos and piercings are not up for discussion."

"Piercings?" Jeff laughed. "How did Henry keep up with you?"

"Henry was so mad when he found out." Harper talked as she buckled Colt into his car seat. "It was the first time I heard him yell and argue with our dad."

"Your dad?" Carter asked in surprise.

"I'm surprised Henry never told you." Harper said as she turned to Carter. "As my 'going away present', dad took me to get my bellybutton and nose pierced. I told him I didn't want to, but he pressured me. I was crying when we got home. Henry helped me take them out and clean the areas. Then he told me to stay in my room and he left. I could hear him yelling at Dad." Carter's eyes widened in shock. Harper cleared her throat. "Are we ready to go?" She asked.

# Chapter 10

Tank and Jeff took Casper down to check the cars. Jeff came back a few minutes later with the 'all clear'. They quickly loaded back into the trucks and headed for the hospital. Carter took her hand in his and rubbed his thumb along the back of her hand. He didn't say anything, but she knew he was trying to show her support.

As soon as they pulled into the hospital entrance, Harper was unbuckling herself. Carter grabbed her hand again and pressed a kiss to her knuckles. "Easy, Dove. We will be pulling up to the entrance, but we need to wait for Jeff and Tank. They will help us unload. Jeff will walk in with us, and Dev will meet us up at the NICU after parking the car." Harper nodded as she tried to ignore the tingles that Carter's kiss left on her hand.

It took everything in her to not tap her fingers impatiently as they waited for Tank and Jeff. Jeff opened Colt's door and got him out at the same time Tank opened up Raider's door and Carter opened his. It was so in sync that Harper couldn't help but be impressed.

They crossed the lobby quickly and entered the elevator without having to wait. Harper shifted anxiously as the elevator climbed to the sixth floor. It was taking forever with multiple people getting on and off at every floor. Carter put his arm around her waist and pulled her to him.

Harper took a deep breath and reminded herself to relax. Only a few more minutes and she would see Bo. It wasn't working and her frustration over the delay was growing. Carter leaned down and whispered for her to calm down as they waited to reach their floor. The doors finally opened on the sixth floor and Devon was waiting for them.

"What took you guys so long?" Devon asked.

"We ended up stopping on every floor for people to get on and off." Jeff said in irritation. "I thought Harper was going to kill someone."

"Don't get in the way of momma bear and her cubs." Devon chuckled as they walked to the reception desk.

"Can I help you?" The nurse looked between the four of them. "Only parents are allowed in and no pets."

Harper stepped forward. "I'm Harper Anderson." The woman just stared at her. "I would like to speak with Dr. Honey." Harper said.

"She is in a meeting." The nurse said with a fake smile.

"You can call her, or I will." Harper stated losing her patience with the rude woman.

"Momma Bear." Devon muttered behind her, but she ignored him.

The nurse just stared at her, so Harper pulled out her cell and quickly dialed the doctor's number. It only rang once before the doctor answered. "Ms. Anderson, I am so glad you called. I was just telling some coworkers about your son's miraculous recovery."

"Good to hear from you, too. I was calling because we seem to be having a bit of a communication error at the front desk." Harper glared at the nurse whose eyes widened.

"I'll be there in just a minute." The line went dead, and Harper put her phone back in her pocket.

Less than five minutes later a door down the hall opened and Dr. Honey walked briskly in Harper's direction. She pulled Harper into a quick hug. "You look so much better than the last time I saw you, and look at this little guy." She gushed. "It's amazing how much they look alike. Follow me and I will take you to him."

Dr. Honey ignored the nurse as she led Harper and Carter into the locked NICU. Raider stayed close to her side as they walked down the hall. They stopped at a door at the end and Harper's heart raced. Dr. Honey stepped aside to allow Harper to enter first.

She slowly approached the crib in the center of the room. A baby, who looked exactly like Colton, lay there wearing a shirt that said, 'Mommy's Lil Man'. Tears blurred her eyes as she picked up her son. She cradled him to her chest as her tears fell. Someone guided her to a couch along the wall and helped her sit. Harper pulled herself together after several minutes. She wiped her eyes as she looked down at her son.

Bo was watching her, and when their eyes met, he smiled. Harper pressed a kiss to his cheek which caused his smile to widen, displaying a dimple. His brown eyes remained fixed on her face as Harper ran her hand over his dark brown hair. Bo and Colt were almost exact copies, except Colt had blue eyes and no dimples.

"I think he remembers you." Dr. Honey said wiping her eyes as she watched Harper and Bo. "Would you like me to take a picture of you before I go?"

"Yes, please." Harper said as she handed Dr. Honey her phone with the camera app open.

The doctor took several with Harper and Bo before suggesting adding Colt to the pictures. Carter smiled as he handed Colt to her. Tears were still wetting Harper's cheeks as she smiled down at her boys. "Would you like to get in the pictures, too?" Dr. Honey asked Carter.

Carter looked at Harper and she gave him a nod. Lexi would like to get a picture of Carter. He sat on the couch next to her. Dr. Honey instructed Carter to take one of the babies and to put his arm around Harper.

Harper closed her eyes as her head rested against Carter's cheek. She turned her face to look at him as he looked at her. Her stomach flipped as their eyes met. Before she registered what was happening, Carter pressed his lips to hers and sparks exploded. The kiss wasn't long, but it stole her breath. Carter pulled back and rested his forehead against Harper's.

A moment later Dr. Honey spoke, causing both of them to jump. "I got several good ones. I'll be back later to talk to you a little more about Bo. I need to return to my meeting. If you need anything, don't be afraid to call me." She handed Harper back her phone and left the room.

Carter kept his arm around her, and she leaned her head on his shoulder. "It's amazing how much they look like each other. Were they identical?" Carter asked.

"They are fraternal twins." Harper smiled.

"How are we going to tell them apart?" Carter asked.

Harper laughed. "Bo has brown eyes and dimples. Colt's eyes are blue, and he has no dimples." Carter made a sound of pondering and she knew he was studying the twins.

Harper remembered she had promised to send pictures to Clara for Lexi and unlocked her phone. She started to flip through the pictures to see which ones to send. Carter's phone buzzed and he pulled his arm away from her to check it. She paused when she got to the ones when Carter had joined her on the couch. Her heart picked up speed as she slowly looked at each picture. Harper sucked in a breath when she made it to the ones where Carter was kissing her. She felt her cheeks heat and quickly returned to the first ones taken of just her and Bo.

"Can you send me a few?" Carter asked while looking at his phone. "The guys are wanting proof the momma bear and her cubs are reunited."

"Uh, sure." Harper said distractedly. "Just let me send a few to Clara for Lexi."

Harper sent off several to Clara of her and both twins and some of just her and Bo. Clara sent back tons of heart emojis and crying faces. Harper smiled as she sent Carter the same ones. When Carter was distracted again, Harper sent Clara a quick message.

**Harper:** Clara? Do you have the phone to yourself?

**Clara:** Yes. What's up?

Stealing a quick glance at Carter, Harper quickly sent several of the pictures of the four of them. There was one with them looking down at the boys, them looking at each other, him kissing her and then resting their foreheads against each other.

**Harper:** Help me understand!!!

**Clara:** Wow. You look like a couple!

**Clara:** Who kissed who?

**Harper:** He did.

**Harper:** I'm so confused.

**Clara:** What's confusing about it? The way he is looking at you is absolutely adorable.

Carter put his phone away and Harper quickly set hers aside. They remained quiet and she just soaked up being able to hold Bo. A few hours later, Colt got fussy. Harper and Carter switched babies and she used the blanket from the crib to cover herself so she could feed Colt. Harper's phone buzzed and she looked at it.

**Jeff:** How's momma bear and her cubs?

**Harper:** Momma bear is no longer in protective mode and feeding cub number 2

**Jeff:** Hahaha glad to have the non-scary momma bear back.

Harper laughed as she set her phone back down. "Was I really that scary when we got here?" she asked Carter.

"You were definitely a force I didn't want to get in the way of." Carter smiled at her. His eyes shifted to something over her shoulder, and he got his thinking face on. "Harper? Does that say Bowman Carter Anderson?"

Harper turned her head to see the nameplate on the side of the crib. She fought the blush that started to rise up her neck. "I didn't tell you?" Harper asked as she turned back to Carter. When he shook his head, she continued. "I named the twins after my two favorite people. Bowman Carter and Colton Henry."

Carter studied her before turning his attention back to Bo. "I'm honored, Harper." Carter whispered. He smiled at her, and she bumped her shoulder against his.

"You look tired. You should rest." Harper suggested.

"And leave you to take care of both these guys?" Carter shook his head. "I'm fine."

Harper didn't press him. She tried to ignore the fact that he was there, but she was hyper-aware of his presence in the room from the moment he kissed her. When Colt was done eating, burped and changed, Harper stood and laid him in the crib. She walked over to the cabinets on the other wall and found what she was looking for. She made a bottle quickly and returned to the couch where Bo was fussing.

Harper lifted Bo out of Carter's arms, and as she sat down, Carter slipped his arm along the back of the couch. He let out a sigh and settled back with his eyes closed. Harper smiled when she heard him start to snore softly. When she was done feeding Bo, Harper took him to the crib as well. A few tears escaped as she stared down at her boys. She pulled out her phone and took a picture. She looked back over at Carter and took a picture of him sleeping.

Someone entered the room, and Carter opened his eyes a crack. Raider got to his feet as Dr. Honey walked back in. She glanced in his direction and kept her voice down as she addressed Harper. "I told your brothers they could go get food, and one of them could bring it to you. The receptionist knows to let only them through."

"Thank you." Harper responded.

"I'm so glad that your little boy survived. Medically speaking, there is no way he should have." Dr. Honey stepped closer to the crib and smiled down at the babies. "Ivy and I were talking about the story behind the twins' names but couldn't remember."

"Colton Henry was named after my brother, Henry. And Bo was named after…a friend." Harper supplied.

"That's right." Dr. Honey smiled and Carter's heart rate picked up. "Bo is the older twin if I remember right." Harper nodded. "But you didn't know about the second baby until after you told Ivy Bo's name."

"You're wondering why I didn't name Bo after my brother." Harper rubbed her arm in an act of self-comfort. "I was a mess when I came in. I thought for sure I was dying. I was in so much pain. When Bo was born and you placed him on my chest, I felt some of the darkness I had been feeling melt away. He was my bright star, my light. Just like his namesake had always been for me. And then Colt came, my second knight in shining armor."

Dr. Honey laughed, and Carter groaned to make it seem like he was just waking up. Harper turned to face him, a look of panic in her eyes. She apparently didn't want him to hear what she just said. He sent her a smile as he stood and joined them at the crib. He placed his hand on her lower back, and she let out a tense breath. Dr. Honey smiled at the two of them.

"I came in to tell you both that all but one of Bo's labs came back early. If you would like, he can go home with you later today." Dr. Honey told them.

Harper leaned against him, and Carter slid his arm the rest of the way around her. "Truly? Bo can go home with us tonight?" Harper asked as tears filled her eyes.

"Truly. I will be back before eight tonight with his discharge papers. Enjoy your boys." Dr. Honey patted Harper's arm before she turned and left.

As soon as they were alone again, Harper turned into Carter, and she felt his other arm come around her. She wouldn't have to leave Bo here tonight. She had been dreading having to, and now she didn't need to worry about it. Carter held her close as she cried in relief. She stayed tucked up against Carter, even after her tears dried. She couldn't bring herself to move away.

"I brought food." Devon's voice broke into Harper's calm.

"Just put it on the couch." Carter said but didn't release her, which she was glad for.

"Wow, which one is which?" Devon asked from beside them, but Harper didn't turn to look at him. She just wanted a few more minutes of this peaceful feeling.

"I had the same question. Bo has brown eyes and Colt has blue, but with them sleeping, I'm not sure." Carter said.

Harper turned her head, so her other cheek rested against Carter's chest, allowing her to see the crib. "Colt is on the right and Bo on the left." She sighed.

"How can you tell?" Devon asked as he studied the twins.

"I just know." Harper shrugged.

"I hope those are happy tears." Devon glanced at her.

"Bo can go home with us tonight." Carter answered.

"That's great! Would I wake him if I held him really quick?" Devon asked excitedly.

Harper laughed and grudgingly stepped away from Carter. She leaned down and picked up Bo. He let out a whimper and she rocked him a little before handing him over to Devon. Devon's smile widened as he took a few steps away. Carter's arms came around her waist as he stood behind her. She leaned back against him as she took a quick picture of Devon and Bo. She sent a quick message to both Jeff and Tank. Her phone immediately buzzed.

**Tank:** I'm going to kill him.

**Jeff:** You weren't supposed to let Devon hold the baby first. I thought I was your favorite.

"I think you just caused some trouble, Dove." Carter whispered in her ear.

"Are you planning on saving me from the wrath of Jeff and Tank?" Harper laughed.

Carter chuckled and let her go. She watched as Carter and Devon spoke quietly together for a few minutes. Devon handed the baby to Carter and left. Carter put Bo back in the crib, studying the twins with a small smile. Harper took a quick picture before sitting on the couch and pulling the food onto her lap.

# Chapter 11

How did he do it? Harper had no idea how Carter could pick out her food so well. Even her unusual and less common preferences he knew. She moaned softly as she took another bite of her beans, cheese, and carne asada burrito. She was in heaven.

Harper heard Carter chuckling beside her, but she ignored him. He bumped her shoulder as he handed her a water bottle from the bag. She accepted it but set it aside as she took another bite. "I don't think I have seen you eat so much in one sitting since we were kids." Carter commented.

"I've been a little stressed the past several weeks." Harper pointed out.

"Fair enough." Carter took a bite of his food.

They ate in silence and Harper scarfed down the rest of her burrito before following it with half her water. She kicked her legs up over Carter's lap, getting an amused chuckle from him as she laid down. She closed her eyes and fell asleep.

Carter watched Harper as she downed her food like she hadn't eaten in weeks, and then pass out. She looked so peaceful as she lay there. Carter smiled as he remembered her walking out of the bathroom that morning, she had literally taken his breath away. He had never seen her in makeup or anything but church or baggy clothes. She still had a tiny waist despite giving birth to three kids, and her blue eyes somehow seemed bluer.

Her story about her tattoo had left him with a burning curiosity to know what it looked like. It was cute how embarrassed she was about it. Not that he wanted her to get anymore, but he was curious about the one she had.

His phone buzzed and he pulled it out of his pocket. A text message from Devon appeared. Unlocking his phone, he read it.

**Devon:** How was lunch?

**Carter:** It was good. Thanks. I don't think I have seen Harper so enthusiastic about eating.

**Devon:** Glad to hear it. Clara's been worried about her not eating enough.

**Devon:** Did you tell her?

**Carter:** Not yet.

**Devon:** You two seemed pretty snuggly when I dropped the food off.

**Carter:** I think she was relieved to be able to bring Bo home early. She nearly collapsed to the floor.

**Devon:** If you don't tell her soon, I might try my hand at her. She is hot, sings like she fell from heaven, feisty and great with kids. She's the perfect woman.

**Carter:** I don't think she is open to a relationship right now. She's been occupied with Luther and now she has the twins.

**Devon:** Challenge accepted

Carter shook his head and laid back on the couch. Jeff seemed to be trying to get close to Harper as well. How long would she keep them in the surrogate brother zone if they really started to pursue her? He knew Devon was just trying to get him to man up and talk with Harper, but Carter didn't know if they were ready for that.

*       *       *

Harper woke to the sound of a cabinet closing softly and Carter talking quietly. "You are as ravenous as your brother. But lucky for you, I can feed you instead of having to wake your mother." Carter was gently bouncing Bo as he shook the bottle. "You will love your sister. She is just as amazing as your mother. And she will adore you. You won't have a fiercer protector than Lexi."

Harper's heart swelled with love for this man. And she was terrified. She pulled out her phone and sent a quick text.

**Harper:** I can't do this. I need to burn the wolf off my skin because I'm not strong enough to do this.

**Jeff:** Slow down, Athena. What can't you do?

**Harper:** Athena? And Carter. I can't tell him.

**Jeff:** Athena, goddess of wisdom and war strategy, not to mention her beauty. I should have known you were Athena when you bloodied my nose.

**Jeff:** why not

**Harper:** I can't. I'm already going to get hurt again when we leave the ranch. Lexi will be too.

**Jeff:** You're leaving the ranch?

**Harper:** When Luther is caught.

**Jeff:** Why won't you stay and try to work things out with Carter?

**Harper:** I'm his best friend's little sister, Jeff. I'm pretty sure I've been in the surrogate sister zone my whole life. Nothing is going to change that.

**Jeff:** If you won't stay to be with Carter, then marry me. I hear Denver has some nice ring shops.

**Harper:** Sorry. I won't marry without love, so it looks like I'm going to be a crazy old cat lady once the kids are grown.

**Jeff:** You're breaking my heart, Athena.

"Hey, I didn't wake you, did I?" Carter asked as he lifted her legs off the couch and sat, setting her legs back over him.

"No. You were just fine." Harper gave him a forced smile. He gave her a quizzical look but didn't ask.

**Harper:** Maybe I should leave after we get back to the ranch regardless. I'll see if Clara knows where I can get a car.

**Jeff:** You better be joking, because if you aren't, I'm getting a marriage license.

Harper set her phone down and closed her eyes. She could feel the start of a headache coming on. How could she and the kids leave without a vehicle? She could do this. The first thing she needed to decide was when she was leaving. Harper rolled so she was facing the back of the couch and Carter shifted to accommodate her change in position. Once she was comfortable, Harper prayed.

She thanked God for healing Bo and for protecting her and her kids. She thanked Him for sending Carter, Jeff, Devon, Tank and Clara into their lives. She prayed for their continued safety and that Luther wouldn't harm the kids. She prayed for a clear head and to know when she should leave the ranch. She asked for guidance in finding a home where she could raise her kids in a loving community and a place where they could go to church. Harper felt a tear slip from her eye as she closed her prayer. She tried to fall back asleep, but Colt woke and started to cry, which caused Bo to start crying.

Harper quickly got up and picked up Colt. She kissed his forehead as she walked back to the couch where Carter was trying to soothe Bo back to sleep. She sat down and covered herself so Colt could eat. Once Colt had settled down, Bo followed suit. How was she going to manage both boys on her own? Where was Henry when she needed his advice?

Harper remained lost in her thoughts until Colt finished. She raised him to her shoulder as she stood. She paced the small room as she burped him. The whole time she could feel Carter watching her. She paced for a good ten minutes before she stopped and changed Colt's diaper.

"Harper, come sit down." Carter said. She looked over at him and thought about refusing, but gave in when she saw the look on his face. He had on his 'don't mess with me' face. So, help her, if Jeff tattled on her, she was going to break his nose.

After she was sitting on the couch, Carter set Bo in her arms. She looked down at her boys and knew at that moment, she couldn't leave the safety of the ranch, not until Luther was arrested. She took a deep breath and let it out slowly. Both boys were watching her, and Harper smiled. A dimple appeared on Bo's cheek, causing her to laugh. Her laughter caused Colt to smile. "You boys are going to be the death of me." Harper told them. "That dimple of yours, Bo, is going to get you out of a lot of the trouble you are no doubt going to cause."

"Are dimples on your list, too?" Carter asked with a smile, and Harper couldn't help but notice the dimples on his cheeks.

"Maybe. My list is quite long. I think I still have the full thing in one of the boxes back at the apartment." Harper shrugged as she turned her attention back to the babies. She repositioned them so they were lying side by side in one arm. They were still so small, they fit in newborn clothes.

"You have it written down?" Carter laughed out loud.

"Of course I do. A girl has to do what a girl has to do in order to protect herself." Harper paused for a moment. "But I'm thinking about burning it. It sure did not help me the first time around."

"Whatever caused you to create such a list?" There was genuine curiosity in Carter's voice that stopped the lie that was forming on her tongue.

Instead, she smiled sadly. "I was young and in love. Then I realized that his world and mine were not meant to mix."

Carter sat quietly for several minutes, and Harper hoped he would drop the subject, but her hopes were dashed. "How old were you? You said you met Luther shortly after starting college."

"How old was I when I fell in love, or how old was I when I had my heart broken?" Harper asked as she kept her eyes on her sons.

"How old were you when you had your heart broken?" He clarified.

Harper took a minute to think about it. Truth be told, her heart broke over Carter more than once. When she was six and he promised to stay with her, but she woke up and he wasn't there. When she was forced into her mom's car, and he just stood there watching, holding onto Henry's arm.

When he didn't show up for graduation. Harper laughed to try to dispel the tension in the room. "Twice when I was a kid and again when I was an adult."

"He broke your heart three times? Do I know him?" Carter sounded frustrated.

Harper looked over at him with a raised brow and straight face. "Yes, you know him and no, I'm not telling you." He looked ready to argue, so she asked a question of her own. "And what about your love life? Any broken hearts sitting over there?"

"Only once." Carter looked away from her as he shifted in his seat.

"Do tell." Harper smiled. It was about time he was the one uncomfortable during their conversations. "How old were you when your heart broke, and did a list ever come from it?"

He gave her a bland look. "No list. And it happened about a year ago." Something in his tone sobered her.

"How long were you together? With your type of military career, I'm sure it was hard to balance a relationship with it." Harper knew a relationship with a special forces man would be incredibly difficult, if not impossible.

"That's the thing, I had been in love with her for over ten years. By the time I figured out what I really wanted out of life, I was too late, and she was married." Carter stared at the door across the room.

"Ouch." Harper watched the muscle in Carter's jaw clench. "Henry didn't know the reason behind my list, but he did know about it. He told me to stop hiding and start living. It took me a while to realize what he meant by that. At first, I had been afraid to get hurt again, but then I became terrified that I would find someone who could replace him in my life. Maybe if we both learn to let go, we can let life happen and everything will all work out."

Harper could feel Carter's eyes on her again and she turned to look at him. "How is that working out for you? Letting life happen and praying it all works out." There was no malice in his voice, just honest curiosity.

"Ah, I fear I am far from that point. I am dangerously close to falling back to square one on my path." Harper shook her head. She could not believe she was having this conversation with the very man she was hopelessly in love with but could not have.

"Why is that?"

"My heart is firmly in four places at the moment. With Lexi. With Bo. With Colt. And with him. And at this point, I don't know if I will ever get it back." Harper watched the sleeping boys, too afraid to look at Carter.

"After all the hurt he put you through, you're still in love with him?" Carter sounded surprised and a little frustrated.

She turned and looked him straight in the eyes as a single tear escaped onto her cheek. "Yes. I am still in love with him."

Carter's stoney expression softened when he saw the tear. He used his thumb to brush it away before putting his arms around her. She leaned against his chest and silently laughed at the irony that Carter, of all people, was comforting her for being in love with him when he could never love her back. Her heart was being shattered and mended all at the same time.

* * *

It was nearing dinner time and the twins had been fed again. They were in the crib together while Harper sat on the couch with her phone. Carter stood leaning against the counter texting Devon.

**Carter:** I can't tell her.

**Devon:** Never thought of you as a coward.

**Carter:** She is in love with someone else.

**Devon:** That's what you thought last time, and look at Luther now.

**Carter:** Well, she just told me her heart was firmly with this other guy, even though he has broken her heart three times.

**Devon:** You should still tell her. Maybe she will realize you are the better choice.

**Carter:** I don't know man.

**Devon:** You should get another wolf tattoo. Maybe then you can be as brave as she is.

**Carter:** Not a bad idea. Back or calf?

A knock came at the door and Raider moved in front of the crib. It slowly opened and a petite blonde woman stepped in the room wearing scrubs. Her eyes landed on Harper and a smile spread across her face as her eyes filled with tears. Carter stood to his full height ready to step in if she turned out to be a threat.

"Harper? I wasn't expecting to see you here." The woman cried as she ran across the room. Harper stood and hugged the woman with a big smile. "You look fantastic, especially having just birthed twins."

"It's good to see you too, Ivy. Beth told me you have been checking in on Bo every day you work." Harper retook her seat and Ivy sat beside her. Out of the corner of her eye, she saw Carter relax back against the counter. His eyes stayed on them while Raider settled on the ground at her feet.

"Where have you been? Beth said you left town after being released from the hospital." Ivy accused. "I knew Dr. Honey shouldn't have discharged you. You had a look about you when you left, and I knew you were not going to listen to the doctor's stipulations."

"Ivy, I was fine." Harper tried to keep her voice down as she sent a glance in Carter's direction. He was definitely listening.

"Fine? You literally almost died, missy. A blood transfusion is no joking matter. I cannot believe you left and missed your follow-up appointment. And you skipped town? Beth made it sound like you drove somewhere." Ivy's voice rose from a whisper to almost yelling by the time she was done talking.

"It wasn't all that bad." Harper tried to ignore the hard look Carter was sending her way.

"I remember specifically telling you that you were not allowed to drive and to be on bedrest for the next two weeks. And that you were supposed to come back in two days to check your levels to see if you needed more blood." Ivy was now on her feet and pacing in front of Harper.

Harper pinched the bridge of her nose. Now she was going to get a lecture from Carter as well, she just knew it. Sure enough, she heard heavy footsteps coming closer. She slowly raised her eyes to meet Carter's fiery gaze. "You were not supposed to be driving? A blood transfusion? Harper…"

"Carter, please. Not now." Harper breathed out a heavy sigh.

"Carter? As in…" Ivy started to say, but Harper cut her off as she stood abruptly. Harper and Ivy talked a lot during the night after the twins were born. Harper had borne her soul to the kind nurse and found a friend.

"Carter, can you go see what is taking the guys so long in bringing us food?" Harper asked, desperately needing a few minutes alone with Ivy.

"I can text them." Carter crossed his arms over his chest as he continued to glare at her.

Harper walked up to him and put a hand on his arm. She lowered her voice so that Ivy couldn't hear her. "Please, Carter. I need only a few minutes of girl talk. Go to the bathroom or something, but all I'm asking for is ten minutes."

"Girl talk?" Carter raised a brow in obvious suspicion. "Sorry, Dove. I am not leaving you alone."

"Please. We are in a locked down section of the hospital with armed guards at the doors and I have Raider." Harper begged. "It's just ten minutes."

"If I give you these ten minutes, you and I are going to have a serious conversation about your near-death experience. I can't believe you drove when your doctor told you not to." Carter shook his head and then uncrossed his arms. "Fine. Ten minutes, but you are taking my gun." He said as he handed Harper his firearm.

"You honestly think I don't have a gun on me?" Harper asked with a smirk. Carter's eyes dropped and she could see him taking her in. "Eyes up here, Carter." Harper smacked his chest.

"I don't see where you could be hiding one." Carter's cheeks pinked slightly as he returned his eyes to her face.

Harper leaned closer to him and lowered her voice. "It wouldn't be a concealed carry if you could easily see it. But if it makes you leave, I will also take yours." Harper grabbed the gun from Carter's hands with a smile and tucked it into the back of her waistband, pulling her shirt over it. "Now, you can leave." Harper pointed to the door.

Carter hesitated as he looked at the door. She could see the indecision in his eyes. He finally stepped close to her and whispered in her ear. "Ten minutes, Dove." And then he walked past Harper and left the room.

Harper was still staring at the closed door when Ivy let out a low whistle. "Wow. The tension between the two of you is intense. Is that 'The Carter'?"

"Yes, that is 'The Carter'." Harper turned to give Ivy a small smile. Then she filled her friend in on everything that had happened over the last six weeks. She also told her about how confused she was when it came to her feelings for Carter. She even showed Ivy the pictures from that morning.

"I can't believe you never told me how hot Carter was. Are those hunks in the waiting area yours too?" Ivy fanned her face.

Harper laughed. They aren't mine, but they are with me. They served with my brother in the military."

"Since Carter is yours, can I have one of the others? Better yet, both?" Ivy and Harper laughed as Ivy grabbed her phone and looked at it. "My brother is bringing up my dinner. I forgot it at home. He is the one that gave Bo the blessing, did you want to meet him?" Harper nodded her head. She would love to thank him for what he did for her and her son.

# Chapter 12

He was only a step in the room when he froze in surprise. Hot fury coursed through Carter's veins as he watched Harper hugging a strange man. Ivy was holding onto Raider's collar several steps away and when she saw him, her eyes widened. Harper noticed him in the next second and quickly stepped away from the man. He had brown hair and dark eyes. He was built like a wrestler and a few inches shorter than Carter. Carter glared at everyone in the room before he settled his eyes on Harper.

"Who is he?" Carter growled out.

Harper's eyes widened for a split second before she narrowed them. "Derek is a friend." She said back evenly.

"I left you with Ivy for ten minutes only to come back to this. You asked me to trust you, Harper. Where did he even come from?" Carter knew he made a mistake the moment the words came out of his mouth. Harper's stance widened and her eyes narrowed even more. She was ready for battle.

"Carter Michaels, you are not my father or my brother. You have no claim on me whatsoever. I am a grown woman and can hold a conversation with anyone I want to without your permission or knowledge." She took a step towards him, eyes blazing.

"Is this the guy?" Carter shot a glare at the guy standing behind Harper. The man looked guilty, which only added to Carter's desire to punch him in the face.

"That is none of your business." She ground out as her hands clenched into fists. "I want you to leave, Carter."

Harper's statement was like a punch to the gut. "I'm not leaving you alone with him." Carter tried to soften his voice, but it didn't work.

"Then you can send in any of the others, but you need to leave. Now." Harper shoved at his chest, and he could see the angry tears in her eyes. His anger only grew. Why was Harper mad? He was the one who walked in on her all over another man. Letting out a growl of frustration, Carter turned and stormed from the room. He barely managed to stop himself from slamming the door as he left.

He burst out into the lobby causing both Jeff and Devon to jump to their feet. "What are you doing out here? Where is Harper?" Devon asked as he reached his side. Carter didn't slow his steps as he stomped down the hallway.

"Send Jeff in there to watch her." Carter snapped.

"What happened?" Devon asked, grabbing Carter's arm, pulling him to a stop.

"A nurse friend stopped in, and Harper asked for ten minutes to have some girl talk. When I got back, Harper was hugging some guy. Then she kicked me out of the room." Carter shrugged off Devon's hand and pushed open the door to the stairs. "I'm going for a walk."

\* \* \*

Harper glared at the closed door. How dare Carter treat her like a child? If she had any doubts before, she now knew that Carter only saw her as a kid needing his protection. She blinked back the tears that threatened to fall. She was so mad at him. He had no right to accuse her of doing anything wrong.

"I'm sorry. I didn't mean to cause any issues between you and your man." Derek said and Harper turned to face him.

"Carter's behavior has nothing to do with you, Derek. And he is not my man." Harper clarified.

"Are you sure? He seemed pretty jealous." Derek shot her a curious look.

Harper shook her head. "It's not like that." She looked back at the door, half expecting Carter to walk back in and apologize.

"Does he know that?" Derek asked with a teasing smile.

Harper wasn't in the mood to discuss Carter anymore. She was furious with him and how he acted. "Thanks again, Derek, for giving Bo the blessing." A light knock sounded at the door and Harper moved to answer it as she continued talking. "And thank you for the number of the real estate agent." She pulled the door open, and Jeff stepped in.

He took in the room quickly. Ivy was standing next to Derek near the couch and Raider was laying on the ground next to the crib. "Hi, I'm Jeff. Harper's brother." Jeff took a few steps across the room and shook Derek's hand.

Derek had a wary look on his face, but he gave Jeff a smile. "I'm Derek. Ivy, here, is my sister. She helped deliver the Anderson Twins."

"Derek is also one of the men that gave Bo a blessing." Harper commented. "He just stopped by to give Ivy her dinner, and I wanted to thank him in person for all he had done for Bo."

Understanding flashed in Jeff's eyes as he glanced between her and Derek, but there was an uncharacteristic stiffness to him that put Harper on her guard. Derek and Jeff chatted for a few more minutes before he and Ivy left to start their shifts. As soon as they left, Harper sank down onto the couch and let out a frustrated growl. She felt Jeff sit next to her, but he remained silent, allowing her to collect her thoughts.

The boys started to cry, and Harper stood. Jeff remained on the couch as she changed both boys and made a bottle. She moved back to the crib as she tucked the bottle under her chin so she could pick up both Bo and Colt. Once back on the couch, she managed to cover herself and Colt so he could eat. Then she offered Bo the bottle. It was a bit awkward, but she was feeding both twins at the same time by herself.

She needed to start learning how to do things on her own, because soon she would be. There was no way she was staying at the ranch with Carter acting like this.

"You could have asked me to help you, you know?" Jeff said, watching her.

"I can't keep relying on you guys for everything. Who knows how long I have until it will be just me and the kids." Harper glanced over at Jeff, and he scowled at her.

"What's up with the real estate agent?" Jeff asked, studying her face.

Harper let out a tired sigh. "Jeff, I told you, I cannot stay. Derek mentioned an old roommate who is a real estate agent in the area I have considered moving to."

"And I thought we already settled on this, Athena. All you have to do is say, yes."

"I'm serious, Jeff. I am not staying at the ranch. Especially after today." Harper's eyes started to burn, but she fought the tears. She was done crying. She was so tired of feeling out of control. Starting today, she was taking back the reins of her own life.

"What happened? Carter looked ready to destroy anything that got in his way." Jeff asked in a quiet voice.

Harper let out a laugh full of frustration. "I am so mad at him. I don't think I have ever been so mad at him in my entire life. He treated me like a disobedient child. He took one step into the room and stopped. He asked who Derek was and I told him he was a friend. Then he started lecturing me about having Derek in the room. That he had only been gone for ten minutes and that he had trusted me." If she wasn't feeding the twins, Harper would be pacing. She was getting worked up all over again. "Derek had literally only been here for a few minutes before Carter came back."

"Did Carter know that Derek was the man who gave the blessing to Bo?" Jeff inquired.

"No. He came in when I gave Derek a side hug as I said thank you. Derek was just about to leave." Harper said frustratedly. "Derek and his sister have done so much for me and the boys. Ivy helped deliver the twins and then she stayed the night with me, so I didn't have to be alone even though she was off the clock. Derek gave the blessing and Ivy has returned every day she has worked to check in on Bo. I was just saying thank you." Jeff made a noise like he was thinking. "When I mentioned wanting to look for a house for me and the kids, Derek gave me his friend's number."

"I really don't think you should leave. At least not yet. Harper, Luther is still out there and very much a threat." Jeff touched her arm, and she looked at him.

"I am looking for a house because as soon as Luther is arrested, I'm gone. I am not staying where I am thought of as a child." Harper was deadly serious, and she could see that Jeff realized it.

She turned her attention back to taking care of the twins. Once she finally had them settle back in the crib, she looked back over at Jeff. He was on his phone and typing furiously. Somehow, she knew he was texting the guys. She didn't even want to know what they were discussing. Her anger had morphed into frustration and hurt, and she did not want to deal with the drama Carter created.

She grabbed her phone and made a call to Derek's real estate friend, Hank. He seemed enthusiastic about helping her. He asked her to send him an email with her must-haves and wants, along with the areas she was wanting to look at.

Throughout the whole call, she could feel Jeff's eyes on her, but she refused to look in his direction. Once the phone call was done, Harper sent a quick text to Clara asking about any vehicles for sale in the area. Price wasn't an obstacle. Luther had way more money than she had been aware of and in the divorce, she got half of it. Over the next hour, Clara sent her four potential choices. Before she could take a closer look at them, the door opened, and Dr. Honey walked in.

"Good evening." Dr. Honey said cheerfully. "Oh. Who's this?"

"Dr. Honey, this is my surrogate brother, Jeff. Jeff, this is Dr. Honey." Harper made the introductions as she patted Raider's head.

"Good to know that you have a good support system, Harper. You are going to need it with twin boys." Dr. Honey laughed as she turned to fully face Harper. "Are you ready to go?"

"Beyond ready." Harper smiled.

"That's what I thought. I am sending all this information with you, but I wanted to also go over it so that if you have any questions, I can answer them for you before you leave." Dr. Honey handed Harper a stack of papers. Harper nodded and the doctor continued. She discussed the injuries Bo had sustained and the treatment that they had done. As for Harper's part, she just needed to take him to a pediatrician in two weeks for a follow-up to make sure he was still doing well.

"Thank you." Harper breathed out, not knowing what else to say.

Dr. Honey gave Harper and each baby a hug goodbye before she left. Harper quickly buckled both boys into their carriers, and before she knew it, she was sitting in the truck with Devon and Carter. Carter was driving this time with Raider in the middle and Devon taking the shotgun seat. Harper didn't even look in Carter's direction, even though she knew he glanced at her frequently.

At the apartment, Devon and Tank once again cleared it before Tank came back down. Carter got out and stood guard next to the truck. Immediately after they were in the apartment, Tank asked if he could hold Bo. Devon and Tank quickly unbuckled the twins and were holding them. Harper glanced around and noticed that Carter wasn't there.

Seeing her confusion, Jeff whispered close to her, so the others didn't overhear. "He went to get formula and bottles for Bo."

Harper couldn't believe her heart still ached to be near him, even though she was mad at him. "While you guys have the boys, I'm going to take a few minutes to myself." She said as she walked into her room and closed the door after Raider entered.

Harper changed into a sports bra, her yoga pants, and wrapped her hands before pulling the punching bag from the closet. She positioned it in the center of the room, put her earphones in, cranked up the music, and began working out her frustration. She had used boxing as an outlet ever since her teen years. She hadn't been able to after she married Luther and it felt good getting back to it.

Thirty minutes later, she was sweaty and still nowhere near ready to face Carter. Someone touched her shoulder. Out of reflex, she turned and threw her weight behind the punch. Her eyes widened as she watched Carter stagger back and crash against the wall.

Tank came running in and looked around. Carter was looking up at her in surprise as he leaned against the wall rubbing his jaw. Harper quickly pulled her earphones out of her ears as she continued to stare at him. She was speechless. She hadn't meant to hit him; it had been a reflex from being scared. Another beat of silence and Tank burst out laughing. His laughter brought in Jeff and Devon, each holding one of the twins.

"I didn't know you boxed." Jeff laughed. "Even though the elbow to the face probably should have clued me in."

"State Champ sophomore year of high school." Harper said breathlessly as her eyes remained glued to Carter. "I'm so sorry."

Carter got to his feet and met her eyes. She looked completely stunned by what had happened. He had called her name twice before tapping her shoulder. When he had walked into her room, he hadn't expected to see her in nothing but a sports bra and yoga pants, boxing. Carter had taken a moment or two to watch her before trying to get her attention. He was sent in to let her know that dinner had arrived. He worked his jaw as he held her gaze. Slowly her stunned look became guarded and wary.

It killed him to see her put up walls between them, but he didn't blame her. After he had cooled down and returned to the waiting room, Devon had let him have it. Jeff had texted Devon the whole story and Carter felt like a complete idiot. He had wanted to apologize, but Jeff suggested giving Harper a little time. Seeing her take out her anger on the punching bag made him glad he had followed the suggestion. She had done nothing wrong, and he had been blinded by his jealousy.

"I deserved that." He told her and her brow rose ever so slightly. "I'm sorry for how I acted. I was out of line, and a complete idiot." She crossed her arms over her chest but didn't say anything. "I'm sorry, Dove." He tried again.

"Don't, Carter. Just don't." She glared at him, and he could see the fire in her eyes growing again. "I am not a child. You have no right to treat me like I am." He opened his mouth to speak, but she cut him off. "Don't say a word. You said plenty earlier. Now, you will listen to me." She took a step towards him, and he swallowed. "Derek was the man that gave Bo a blessing. I was thanking him for being willing to get fired in order to do it, since no one was allowed in Bo's room." Harper took a deep breath. "I know I have made a lot of mistakes in my life, but I am not the kind of girl to just throw herself at any man that walks by. Other than my brother, I have only loved one man in my life, and convinced myself to settle for less when it came to Luther. It hurts that you would think so little of me."

"Harper, I don't…" Carter tried to reach out and touch her arm, but she stepped back.

"I am so mad at you right now, Carter." Her voice had softened, and she took another breath. "I think I need some space."

The silence in the room was deafening and Harper swallowed down the tears that wanted to come. She had seen the hurt and regret in Carter's eyes as she had berated him. He didn't try to say anything else, only nodded, and hung his head. She fought against the urge to wrap her arms around him. She needed comfort, and she knew she could find it with him. Instead, she grabbed Carter's hoodie and slipped it on before she turned to the door and shoved past Jeff and Devon. She went to the kitchen, pulled out an ice pack and shoved it into Carter's chest as he slowly walked in. He looked up at her surprised, but she quickly looked away. The food was passed around, and the silence from her speech continued to stretch on.

"I was wondering if we can pack the trucks tonight? Now that we have Bo, I would feel more comfortable getting back to the ranch as quickly as possible. This place brings back...memories." Harper broke the silence and all attention turned to her.

"Sure thing, Athena." Jeff gave her a small smile. "One of us can stay up here with you and the twins while the rest of us load the trucks."

Harper thanked them and finished eating. Tank helped her take the babies and their things into the bedroom so she could feed them. Devon opted to stay behind, and the others made quick work of the meager belongings she and Lexi had. As the guys returned, Harper's phone rang, and she answered it with a smile. She was still in the back room alone but the door was open.

"Mommy!" Lexi's cheerful voice rang through the line.

"Lexi, baby." Harper said as she burped Bo. "Oh, it's good to hear your voice."

"Are you okay, mommy?" Lexi's joy morphed into worry.

"I'm better now that I get to hear your voice. How are you doing? What have you been up to?" Harper asked. She put the phone on speaker, as she sat on the floor so she could change Bo's diaper.

"I'm doing good. Peter and two of the policemen took me to go see some cars. Clara said we needed one for when it was time to go away." Lexi gushed out, but then paused. Harper could almost see the frown on her daughter's face. "Are we going away?"

"Not yet, but hopefully soon." Harper glanced at the open door and prayed no one could hear her. "We talked about this, remember? As soon as he is arrested, we need to leave."

Lexi was quiet for a long time. Harper was able to finish the diaper change and pick the phone back up, turning the speaker off by the time Lexi spoke. "Because God doesn't want a man and woman to live together unless they are married?"

"That's right, baby." Harper smiled.

"Then why can't you marry Carter? I like Carter. He tucks me in at night and he makes you feel better when you are sad. I don't want to go!" Lexi yelled. Harper had never heard her daughter raise her voice before.

"That's not how it works, sweetheart." Harper tried to explain, but Lexi started to cry.

"It's not fair. I don't want to go. What about Bella and my pony?" Harper tried to calm her daughter, but Lexi just kept yelling until the call was disconnected.

Harper stared at the phone and jumped when it started to ring again. Harper answered it immediately. "Lexi, honey. I need you to listen."

"Sorry, Harper. Lexi locked herself in her room." Clara apologized softly.

"Okay." Harper whispered as she pulled her knees to her chest.

"Everything will be okay. She'll understand. Just give her a little time." Clara said and Harper sucked in a shaky breath. "Do you know when you will get back?"

"Tomorrow night." Harper sniffled.

"Get some sleep, Harper. Things will look better in the morning."

"Thank you, Clara." Harper hung up the phone and set it on the charger.

She hoped that Clara was right, and that Lexi wouldn't hate her when it came time for them to leave. Harper looked over at Bo and Colt who were sleeping in their bassinets. She wrapped her arms around her legs and pulled her knees closer to her chest. She laid her head back on the bed and closed her eyes as she fought her tears. She could do this. She was strong and capable. It wasn't going to be easy, but Harper was determined to make it work. For both her and for her kids.

Harper sat there for a long time but did not have the energy to climb into bed. She was emotionally and physically exhausted. She regretted boxing earlier. Her muscles were already sore and becoming stiff. She heard several sets of footsteps approaching her bedroom door, but didn't care to look.

"I can't believe she fell asleep like that." Tank said quietly.

"Colt kept her up most of the night before, and she was up the majority of the day with both boys. I'm surprised she lasted so long. She has to be completely exhausted." Carter whispered back. She hated that just the sound of his voice caused her to feel more at peace and relaxed.

"I've got to take the dogs out. Get her in bed so she is more comfortable." Tank ordered softly. "Come, Raider."

There was a moment of silence before strong arms scooped her off the floor before gently setting her on the bed. Her blanket was pulled up over her and she curled into a ball. She knew it had been Carter who had tucked her in, even though she had kept her eyes shut the whole time. A hand brushed the hair off her forehead and then moved slowly, stroking her hair. Harper let out a soft sigh as she started to drift off to sleep.

"Goodnight, Harper." Carter's whisper was so soft she almost didn't hear it before he pressed a kiss to her temple. As he leaned away, he said something else, but Harper wasn't able to catch it as sleep overtook her.

# Chapter 13

Harper was so glad she had talked the guys into letting her and the twins have the room to themselves. Tank had insisted on both Casper and Raider staying with her, which she heartily agreed to. Both Colt and Bo were incredibly fussy for hours. She had just fed them and changed their diapers. Whenever Lexi had gotten this way, she would pace her room and sing softly to her. Harper hadn't wanted to sing because she knew the men down the hall would hear her, and she didn't like people listening to her, but she was desperate at this point.

She closed the door, leaving it cracked. That was another stipulation of her being alone in the room, the door remained open. Holding both babies up to her chest, Harper began to sing softly. After several songs, Bo began to fall asleep. Colt followed a few minutes later, but she was worried that if she stopped or put them down, they would wake up again.

The door creaked open. Harper glanced over to see Carter stepping into the room. He moved slowly over to her and placed a hand on her back. "Harper, let me take one of the boys. It's almost 3:00. You should get some rest."

Harper hesitated for a moment as she continued to sing softly. She was so tired. She gave Carter a small nod and he carefully lifted Colt from her arms. Colt started to whimper. Carter lifted the baby up to his shoulder as Harper continued her lullaby, and Colt fell back asleep. Their eyes met and Harper could barely see the relieved look in Carter's eyes as he watched her. He and Jeff had come in a couple of times earlier and offered to help her, but Harper had sent them away. Each time Carter had looked pained but respected her wishes to be left alone.

Lexi's plea for her to marry Carter flashed back into her mind, and she quickly looked away. Another hour passed before Harper was brave enough to try to sit on the bed. She wasn't singing anymore, but she was humming. Carter sat slowly beside her before putting the pillow behind Harper's back. She gratefully sagged back against it and closed her eyes. She was definitely less confident in her ability to do this on her own, now. One baby was hard enough, but two were proving impossible. Carter had moved Colt from his shoulder and was cradling him. Harper felt her body going heavy just before falling asleep.

Harper groaned as she pressed her face into her pillow. She froze for a second when she realized she was no longer holding Bo, and then jerked upright. She frantically scanned her room for her son but came face to face with a startled Carter lying next to her. She let out a squeak of surprise as she fell off the bed in her haste to put some distance between them.

Her mind raced through the previous night. Carter had been sitting next to her on the bed, each of them holding a baby. Carter was still in a somewhat sitting position, but how did she end up curled up against him, using his chest for a pillow?

"Harper!" Carter called as he climbed off the bed and knelt by her side. "Are you okay? Where are the boys?" he asked, his eyes raking over her for any injuries.

"Oh good. You two are awake." Harper and Carter's heads snapped in the direction of the door to find Devon smiling at them. "I was just coming to get you Harper, Colt is getting hungry."

"You have them?" Harper asked in disbelief as her sleepy brain was still trying to make sense of what was going on.

"Yeah, Tank came to check on you all. He found you and Carter passed out while holding the twins. We thought we could take them for a while, so you could get some sleep." Devon shrugged. "You were up past four."

"Why didn't you wake me?" Harper asked. "You should have told me you were taking them. I nearly had a heart attack when I woke up and saw them gone." Harper's brain was finally starting to wake up and clear.

Carter ran his hand down his face and Harper could see the exhaustion in his features. "And how did I end up..." His voice trailed off as he glanced over at Harper.

"Don't blame us for that." Devon raised his hands in a show of innocence. "Harper was already using you as a pillow when we got the boys." Harper's face heated. "I wouldn't say we can blame you two either, though, you looked like you literally passed out and slumped to the side and Carter just happened to be there." Devon gave her a smile as his eyes twinkled.

Harper glared at him as she got to her feet. She was so tired and mad. She stormed from the room. She could hear Carter's quiet voice lecturing Devon as she left.

She found Jeff pacing and patting Colt's back in the kitchen. She marched right up to him, took Colt, and then locked herself in the bathroom. Not the most ideal place to nurse a baby, but she didn't want to see any of the men at the moment. She had even locked Raider out. She needed a moment to process all the swirling emotions inside of her.

Even being up all night, Harper felt well rested after only getting two hours of sleep. Before realizing her son was no longer in her arms, she had felt so comfortable. She could not believe she was sleeping with Carter. Embarrassment flooded her as she remembered the same surprise and confusion in Carter's eyes that she had been feeling. Harper reminded herself that it had been an accident. Neither one of them had planned it. They had been up all night with the twins and had fallen asleep. The only people in the wrong were the ones who had allowed it to continue.

She opened the bathroom door as she was burping Colt and walked out into the kitchen. Carter was leaning up against the counter glaring at Jeff, Devon, and Tank. All three men were looking at the ground and looked like they had just experienced a lecture from a disappointed father.

Even though she was mad at them, she couldn't help the smile that tried to surface as she took in the scene in front of her. As she approached, apologies started to fill the air and she held up her hand to stop them.

"First, I want you all to realize that you are firmly in the doghouse at the moment. Seriously, what were you thinking?" Harper swayed as she patted Colt's back, but her voice was stern. "Regardless of the door being open, you three allowed me to break one of my promises to Lexi. Thankfully, she wasn't here to see her mother in bed with a man she isn't married to. Especially after I have had to explain that it is against God's commandments when she started asking about Luther and all of his many lady friends." The wide-eyed looks of surprise and guilt almost made her laugh. Man was she tired if everything was becoming funny. "I know it is partially my fault for falling asleep, but you all should have woken us up when you took the boys."

"We're sorry, Harper." Jeff said penitently. "We were only thinking about giving you a break and allowing you to get some rest. We hadn't even taken any of that into consideration."

Harper shook her head and sighed. "When was the last time Bo was fed?"

"I was just about to make him a bottle." Tank looked down at the baby in his arms.

Harper moved to Carter's side, and she passed Colt over to him. Carter didn't even hesitate to take the child. She was hit with how easy and natural she and Carter had become with the kids. Panic once again started to settle in on how much she had allowed Carter into her life. She pulled her eyes from Carter's and faced the others. "I'm jumping in the shower before we leave."

She stood in the hot spray, having the water wash away her exhaustion, allowing her to think. Looking back on the last six weeks, she could see how effortless it had been for her to trust and put her faith in Carter. He had been her rock during childhood, until the day her father had picked her up and tossed her into the back seat of her mother's car. She had been screaming for Carter and Henry to help her. To save her. Henry had tears on his face as he watched her. Carter had a stoney expression as he held Henry's arm, holding him back from chasing the car. Seeing them standing in the middle of the road, watching her being taken away, was the last time she had seen him.

Harper apparently hadn't learned her lesson. Allowing herself to have feelings for him only led to hurt. She couldn't help the fact that she was hopelessly in love with him, but she had thought she had put up protective walls so she wouldn't fall any deeper.

Now, she was drowning. And worst of all, Lexi was going to be crushed as well. Being with Carter was so natural and easy. She hadn't realized just how much they had blended together until she had instinctively passed her son over to him, even though she was still upset with him.

A knock came at the door and Harper tensed. "Everything okay in there?" Jeff called through the closed door. "Both babies are fed, clean and ready to go."

"Give me a minute." Harper called back as she quickly turned off the water and dried off. Because they were traveling today, she decided to dress in some comfy clothes. She wore her yoga pants with pockets and a sky-blue V-neck shirt. She quickly French braided her hair and opened the door. "Sorry." she said as she sat on the counter to lace up her tennis shoes.

"No worries. Tank took the dogs down to use the bathroom and decided to check the cars. He is waiting for us." Devon picked up Bo's car seat and gave her a small smile.

"Devon and Jeff will carry the twins, while I take down the last few things." Carter stepped close to her and put a hand on her elbow. "I need you to stay close. We will be moving fast. I don't like the idea of you and the twins being so exposed."

Less than five minutes later they were leaving the apartment. Tank had insisted on Harper wearing her bulletproof vest whenever she was not feeding the baby, until they were back on the ranch. So, she was once again wearing Carter's hoodie over it.

Habit had her pausing and locking the apartment. She turned to find that the guys were halfway to the elevator. Harper's heart rate increased. She needed to catch up to them. She only made it a few steps when her elderly neighbor opened her door and stopped her.

"Where is your precious little girl?" The old woman asked.

Harper glanced anxiously down the hall. The guys hadn't seemed to notice that she wasn't right behind them. "She is with a friend." Harper took a step farther down the hall. "I'm sorry but I really need to get going." Harper ran as she saw them step into the elevator. The doors were closing and there was no way she was going to make it. "Carter!" She called out just as the doors closed.

Harper's anxiety skyrocketed as she looked up and down the hall. She debated waiting for the elevator to come back up or taking the stairs. The elevator was situated in the center of the building with a hallway branching on either side; the stairs were at the far ends in both directions. Unease filled her as she stood in the empty hallway. She jumped when her phone rang. With shaky hands she answered it without looking at the caller.

"Harper? What happened?" Carter's worried voice came through the line.

"I don't know. I locked the door, then my neighbor, and I couldn't catch up." Harper's voice was even shaking. Harper glanced back down the hall as the feeling of being watched caused the hair on the back of her neck to stand on end. She lowered her voice to a whisper. "I'm scared, Carter. Something doesn't feel right."

"I know, baby. Go back to the apartment and lock the door. We will be there as soon as we can." Carter's normally soothing voice was filled with tension.

"What about the boys?" Harper asked, fear causing her voice to tremble.

"We are almost to the truck with them now. Tank and Jeff will stay with them." Carter told her calmly. "Harper, have you made it to the apartment yet?"

"Almost." Harper sprinted back down the hallway.

"Jeff says to keep the phone on. Don't hang up." Harper heard voices and a closing car door in the background as Carter instructed her. "Put the phone in your pocket and get inside. We are on our way."

Harper put the phone on speaker and slid the phone into the pocket on her thigh. She fumbled with the keys as she unlocked the door and quickly entered. Before she could fully close the door behind her, it slammed into her, causing her to fall backwards into the wall. The door slammed closed, and she looked up to see Luther standing over her. He slowly turned the deadbolt as he gave her a triumphant smile.

"Luther." Harper breathed out as she scooted back across the floor.

"Thought you could just walk away from me, did you?" He sneered at her. "You are mine. I knew from the first time I saw you that I had to have you." He took a slow, predatory step towards her. "You belong to me."

"The first time we met, I threw my drink in your face and told you to buzz off." Harper glared at the man she had come to loath.

Luther laughed as he took another step. "The first time I saw you, you were stepping off a bus wearing a white jacket and light blue beanie. You were smiling and laughing with a fellow passenger, and I knew at that moment that you were mine."

It took her a second to remember the moment he was talking about. She blinked in surprise. "That was here in Denver. The bus was at a pit stop while I was on my way to college."

"Yes, that provided a challenge. I had to call work so I could work remotely for a few months. But by that time, I had already purchased my bus ticket and I watched you the rest of the way."

"You followed me from a gas station?" Harper yelled.

"Then you went and turned me down several times." Luther's eyes had gone cold. "I watched you and learned your preferences and dislikes. I started to act in the way that you liked, and I purposely bumped into you around campus." Harper's mind whirled as she tried to make sense of everything Luther was saying. "I even participated in that cult of yours. You were so stubborn. You told me you would never love me and that you could only offer friendship."

"You lied to me." Harper snapped at him. He had manipulated her the whole time. Disbelief and anger filled her as she slowly got to her feet.

"I told you what you wanted to hear." Luther growled out. "You were mine, and yet you were holding out for some soldier boy, who wasn't even around."

"I wasn't yours then, and I am not yours now. I told you when you asked me to marry you that I didn't think I was capable of loving anyone else at the time. You said you didn't care." Harper took a small step to the side so that the kitchen island was between her and Luther. "I even asked for an annulment after we had been married for a month."

"I don't care if you love me, babe. All I care about is that you are mine and only mine. You belong to me no matter who your heart belongs to." Luther pulled a gun from the waistband of his pants. "Yet you left." Harper's eyes darted to the gun, and she felt cold. "I find you in a house, with not only one man, but four. Tell me Harper, which one of those men is the father of that little brat you insisted on keeping."

"Luther, what are you doing?" Harper asked breathlessly as he fiddled with the gun in his hand.

"You need to be reminded who you belong to, Harper." Luther pointed the gun at her, and she swallowed. "Get in the bedroom, babe. You will be willing this time. Unlike the first time, when I had to slip something in your drink to get you to even let me kiss you without you flinching away from me." Acid churned in her stomach. Had he really drugged her? Thinking back, she could not remember sharing a bed with him. They had slept in different rooms from the beginning.

His voice was cold and filled with a threat. Harper didn't feel like she had a choice. She backed towards the bedroom and Luther gave her body a long look. Shivers of disgust ran down her spine. She bumped against the closed door, and she fumbled to try to open it, but she wasn't willing to take her eyes off Luther. He stepped closer to her and pressed the barrel of the gun to her temple. She tried to turn away from it, but he grabbed her face, holding her in place.

"You are hurting me, Luther." She whimpered and he pressed the gun harder against her, causing her to gasp in pain.

"Kiss me." He growled out.

"Luther, please. Stop." Harper begged as she tried to push him away.

Luther ignored her protests and kissed her hard. The metallic taste of blood filled her mouth as she struggled against him. Harper fumbled with the door handle again. The door finally gave way behind her, and she fell backwards. Luther swore as he stumbled several steps. When he looked back at her, Harper knew she had pushed him too far. Pure hatred filled his eyes. He reached down and grabbed her by her hair and shoved her towards the bed.

"You have been refusing to kiss me since we met. You are mine!" He raged as he paced in front of her. Harper moved slowly, trying not to draw his attention while he waved his gun around as he yelled at her. As soon as she got to her feet, he whirled to face her. "You are mine." He said again. "No one else can have you." Luther raised the gun and fired two shots into her chest causing her to fall back on the bed as pain stole her breath.

# Chapter 14

Carter put an earbud connected to his phone in one ear and a com bud in his other. Devon had the other set. Luther had Harper trapped in the apartment and Carter was beside himself with fear. He had suspected that Luther was a crazy stalker, but he hadn't realized how insane he was. Devon was on his heels as they ran up the stairs. He listened to Luther and Harper's conversation with more and more dread.

The connection to the phone periodically cut out as they climbed. They reached Harper's floor as he heard Harper begging Luther to let her go. Carter's training was the only thing keeping him from racing down the hall and crashing into the apartment.

"What's the plan?" Devon asked quietly as they cautiously approached the door with guns drawn.

"He's taken her to the bedroom." Carter whispered. "The phone cut out and we can't hear the conversation anymore." He said for Jeff and Tank's benefit. His inability to hear what was going on with Harper was sending his anxiety through the roof. He paused listening. A door burst open, and Luther swore before he started yelling at Harper. "I think she pissed him off." Carter looked anxiously at Devon.

Two gunshots rang out and Carter couldn't breathe. Devon recovered first and kicked the door in as a third shot filled the air. Carter followed Devon as he moved quickly and carefully to the bedroom.

Luther was on the floor, but it was Harper lying on the bed that caught Carter's attention. He knew Devon would make sure Luther was no longer a threat, so he ran directly to Harper's side. She was gasping for air as he knelt next to her.

He cupped her face, and her eyes flew open. "Harper, honey. Where are you hurt?" Carter asked desperately. Her fearful eyes settled on him as she struggled to pull in a breath. Tears leaked out of the corners of her eyes. He turned his attention to looking for any injuries. Two holes were in the hoodie she wore. His mind couldn't function as he struggled to know what to do.

"We need to get the hoodie off." Devon knelt on her other side as sirens sounded in the distance.

Devon pulled out a knife and cut the fabric so they could see what they were dealing with. They could easily see where each of the bullets had struck her vest. Relief filled him until Harper shoved at their hands.

"Can't breathe." She wheezed as her eyes pleaded.

Carter immediately started unstrapping the vest, and as soon as the vest was off, Harper's hand reached to touch her chest. There was no blood, but she could still be injured. Carter grabbed her hand and pressed a kiss to her knuckles as he sent up a prayer of thanks that the vest had stopped the bullets.

Harper watched Carter as he squeezed his eyes closed and kissed her hand. She could breathe better now, but her chest still hurt like crazy. She closed her eyes as she tried to slow her breathing. "No, Sweetheart. I need you to stay awake for me." Carter said as he touched her face. Harper opened her eyes and looked into his worried ones. "Harper, we are going to need to cut your shirt off to make sure that you aren't seriously hurt." There was a question in his voice.

Not quite sure if she could speak yet, she nodded. Carter leaned forward and pressed a kiss to her forehead as she felt her shirt being cut. Cold fingers touched her skin, and she hissed in pain as the stinging increased. Carter whispered soothing words and cupped her face. Harper gripped his wrist tightly as she fought the urge to cry.

"Almost done." Carter stroked her cheek with his thumb as he looked into her eyes.

"Carter? Where's Luther?" Harper asked, but a commotion came from the front of the apartment, stopping him from replying. She tightened her grip on his wrist as she let out a whimper.

Carter's head whipped to the side as he looked over at the door. "It's the police. Jeff called as soon as we heard Luther's voice." Carter looked back down at her.

Harper was relieved that Carter refused to leave her side and had covered her with a blanket. She was wearing a bra, but still, she didn't like being so exposed. Paramedics showed up shortly after the police had cleared the apartment. Devon was talking with the officers about what had happened, and Harper tuned out the chaos. The stinging pain was fading with each passing minute. It still hurt, but not nearly as much as it did when Carter showed up. She sent up a prayer of thanks that she had been protected and that no one was seriously hurt.

"Ma'am?" The female paramedic that had examined her earlier walked back over to her. "You only appear to have bruising, but we want to take you to the hospital to run some tests."

Harper groaned as she sat up. Both the paramedic and Carter protested, but she ignored them. "I am not going to the hospital." she said firmly.

"Harper, I think it would be a good idea. It won't hurt to have a few tests done." Carter put an arm around her waist, pulling her closer to him. She laid her head against his shoulder.

"I agree with your husband, it would be better safe than sorry." The paramedic said.

Harper shook her head, too tired to correct the 'husband' comment. "No, what I need to do is get out of here."

"I am afraid we have a few questions for you." A police officer walked up.

Harper wanted to cry. Carter wrapped his other arm around her and she buried her face in his shoulder. "I'm sorry, sir, but Harper isn't going to be answering any more questions right now. You have both mine and Devon's reports, as well as every communication we have had with the Denver Police for the last six weeks." Carter said firmly. "If you need to get a hold of us, our contact information is all throughout the file."

"With all due respect, Mr. Michaels, you are not in charge." The officer crossed his arms over his chest.

"With all due respect, Officer Daniels, it is my job to protect Harper from anything that will hurt her in any way. She needs time before answering any questions. You have the phone call recording and reports. Plus, Harper is a nursing mother with twins. She needs to get back to them." His arms tightened around her.

Harper peeked over at the officer and leaned heavier against Carter. And then stiffened. The twins. Devon caught her frantic look and walked over to their little group. "The twins are still with Tank, Jeff, and the dogs. Both are sleeping and safe." He whispered, and Harper let out a sigh of relief.

A tall man with short greying hair walked into the crowded room. He scanned the scene slowly, taking in every detail. His eyes caught on Harper, and she gasped. Her father? What was he doing here? As he reached their group, he dismissed the officer before studying her. Shock gave way to hurt and confusion.

"It's good to see you, Harper. I wish it was under better circumstances though." Her father said.

Her breathing turned ragged as she stared at the man that had forced her to leave the only home she had ever known. Sensing her distress, Carter shifted so that his body partially blocked her from her father, while Devon moved to stand in front of them. "Mr. Anderson." Carter said dryly. "It's been a while."

"I see you and my daughter have gotten close." Her dad glared at them.

Harper stiffened. She rotated in Carter's arms so that she could face her father. "You stopped being my father the moment you shoved me into that car and sent me away with that woman." Harper snapped. "Do you even know what she put me through?"

"Harper, it's not that simple." Her father's expression softened as he looked at her.

"No, it is that simple. Mom was unfaithful. She was done with wanting a family life, so she asked for a divorce. You fought because you wanted to make it work, but she didn't." Harper grabbed Carter's hands that were still around her. "I begged you to let me stay with you and Henry, but you refused. You tried to make it up to me by taking me to do something mom said I wanted to do. Mom didn't know what I wanted. She never had." This confrontation was a long time coming and she had passed her threshold of control for the day. "The first night on the road, she locked me out of the hotel because she had several guys over. I slept in the pool area on a deck chair." Harper saw all of the men wince. "She got into drugs and all sorts of stuff. I used to have to lock myself in my room because the men she had over scared me. I started spending more and more time away from that place. I would get into trouble so I wouldn't have to go back there."

"Harper, I didn't know." Her father whispered as pain filled his eyes. "Your mother never stayed in contact with me."  "You seem in charge here, so let's get a few things straight." Harper stepped away from Carter but kept hold of his hand. "Luther is my ex-husband who attacked me and put me into labor six weeks ago, almost killing me and my baby. Since then, he has been stalking and threatening me. Tonight, he tried to kill me. That is my report, sir. I'm going now." Harper started pulling Carter toward the door. "Carter's and Devon's numbers are on the reports so if you have any more questions, contact one of them."

No one tried to stop them as they left. By the time they reached the elevator, Harper put a hand on her chest and took a slow breath. Carter put an arm around her, and she leaned against him. Devon came jogging down the hall as the elevator opened for them. No one spoke as they made their way to the trucks. Jeff jumped from the truck and pulled her into a hug when he saw them.

"Are you okay?" Jeff asked as he stepped back and looked her up and down. "What's with the blanket?"

Harper's face flushed as she looked at the blanket she had wrapped around her. Carter guided her to the truck and opened the back door. Leaning in, he unzipped a bag, pulled out something and handed it to her. "Put this on." He said quietly before turning his back to her, using his body to shield her. The wind blew as she pulled the shirt over her head. Shivering, Harper pulled the blanket back around her.

"Okay." She said and he turned back around to face her. He gave her a smile as he grabbed her hand and led her back to the front of the truck where Tank stood with Raider and Casper.

"I'm so sorry. I shouldn't have taken both dogs." Tank said as he gave her a hug.

Harper pulled back sharply so she could see his face. "Don't you dare start with that nonsense." She chastised. "This was all my fault. I had gotten into the habit of locking my doors. Without thinking about it, that's what I did. When I looked down the hall, everyone was almost to the elevator, and then my neighbor asked about Lexi. It slowed me down enough that I missed the elevator." Harper rubbed her head as exhaustion started to take over.

"We can talk about what happened later. Let's get you in the truck so you can rest." Carter touched her elbow.

"Aren't we going to the hospital?" Tank asked in confusion.

"Harper wants to get on the road. She declined going to the hospital." Devon huffed out. Clearly, he agreed with Carter and the paramedic. Judging by the frowns on Tank and Jeff, they didn't like her choice either.

"The twins will need to be fed soon, and I would prefer to be as far away from here as possible." Harper said as she followed Carter.

Instead of opening the back like she had assumed, he opened up the front passenger seat. Carter helped her up and pointed to the middle. She scooted to the center, and he climbed in beside her. Devon got in the driver's seat and Jeff in the back by the twins. Harper watched Tank load up the dogs in the front of the other truck before climbing behind the wheel.

Harper waited until they were well on their way before looking over at Devon. "Dev, do you have any of those pills your sister recommended for me after the accident?"

He shot her a glare. "I would prefer to take you to the hospital."

"Never mind." Harper whispered as she closed her eyes and leaned her head back. She was hurting and too tired to argue with them. And if that meant waiting until they got back to the ranch to take something, she would.

Devon growled before directing Jeff on where to find the medication. She gratefully accepted the pills and quickly swallowed them. Carter slid his arm behind her and guided her head to his shoulder. "Try to rest, Dove." He whispered before pressing a kiss to her forehead.

Closing her eyes, Harper replayed the entire event over and over. Could she have done anything different? If she had, would it have turned out better or worse? She had honestly thought she had been shot. The pain that came with each round that hit her vest had scared her. She had three kids that depended on her, and she needed to be there for them. Then Carter was there. She had instantly known that she was going to be okay. With the fear and the pain and then seeing Carter, Harper's mental state was not fully functioning, but she could have sworn he had called her 'baby' and 'honey'. But that didn't make sense. Neither did his kisses.

They hit a bump in the road and Harper groaned. Her stomach pitched and her eyes flew open. "Pull over." she demanded. Devon glanced at her as he moved to the shoulder.

She nearly dove over Carter to get out of the cab. She stumbled a step before throwing up. A comforting hand settled on her back, and when she was finished, a baby wipe was pressed into her hand. She wiped her mouth and looked up at Carter. He was studying her with so much concern, it nearly undid her fragile control of her emotions. She put her arms around his waist, and he pulled her close.

"We need to get you to a hospital." Devon said through Carter's open door.

"We do not need a flipping hospital. I just need to eat something." Harper said as she stepped out of Carter's embrace and climbed back into the truck with a wince.

"Let me see, to make sure you aren't bleeding internally." Devon said sternly. Harper pulled down the collar of her shirt to show one of the spots where she had been shot. He gently touched it as he observed her face. "Not as tender as before." He muttered to himself. "Carter, you will need to check the other side. It's along her ribs." Carter lifted the bottom of her shirt, just enough to see the mark. Everywhere his fingers grazed her skin left goosebumps and the sensation of electricity tingling her skin. "Well?"

Carter looked at her and the corner of his lips curved up. "The bruising looks about the same." Carter told Devon without taking his eyes off Harper. He waited until Devon had pulled back onto the road before saying anything. "I thought you said there was *a* wolf."

"No. You said a wolf. I said I liked what wolves stood for." Harper clarified.

"You saw her tattoo?" Jeff asked as he sat forward. "What does it look like?"

Harper took a sip of water from the bottle Jeff handed to her over the seat. "Devon, pull off at the next town so we can feed the twins and find something for us to eat." Harper turned in her seat to see both Jeff and Carter. "I have a few wolves walking in a line." She desperately wished Jeff would drop it, but the interest in his eyes dashed her hopes.

"It looked like the wolf was looking at something in the sky." Carter smiled at her.

She glared at him. "I thought you were checking the bruising?"

"It looked like a small white bird." Devon supplied with a chuckle. "Almost like a dove."

Harper turned back around. These men were impossible. It was like being in a car with Henry and his constant teasing. It was only going to get worse until she gave them all they wanted to know. Taking a deep breath she explained. "The middle wolf represents me and yes, it is a dove. At the time it was the best nickname I had. Dove sure beats Jailbait or Eye Candy. The other wolf has dog tags and his position at the back of the pack makes him the protector of the group. Satisfied?" She asked.

"Now I want to see them. They sound cool." Jeff sat back in his seat.

Thankfully, talk about her tattoo ceased when Devon took the next exit and pulled into a fast-food restaurant parking lot. Carter ran inside with Tank to order them food, while Jeff passed Colt up to Harper to feed, and Devon made a bottle. It was an hour before Devon was pulling back onto the highway. She hadn't eaten much, but the small amount she managed to swallow settled her stomach for the most part. She leaned her head back again and closed her eyes.

Harper listened to the radio as the men's conversation eventually died down. She opened her eyes and looked around the occupants of the truck. Jeff and Carter were both asleep. Devon glanced over at her and gave her a thoughtful look. "What?" she asked quietly.

He shrugged and turned his attention back to the road. "I have treated you twice now and have had a decent view of your tattoo after the gunshot." He glanced over at her again. "You mentioned you being the wolf that is looking up at the sky, does the soldier wolf represent Henry or the 'soldier boy' Luther mentioned you were in love with?" he asked curiously.

She glanced back at Jeff and then at Carter before answering. "Who do you think it represents?" She returned the question to him in hopes she could avoid lying to Devon. There was no way she was going to admit she got a tattoo to represent Carter.

"I'm not sure, because there is a third wolf. I have only seen the back half of it." Devon smiled. "You didn't want to tell us about the third one."

"The third wolf is special to me. He is my compass. My personal guide. He always led me down the right path." Harper said quietly. The wolf also wore a baseball cap because Henry was rarely without his. She had even taken to calling him Cap.

"So, you have a guide leading you and a protector following you to make sure you are safe while you are looking to the skies." Devon asked. "Now which one is Henry, and which one is your beau?"

"Who says the other wolves represent specific people? At that time in my life, I felt lost and alone. This tattoo just shows that I was impulsive, immature and needing guidance." Harper said as she absentmindedly rubbed her sore ribs.

"I think your tattoo has a much deeper meaning than you are wanting to share. It seems very thought out and well put together." Devon grabbed her hand and gave it a quick squeeze before returning his to the steering wheel. They were both quiet for a long time, and Harper had assumed Devon was happy to listen to the radio, but what he asked next surprised her. "Do you think you will ever marry again?"

Harper was quiet for so long that Devon looked over at her. "I am not completely opposed to the idea of marriage, but I'm not willing to put myself or my kids into a situation like Luther again. I can't risk it. I had always seen myself with a large family, but after everything, I think I can live with the three kids I have and die happy as an old cat lady." She shrugged and gave him a smile.

"You don't ever want to fall in love?" Devon asked in surprise.

"I have been in love, Devon. Correction, I still am in love, and it sucks. It is such a curse. Hurt and loneliness are the only things that come from romantic love." Harper huffed. "Lucky me, my heart has decided on someone that can never feel the same. Yet my heart refuses to come back to me. I made a promise to myself that I would never marry without love again." Harper fought back her rising frustration that she could not seem to get rid of her feelings for Carter, even after he wasn't in her life for over ten years. "My lot in life is to raise my kids and to find happiness in their joy."

"That seems like a pretty lonely life." Jeff yawned from the back seat. Harper cringed. Apparently, she wasn't as quiet as she had thought she was. "Want some advice?"

"I have a feeling you are going to give it regardless." Harper growled out.

Jeff laughed. "You need to not be scared to put yourself out there. Love can be a wonderful thing if you let it." Harper rolled her eyes as she turned to face him. "I'm telling you, Athena, we could be great together. My offer still stands." The playful spark was in his eyes.

"You're still asking me to marry you, Jeff?" Harper smiled back. "And what would you do if I actually agreed?"

"You wound me, Athena. Do you think I'm a coward and would back out?" Jeff's smile was wide.

Carter opened his eyes and looked around the cab of the truck as he blinked sleep from them. "Not a coward, Jeff. Just someone who is wanting to get married for the wrong reasons. So again, my answer is no." Harper was saying to Jeff. What were they talking about? Marriage? What had he missed?

"I don't want you to go, and now that Luther is no longer a problem, I figured I would ask again." Jeff commented.

"What did happen to Luther?" Harper asked as she looked at Carter, but he couldn't find the words to speak. His mind was still caught up on Jeff asking Harper to marry him. And, by the sounds of it, it was not the first time.

Devon thankfully informed Harper that Luther had shot himself in the head. He was still alive by the time the police arrived, but it hadn't looked good. Harper sat there staring at the windshield for several minutes without speaking. "I'm a horrible person." She mumbled to herself. She looked up at Carter with guilt. "I feel nothing but relief. Like a weight has been lifted. What kind of person does that make me?"

The turmoil in her eyes tore at Carter. He grabbed her face gently with both hands so that she was forced to look at him. "You are not a horrible person, Dove. Luther did terrible things to you, and you are not relieved that a human life may end, but you are relieved that the person's actions are going to stop." Her eyes became wet, but she blinked hard, keeping the tears back. "You feeling guilty over this just shows how good of a person you are." He held her gaze until she nodded, and he slowly released her.

The twins woke up a few minutes later, and Devon quickly found somewhere to pull off to feed them. Jeff and Devon switched seats and thirty minutes later, they were back on the road. Harper was talking with Jeff about the surrounding area and Carter was trying to figure out why Jeff was acting like a tour guide, when his phone vibrated in his pocket. Pulling it out he saw a text from Devon.

**Devon:** Your girl is as bitter as they come.

Carter glanced over at Harper and then back down at his phone.

**Carter:** Bitter? About what?

**Devon:** Love. You are going to have a lot of work to do in order to win her over.

**Carter:** She told me about the man she feels she is still in love with. A soldier if I remember right.

**Devon:** She thinks she is going to die an old cat lady.

**Carter:** Not if I can help it.

**Devon:** You better move fast. Clara told me Peter just helped Harper purchase a truck, and Jeff says she is speaking to a real estate agent about purchasing a house.

Carter felt like someone punched him in the gut. Harper leaving the ranch had never crossed his mind. After her blow up at the guys this morning about sharing a bed, he guessed it made sense. Harper wanted to teach Lexi that living with a man without being married was wrong. He whole heartily agreed with her, but the thought of them leaving had him reaching for her hand. She glanced at him, then at their joined hands, and then back at him; but he didn't react. A small smile spread on his lips as she turned back to Jeff and continued their conversation without skipping a beat or pulling away.

**Carter:** Where? When?

**Devon:** Jeff seems to think almost right away.

**Carter:** I can't let her go. Not again.

**Devon:** Then do something.

# Chapter 15

"Harper, wake up." Carter's voice whispered in her ear. "We're home."

Harper bolted upright and winced. She grabbed her side as she looked around. They were pulling up in front of the ranch house. Horses grazed in the pasture to the south of the barn, and she smiled. Carter opened his door and stepped out. He extended his hand to her, and she allowed him to assist her down. Harper took another look around, but a wave of disappointment filled her. "Where's Lexi?" She asked.

"Clara said they would be here around the time we arrived." Devon said from the other side of the truck. "Should we take these little guys inside?"

Harper nodded as her eyes looked down the empty lane. Carter put a hand on her lower back and guided her towards the house. "She will be here soon." Carter softly told her.

By the time they got inside, Jeff and Devon had both babies out of their car seats and were playing with them. Harper smiled sadly at the sight. She pulled out her phone as she began to walk slowly around the living room, stretching her legs. An email from Hank was on her notifications and she quickly opened it.

*Miss Anderson,*

*I got your message about switching to a rental instead of purchasing. I think I have found several that fit what you are looking for. The first listing I feel is the most promising. It is also not far from where you said you are currently staying. Let me know what you want me to do.*

*Hank Trevors*

Harper looked at the listings. The first one was a decent sized home on five acres. The house had three bedrooms, two baths, and a fenced backyard. It also had a two-stall barn and a small pasture.

Looking through the pictures, Harper knew that the house would be perfect for her and the kids. She copied and pasted the address into her maps app to find that the house was only forty minutes from the ranch, and twenty minutes from Clara's house. Looking back at everyone in the living room, she knew she didn't want to leave them. They were family, and she couldn't take Lexi away from the only real family she had ever known.

She walked into the kitchen and pressed Hank's name on her contacts. The phone rang three times before he answered. "Hank Trevors."

"Hi, Hank. It's Harper." She said softly, not wanting to be overheard. "I just took a look at the listings."

"What did you think?" Hank asked with enthusiasm.

"I really like the first one you sent me. I feel like it would be perfect for me and the kids." She told him glancing at the doorway to the living room.

"Great!" He said and she could hear him typing on his computer. "This property is available immediately and is a month-to-month contract. The landlords are an older couple who have gone out of state for the time being and are crazy nice, if I do say so myself."

"Why is that?" Harper couldn't help the smile that appeared on her lips as she leaned back against the counter.

"They are my grandparents." Hank laughed. "Do you have any questions about the property before I send you the lease to sign?"

"What is their pet policy?" Harper was going to try her best to convince Tank to let Lexi keep Bella. That girl was going to have a hard enough time leaving the ranch and the guys, Bella might be able to soften the blow just a little.

"You can have any pet you want as long as it doesn't destroy the place. If there are any damages, all they ask is that you repair them." Hank answered.

"Perfect. I will take it." Harper said with more confidence than she felt.

"Sending the lease over now. Sign it and send it back. I have also sent you an address to send the deposit and first month's rent. As soon as that happens, I will send you a text with the location of the key." Hank said goodbye and hung up.

Her phone buzzed a minute later. She turned around and leaned over the counter and read through the lease. She signed it electronically and sent it back. She let out a sigh as she turned around. Jeff stood in the doorway with his arms folded. Harper froze when she saw him. He stalked towards her and lowered his voice. "You're leaving?" He growled out.

"I told you this before, Jeff. I cannot stay here now that Luther is no longer a threat." Harper pushed off the counter and headed for the living room. Just as she was entering the room, she saw Clara's truck driving up the lane with a second truck following behind it. "Lexi." She breathed out as she bolted for the door, ignoring Carter and Tank's call for her to wait. As soon as the truck stopped, Harper yanked open the back door.

Lexi launched herself into Harper's arms. She stumbled back a few steps before dropping to her knees. The pain that shot through her chest caused her to bite the inside of her cheeks to keep from crying out. Men's voices shouted, but she ignored them and pressed a kiss to her daughter's face. "I missed you, baby girl." Harper whispered.

"I missed you too, mommy!" Lexi cried as she squeezed Harper's neck tighter before she was lifted from Harper's arms. "Carter, put me down. I want my mommy." Lexi yelled.

"I know, Princess. But you have to be careful with your mommy. She was hurt earlier today." Carter explained and Lexi stopped struggling against Carter's hold.

Lexi looked down at Harper with wide eyes. "You are hurt?" Lexi asked and Carter put her down. Harper was still kneeling as Lexi slowly approached her.

Harper pulled her back into her arms. "Just a little sore, Lexi. Nothing to be worried about." Devon scoffed but didn't say anything. "Now, are you ready to meet your brother? He is inside." Harper asked as she gave Lexi a big smile.

Carter helped Harper stand and gave her an unhappy look as Lexi ran for the house. "Sore? Is that what you call being shot twice in the chest?" Devon growled at her.

"You were shot?" Clara came rushing over to her and looked her up and down as if assuring herself that Harper was okay.

"We can talk about this later, right now I am going inside and holding my kids." Harper walked away from everyone and followed Lexi inside.

Lexi was standing next to Tank, looking at both of her brothers with a look of wonder. Harper crossed the room and lifted Bo before sitting on the couch. Lexi followed her and Harper put Bo in Lexi's arms. Tank handed Colt over to Harper with a smile before heading for the front door.

"He is so cute." Lexi giggled. "He looks like Colt."

Harper put an arm around her daughter and watched as Bo smiled up at his sister. She kissed Lexi's head as she fought back the tears that wanted to come. She was holding all of her kids for the first time. She never thought she would have this opportunity. Several minutes passed before the rest of the adults came back into the room. Harper was enjoying her time with her kids, but when she saw the faces of everyone, she knew something was wrong. Everything about Carter, Jeff, Devon and Tank screamed tension.

"Harper, can I speak with you really quick please?" Devon asked and walked into the kitchen, not waiting for her to respond.

Harper kissed Lexi's head one more time as she carefully got to her feet. Carter was right there and took Colt from her. He gave her a look full of pain and determination as their eyes met. What was going on? She watched as Carter took her seat next to Lexi. Shaking her head, Harper walked to the kitchen. She wasn't really surprised to see Clara there as well. Harper was pretty sure Devon had filled his sister in on the gunshots.

"Police Chief Anderson called." Devon looked straight at her, and Harper's stomach knotted. "Luther died from his injuries an hour ago." The air rushed from her lungs, and she sat down slowly in the nearest chair. Luther was dead? She felt emotionless. There was no pity, no regret, no sadness. Just nothing.

"Harper, Dev told me about you getting shot, and about you not wanting to go to the hospital. Will you allow me to look at you to make sure you don't have any internal bleeding or possible fractured bones?" Clara asked softly.

Harper looked up at her friend and then over to Devon. "You might as well come too, Devon. You will know if there are any major changes from the last time you looked at them." She stood and walked straight upstairs to her room.

Devon closed the door behind them and looked down as Harper pulled Carter's borrowed shirt off. Clara gasped as she saw the bruising on Harper. The bullet had struck her sternum. Bruising spread from the impact point. It was the size of a large grapefruit. The second bullet had hit her ribs near her side. The bruise wrapped around her side to her back. Clara took her time to examine each spot, gently pushing here and there.

"What do you think, Devon?" Clara asked, glancing back at her brother.

"The bruising is a little worse than before." He answered. "But that is expected with the injury being so fresh."

"I do not think you are in any real danger, but I would like to do some x-rays. Come to my office first thing in the morning and we will get them done." Clara said as she helped Harper put the shirt back on. Devon left, but Clara held Harper back. "Jeff said you are leaving."

Harper let out a sigh and sat on the bed. "I can't stay here, Clara. The threat to me and the kids is gone, which means I have no reason to stay here." She saw Clara start to protest and rushed on. "And don't say that I am family and have every right to be here. I don't want to go. I love all of you, but I can't stay on the ranch."

"I am positive that no one would mind if you did, Harper. You aren't alone and we can help support you and the kids." Clara argued.

"I will not live with men that are not my blood relations, or to whom I'm not married. I will be a better example to my kids than my mother was to me." Clara remained silent as she moved to Harper's side and sat. "That is why I can't stay here." Harper lowered her voice.

"Where are you going to go?" Clara had tears in her eyes, but she didn't argue anymore.

Harper smiled. "Not far actually." Harper told Clara about the house she was going to be renting. They discussed when to start taking her things over, and all the fun things they could do living closer together. "I would actually like it if the guys didn't know where I was going." Harper said. Clara gave her a look of surprise. "At least not for a while. Lexi and I have lived under Luther's influence for Lexi's whole life. Then we moved here, which has been great but…" Harper paused trying to put her thoughts into words that made sense.

"You and Lexi need to find yourselves." Clara finished for her with a small smile. "I get that. Maybe you should also have little contact with them. You and Lexi deserve to heal privately for a bit."

"I agree. I need some space to process some things, and to know if my feelings for Carter are real or if I am dealing with transference." Harper shrugged. "Lexi also needs to keep her positive male role models."

"They will see you at church and know you haven't gone far." Clara warned.

"I am not going to hide from them. I just want to wait as long as possible for them to know where I will be. If they knew, they would show up at the house constantly." Harper covered her face with her hands. "I just need a little time."

"Why don't you borrow Tank's truck when you come in the morning, and I can help you unload your things? That way they won't know where your new place is." Clara suggested.

Harper gave Clara a hug. "Thank you." They stood and headed for the door. "I need to talk with Lexi about everything." Clara agreed and suggested going for a walk. She would make dinner while they were out.

Harper fed Colt before she grabbed Lexi's hand. As they stepped out onto the porch, she heard Clara explaining that Harper needed to have a private talk with Lexi. She sent up a prayer thanking the heavens for Clara. They stepped into the barn and Mozart's soft knicker greeted her. "Would you like to go for a ride?" Harper asked Lexi, who eagerly agreed.

It took her longer to saddle Mozart than it had the last time. She was going to have to take some pain medicine again tonight. She helped Lexi with her riding helmet before lifting her into the saddle. Harper swung up behind her daughter, then nudged Mozart into a canter.

They rode in silence for several minutes before Lexi looked back at Harper. "Mommy?"

"Yes?" Harper smiled down at her.

"Are we leaving?" Lexi asked.

Harper pulled Mozart to a stop and got down. She reached up and lifted Lexi from the saddle. Tying Mozart to a thick branch, Harper led Lexi to a fallen tree and sat. "Do you remember when we first got here, and you were concerned about us living here? Do you remember what I said?"

"You said we were just visiting, so we could be safe from him." Lexi answered as she climbed onto Harper's lap.

"We cannot stay at the ranch, Sweetheart. We were only visiting so that Carter, Jeff, Devon, and Tank could protect us. Luther is no longer going to hurt us, so we do not need to be protected anymore." Harper tried to explain. She prayed that Lexi would understand.

"What happened to him?"

"He got hurt and died today." Harper wanted Lexi to understand that they didn't have to worry about Luther anymore, but she also didn't want to scare her with the events of the day.

Lexi was quiet for a long time. "Mommy?" Lexi's little voice finally said. "I don't want to leave my uncles and Carter."

Harper hugged Lexi close. "Neither do I, baby. But we don't have a choice. We need to spend some time together; just you, me, and your brothers. And maybe after a little while we can come back for a visit."

"I like that plan." Lexi said as she jumped off Harper's lap. "Can we go back home now? I want to hold my brothers." Harper laughed as she followed Lexi back to Mozart. They rode back and Lexi filled the evening air with her chatter. She told Harper about all the fun things she got to do with Hannah.

Harper let out a groan when she saw Carter and Devon waiting in the barn for them. She dismounted, but before she could reach for Lexi, Devon lifted her down. "Can you go inside with Devon?" Carter asked Lexi with a smile. "I'm going to help your mom unsaddle her horse." Lexi nodded her head and skipped off with Devon following behind her. Carter didn't say anything until they saw Lexi and Devon enter the house. "Have a good ride?" He asked.

Harper let out a tired sigh. "The ride was fine."

Carter started unbuckling the saddle. His silence was making her anxious. She had thought he would be lecturing her about riding or trying to convince her to not leave like everyone else had. But he remained quiet. Harper wrapped her arms around herself as she watched him pull the saddle and blanket off Mozart's back. While he was returning them to the tack room, Harper untied Mozart and led him to his stall. She closed the door and started to unbuckle his bridle.

"Are you really leaving?" Carter asked from behind her.

Harper's hands stilled and then she dropped them to her sides. She turned to face him, and her heart slammed painfully in her chest. She really didn't want to leave this man, but she had to. "Carter, I have to put Lexi and the boys first. I have to be willing to do what I am teaching them to do."

Carter took a step closer to her and slipped a hand around her waist while the other cupped the back of her neck. His eyes bore into her with such intensity, it stole her breath. "You are a great mother." He whispered before pressing his lips to hers.

Harper closed her eyes and melted against Carter. He deepened the kiss, and she circled her arms around his neck. He pulled her closer to him and she gasped as his hand pressed the bruise on her side. Carter released her quickly. "I'm sorry." he said quickly.

Harper ran a shaking hand through her hair. She was sorry too. Sorry that the kiss ended. She was too afraid to look at him. What had she been thinking? This was a mistake. She is supposed to be putting distance between her and Carter so she could figure out if her feelings for him were real, not kissing him. Now she was more confused than ever.

"I'm going to go check on Lexi and the boys." She muttered before turning and walking out of the barn. She knew Carter would finish taking

Mozart's bridle off, so she didn't stop, even when she heard him call after her.

Dinner was a quiet affair and Harper was relieved when no one protested when she and the kids went to bed early. Both Bo and Colt slept peacefully, and Lexi fell asleep to Harper reading to her out of the scriptures. All was quiet, but Harper just kept replaying that kiss in the barn. She hadn't even hesitated when Carter had kissed her. Unlike every other time someone had kissed her, Harper hadn't wanted it to stop. Her dang side had ended it. Harper buried her face in her blankets. It was a good thing she was leaving tomorrow.

# Chapter 16

Harper watched in amusement as the guys scarfed down their breakfasts and held several different conversations. From what she had gathered; feed needed to be taken to the south field, cows needed to be moved and a pipe broke out near the west field. Tank left first but came running back a minute later.

"Harper, can I borrow your truck?" Tank asked. "Mine still has the car seats and all your stuff from your apartment in it."

"Go ahead. Just leave me your keys." Harper looked up and saw the guys watching her curiously. "I have an appointment with Clara to get x-rays done. I thought you all would be happy that I was seeing a doctor."

"We are, Dove." Carter stood and cleared his dishes.

"We are just concerned that you aren't going to be here when we get back." Jeff commented as he pulled his coat on.

Harper stood and followed the four men as they stepped out onto the porch. She couldn't believe that two feet of snow had been dumped overnight. She held both Bo and Colt close to her as a cold wind blew. "Don't worry, we plan on being here for an early dinner." Harper said with a smile.

Carter stayed back on the porch while Tank and Devon climbed into her truck and Jeff headed inside the barn. He knelt down and kissed Lexi's cheek. "See you tonight, kiddo."

"Bye, Carter." Lexi gave him a hug and kissed his cheek before she slowly walked inside, out of the cold.

Carter stood to face Harper. He kissed both Bo and Colt. "You two, be good for your mom." Harper's heart stammered when their eyes met. He shifted slightly closer, and his eyes dropped to her lips. Jeff called for Carter from the barn and Carter looked over his shoulder before looking back at her. "Drive safe today, Dove." He said as he turned and walked over to Jeff. Harper watched as he swung up into the saddle. He looked back at her, waved and then he was gone.

Disappointment filled her. She shook her head and went back inside. She cleaned the kitchen and packed a lot of their stuff. She loaded Tank's truck and then got the kids ready to brave the cold snowy day. She drove carefully and made it to Clara's office shortly after nine. Harper's pain flared up as she carried both baby car seats.

As soon as they entered, Clara rushed over and took the car seats from her before leading them into a room. Clara had a nurse sit with the kids while Harper got the x-rays done. While she was waiting for Clara to take a look at them, Harper sat in the exam room chair to feed Colt. Lexi was sitting on the ground holding Bo's bottle for him. The little girl was a little lethargic today, and Harper worried Lexi was sad about their upcoming move. Her phone buzzed in her pocket, and she pulled it out to see who had texted her.

**Carter:** How are things going?

**Harper:** Miss us already?

**Carter:** Always, Dove. Did you make it to Clara's office safely?

**Harper:** We did. Roads were a bit slick so we might go to Clara's for a little while before heading back to the ranch.

**Carter:** Stay safe, Dove. Let me know when you are heading back and when you arrive.

**Carter:** Let me know what Clara says.

Harper smiled. Carter worried too much. Colt finished eating and Harper rotated in her seat. She snapped a selfie of her and the kids, Lexi still feeding Bo, and sent it to Carter.

**Carter:** Wish I could be there with you guys.

**Harper:** Get back to work, cowboy or you'll be late for dinner.

The door opened and Clara walked in. "Good news, no breaks. You are just bruised and going to be really tender for several weeks. You need to take it easy and no heavy lifting when at all possible."

"That's a relief. Now the guys can get off my back." Harper placed Colt in his car seat and buckled him in. "I am heading over to the house to see if I can get some things settled before I have to go back."

"I don't work today. If you want, I can help." Clara offered.

Harper looked at her friend confused. "I thought you were working?"

"Oh no. I only came in for you." Clara laughed. "Those kinds of injuries are no joke. We needed to make sure you were okay."

Harper laughed and accepted Clara's offer of help. Clara helped get the twins and Lexi to the truck and then headed to the sitter to pick up her kids. She promised to meet Harper at the rental in an hour.

The house was not hard to find, and it was positively charming. The exterior was a cheerful yellow with white trim and a wrap-a-round porch. Lexi excitedly ran to the door. As soon as Harper got the door open, Lexi ran through the house and pointed at everything. True to Hank's word, the house was mostly furnished.

The kitchen and living room were open concept with an island as the divider. The table was big enough to seat four people. The counters were granite and there was a farm style sink beneath a window that overlooked the backyard. The couch in the living room was clean and looked comfortable. It faced a small TV that was mounted on the wall. A gas fireplace stood in the corner.

Harper put the twins down on the living room floor before following Lexi down the hall. The first door on the left was a bathroom. The master bedroom had its own ensuite and was on the right. At the far end of the hall, two doors faced each other with matching sized rooms.

Lexi claimed the room on the left because she liked the stars on the ceiling. Harper smiled at the excitement and happiness Lexi exuded, even though her normal level of enthusiasm wasn't there.

She loved the house, but there seemed to be something missing. Harper went out to the truck and pulled out the two bassinets that she had used in the kitchen at the ranch house. She put the babies in them and put a movie on for Lexi so she could start bringing things in. By the time Clara showed up, Harper was halfway done unloading the truck.

"Wow. This place is great!" Clara exclaimed. "I have lived in this area for years and have never seen it."

"It is tucked back and away from the main road." Harper smiled. "Lexi seems to like it."

Clara looked over at Lexi and Hannah as Lexi was showing Hannah everything. Harper and Clara laughed as they headed outside to finish unloading the truck. With the two of them it took less than twenty minutes to bring in the rest of the boxes. Harper lit the fireplace before sitting on the couch next to Clara. The girls were playing in the back room and the twins were still sleeping in their bassinets. A sigh escaped Harper as she leaned back. This place, this move, felt right. She had prayed hard about this decision, and she felt like she was where she was meant to be.

"Mommy!" Lexi screamed. Harper ran down the hall and entered Lexi's room in time to see her daughter throw up all over the floor. She scooped up the crying child and ran to the bathroom. Lexi had never been sick before, and Harper didn't know what to do. "My tummy hurts." Lexi sobbed.

"I know, baby." Harper tried to soothe her, even though she herself was freaking out. "It's going to be okay."

"Oh dear." Clara whispered from the bathroom door. "My kids were sick earlier this week. I thought I had cleaned everything before Lexi got to our house."

"What do I do?" Harper asked desperately looking up from where she sat with Lexi on the floor.

Clara gave her a sympathetic smile. "Try to keep her hydrated and comfortable. Since you just moved in, I doubt you have any Gatorade or any other food." Harper shook her head. "I'll take my kids with me, and we will run to the store and pick you up some groceries after I clean up the mess in the other room. You worry about cleaning Lexi up. Try to keep her away from the twins as much as possible."

By the time Harper had finished giving Lexi a bath, Clara was gone. Lexi had thrown up once more in the toilet during her bath, and Harper was close to tears. She got Lexi tucked into her bed with a bowl close by and went to check on the twins. They were just waking up, but hadn't started to cry yet, so she left them in their bassinets. She saw her phone sitting on the couch and snatched it up. She needed to make a call.

"Michaels." Carter's strong voice came through the line. He sounded distracted and she could tell he was still out with Jeff checking on the cattle.

"Carter." Harper swallowed the lump in her throat. She desperately wanted Carter to be there with her, to tell her everything was going to be okay.

"Hey, Harper. You on your way back to the ranch?" His question was followed by him calling out to the others with him about one of the cows breaking free.

Harper gnawed on her lower lip. "I'm not going to make it back to the ranch tonight." She said softly, fighting the tears that stung her eyes. This was not how she had wanted things to go today.

Carter was quiet for a second before he shouted out to several of the men and then he spoke to her. "What's going on, Harper?" She had his full attention now. Even the wind she could hear from his side of the call a moment ago was absent.

Her control slipped and she started rambling. "This isn't how I wanted today to go. We were supposed to be home for dinner tonight. We were supposed to sit down and all talk together, but then Lexi. And I don't know what to do. I just don't know." Harper spoke so fast she didn't know if he even understood any of what she had said.

"Slow down, hun. Take a deep breath and let's try this again." Carter sounded worried and the guilt Harper was already feeling magnified.

She took a deep breath and sat on the couch. "Lexi is sick. She started throwing up thirty minutes ago. Clara ran to the store to get her some Gatorade, but we won't make it back to the ranch tonight."

"Where are you? I can come and get you." Carter asked.

"Carter, Lexi is throwing up. She won't be able to make the car ride back to the ranch." Another deep breath. "And then back here."

"Where is here, Harper?" Carter's tone instantly became guarded. "You left." He said quietly.

"I hadn't meant to 'just leave', Carter. We went to get the x-rays and then stopped by the house. I was planning on coming back to the ranch to talk with everyone about it. But then Lexi got sick." Her voice broke. "I'm sorry. I didn't...I wanted..." Tears leaked down her cheeks and she buried her face in her hands. "So much has happened. Living with Luther for five years. Lexi. The abuse. Henry and the twins. Being shot. My father. I needed a place to process."

"Harper, why won't you tell me where you are?" Carter sounded hurt and frustrated.

"Because you will show up and I need time to work through some things."

"If you were planning on coming for dinner and then going back, you are close then." Carter said and Harper couldn't stop the smile and laugh that came out.

"Slow down, Cowboy. We are far enough away you cannot just ride up on that horse of yours, but close enough that Lexi can still have her favorite uncles and her Carter."

"Hmm." Carter said after a few moments of silence. "I think we can work with that for now. When will we see you again?"

"I'm not sure. It depends on how long Lexi is sick for and if anyone else gets it." Harper sighed. "She has never been sick, Carter. I don't know what to do."

"Everything will be okay, Dove. If you need anything, we are just a phone call away." Carter's tone softened and Harper started to feel calmer.

"A phone call and a good chunk of the day." Harper muttered, and she heard Carter chuckle.

"Mommy!" Lexi called from the back room. Harper went back to Lexi. The girl was pale and Harper's heart broke. "You left me."

"I had to check on your brothers, sweetheart. How are you feeling?" Harper sat on the bed next to her daughter and brushed the hair off her face. She still held the phone to her ear. She could hear the wind and calls of men in the distance through the line. It was comforting to know that Carter was still on the line with her.

"I'm sorry, mommy."

"Love, there is nothing to be sorry about. Everyone gets sick sometimes." Harper soothed.

"Can I talk to her?" Carter asked.

"Carter wants to talk to you. Are you feeling up to it?" Harper grinned at Lexi's instant smile and handed her the phone.

A cry from the front room had Harper standing. She glanced back at Lexi who was happily talking with Carter and left the room. He could keep her entertained while Harper fed the twins. It was nearly an hour later before Harper was done feeding and changing both boys. She peeked back into the room to see Lexi nearly asleep holding tightly to the phone. Harper kissed her daughter's head and carefully pulled her phone from Lexi's grasp.

She left the light on and the door open as she walked back out to the front room. She sat on the couch with a tired sigh. She looked down at her phone to see if Clara had messaged her and saw that the call with Carter was still going. Lifting it to her ear she heard the sound of Carter calling out to Jeff. "Carter?" She asked. She could not believe he had stayed on the phone this whole time.

"Hey, Dove. I think Lexi fell asleep on me." Carter said. "You sound exhausted."

"She very nearly did, and I am exhausted, and I have a feeling tonight is going to be a long one." Harper settled more comfortably onto the couch and stared into the fire.

"Wish I could be there to help, but someone won't give me an address." She could tell Carter was smirking by the tone of his voice.

Harper smiled. "Alright cowboy, if that is how things are going to be, I'm going to hang up."

"I was teasing, Dove. No need to hang up on me." Carter said.

A knock on the door preceded Clara and her kids walking in. "I have to go, Clara just got back, and I need to help bring in the groceries." Harper felt disappointed that her call with Carter was coming to an end. She was reluctant to hang up the phone, afraid of losing the connection she had with him. Just hearing his voice had helped her keep calm.

"I should go too. Jeff is getting irritated that he has been pulling most of the weight. I'll call you later." Carter said and then the line went dead.

Harper put the phone down and pulled her coat on. She helped unload the groceries and put them away. Clara gave her a rundown of what to do to help Lexi feel better and what to do if the twins caught it. It had gotten late, and Clara headed back home with the promise to call in the morning.

The house felt too quiet as Harper curled up on the couch with a blanket and mug of hot chocolate. Not used to the quiet, Harper turned on a chick-flick. She hadn't watched TV since Lexi was born. Luther had become so controlling over every aspect of her life, and she had let him in order to keep the peace. When she complied, Lexi was left alone for the most part.

She was on her third movie when she started to doze off. Lexi had woken up several times during the first two movies but was resting peacefully now. Her phone ringing woke her up with a start. She scrambled to answer it before it woke any of the kids. "Hello." she said breathlessly.

"Is this a bad time?" Carter asked.

"Hey." Harper sighed as she settled back against the couch and closed her eyes. "No. It's fine."

"How are things going over there? How's Lexi doing?"

"I think she is doing better. She hasn't thrown up in a while. I'm hoping she is over the worst of it." Harper yawned.

"I hope so, too. She sounded miserable earlier." They talked for the next two hours, and Harper found herself dozing off as she listened to the sound of his voice. She yawned again. "Harper, are you falling asleep? You should go to bed." Carter's voice was soft, and Harper made a sound of protest. "Come on, Harper. You need to sleep while you can."

"But I still have to put the twins in the crib and check on Lexi before I can go to bed." Harper whined, but she stood up and carried the boys to the pack-n-play Clara had let her borrow. She peeked in on Lexi to find her still asleep and changed into her pajamas while she listened to Carter teasing her about not giving him the address, otherwise, he would have gladly helped. She climbed under the covers and closed her eyes. "I'm in bed. Happy?"

Carter laughed. "I'll check on you in the morning. Good night, Sweetheart."

"Hmm?" Harper tried to ask what Carter had said, not sure if she heard him right, but fell asleep before she heard his answer.

# Chapter 17

Carter was smiling as he stepped into the kitchen the next morning. He had spent a good part of the night talking with Harper. Even though he hated that she had left, he understood her reasoning behind it. He was just glad she hadn't gone far and that she was still answering his calls. Jeff and Tank were sitting at the table when he walked in.

"You look awfully happy for a man whose woman ditched him." Jeff commented dryly.

The guys hadn't been happy when they found out that Harper and the kids had moved out. Jeff and Harper had gotten close, and he seemed to be taking it the hardest. Carter hadn't had the chance to tell them her reasons before they stormed out of the room when he told them they weren't coming back that night.

"Harper didn't run off, Jeff." Carter rolled his eyes. "She was planning on coming back to explain her decision, but Lexi got sick." Jeff and Tank's heads snapped in his direction. He had their full attention. Good. "We all know that Harper had never liked the idea of staying here. She had always said that she wouldn't live with a man she wasn't married to. But yesterday when she called, she mentioned she needed time to process everything that has happened. She wanted to sit down and talk with all of us at dinner last night, but Lexi started throwing up."

"She is close then. If she had planned on coming back here for dinner." Tank commented as he sat back in his chair. "Where is she staying?"

"She wouldn't tell me. She does not want us just dropping by right now. Clara was helping her get settled when she called." Carter sat at the table and took a bite of an apple. He missed Harper's warm breakfasts.

"I checked my truck's location last night and it is at Clara's house." Tank said.

Carter thought about it for a minute. "That doesn't make sense. Lexi was telling me all about the new house and it sounds nothing like Clara's place."

"Harper switched cars with Clara because she had a feeling you would track your truck." Devon said as he walked into the kitchen. "Clara wouldn't tell me Harper's location either. Clara is the one that suggested Harper have limited contact with us for a while. According to Dr. Clara McCall, Harper's experiences over the last five years, at the very least, have made her lose her self-identity and self-confidence. Harper needs some time away from us in order to process all that has happened and to know where she wants her life to go."

He didn't know Clara was the one that suggested this distance. "Harper said they were far enough away to not easily stop by, but close enough that Lexi could still see us." Carter thought out loud. "At least she is taking our calls."

"Did she say when we were going to see them again?" Jeff asked.

"She wasn't sure. Lexi was pretty sick last night, and Harper was worried about the twins getting it." Carter ran his hand through his hair. He prayed they wouldn't get sick, too.

The guys seemed appeased that Harper hadn't gone far and planned on staying in contact. The day got underway, and Carter was back in the saddle. This time Devon came with him as he checked the fences.

Carter checked his watch for what felt like the millionth time. He didn't want to wake Harper by calling too early, especially if she had had a rough night with Lexi.

"Just send her a text." Devon broke the silence between them. "It would be nice if you would focus, and I don't think that is going to happen until you talk to her." Carter smiled and pulled out his phone. Devon was right, he was desperate to talk with Harper.

**Carter:** Morning, Dove.

**Harper:** Howdy, Cowboy. Up with the sun again?

**Carter:** Always. How's my Princess this morning?

**Harper:** Your Princess? You have claimed her just like she has claimed you. It is always 'her Carter this' and 'her Carter that'.

**Harper:** She is doing a lot better. Still a bit lethargic but no longer throwing up.

**Carter:** I'm so glad she is doing better. How is everyone else?

**Harper:** So far so good. How did the guys take it?

**Carter:** They are mad. Tank tried tracking his truck. Devon tried to get info from Clara. Jeff is more hurt than anything. He has adopted you as his little sister.

**Harper:** He reminds me a lot of Henry. And what of you? Are you mad at me, too?

**Carter:** I'm not mad. Disappointed that you weren't able to come home last night, but not mad. I understand.

"Did you get your fix?" Devon asked. Carter looked up and remembered they were just sitting in the cold and still had a ton they needed to do.

**Harper:** Thank you for keeping Lexi company while I was busy with the twins and for talking with me last night. I wasn't handling Lexi being sick very well.

**Carter:** Glad to help, Dove. Devon's waiting for me to continue checking fences. I'll call you later.

**Harper:** Stay safe, Cowboy.

Carter was grinning as he zipped his phone into his pocket. Devon tried to glare at him but ended up laughing. "You are sunk, man." Devon kicked his horse into a gallop.

"I'm okay with that." Carter grinned and followed Devon. He knew he was head over heels in love with Harper.

It was killing him that she moved out, but he understood. She was right. They should not be living together now that Luther was no longer a threat. At least not yet. Carter fully intended to have Harper move back in as his wife. At the moment, she needed time, and he would give it to her. He would be here whenever she needed him. And when she worked through whatever she needed to, he would ask her to marry him.

The day passed quickly as Carter worked the ranch. They got in earlier than they had the day before, and he quickly jumped in the shower before reaching for his phone to call Harper. They talked for an hour before the crying of the twins caused Harper to go. He made his way downstairs and endured the teasing the others dished out.

To everyone's disappointment, meals went back to the simple boring ones they had been eating before Harper had shown up. Lexi's bedtime rolled around, and he received a call from her. Lexi insisted he read her a story, even if she couldn't see the book, before she would go to sleep. The rest of the night he spent planning with the guys for the next day while texting Harper.

For the next two weeks, Carter's days followed the same pattern. He woke up and texted Harper, did chores around the ranch, took a shower and texted Harper. Followed by a phone call with Lexi, dinner and then he spent an hour or two talking with Harper on the phone.

Sundays were different. They met up at the church and he helped her with the kids. After church, everyone drove over to Clara's for Sunday dinner. He was half tempted to follow her home to see where she lived but refrained from breaking her trust.

His feelings for Harper only deepened over the weeks since she moved out. He grudgingly admitted that she was right to have left. He really needed to talk with Harper about how he felt. Carter started making a plan to do so at Christmas.

# Chapter 18

Christmas was a few days away and it would not only be Bo and Colt's first Christmas, but also Lexi's. Luther had refused to even have a Christmas tree. Harper and Lexi set up a small tree in the corner. Lexi was so excited about it, but Harper had mixed feelings.

She had always loved Christmas. The lights and music and holiday spirit were magical. This year, however, seemed to be lacking something. It wasn't until Carter had asked if they would like to go to the ranch for Christmas dinner, that she realized what was missing. She wanted to spend it with Carter.

The whole distance thing Clara had suggested only drove home the fact that her feelings for Carter were real. She loved him. She was terrified and unsure of how to proceed with this knowledge. Her phone buzzed and she looked at it.

**Carter:** Would it be possible to stop by tomorrow and steal Lexi for a few hours?

**Harper:** Why are you wanting to steal my daughter?

**Carter:** We talked about some things last night while I was reading her a book, and I made a promise.

**Harper:** And what promise is that?

**Carter:** Part of the promise involves a secret, which I am unable to share. Come on, Dove, it is Christmas.

**Harper:** I think that should work, but you have to promise me something.

**Carter:** You Anderson girls make me promise a lot of things.

**Harper:** That's fine, Cowboy. You can find someone else to go shopping with tomorrow.

**Carter:** What is the promise?

**Harper:** I need you to keep her until dinner

**Carter:** Not that I'm complaining about spending more time with my favorite little girl, but why?

**Harper:** I have someone coming by and I don't want her to see him. At least not yet.

**Carter:** Him? Not yet? Who are you introducing to my little girl?

**Carter:** Do I get to meet him?

**Harper:** Are you shopping with Lexi tomorrow or not, Cowboy?

**Carter:** Be there by nine. What's the address?

Harper reread their conversation and laughed before sending him her address. Did he think she was bringing over a guy she was dating? She didn't have time to go on dates. Even if she did, Carter made it so she didn't want to date.

Harper wanted to make this Christmas special for Lexi, and she hoped she would be able to accomplish that with what she wanted to get her daughter. She only had two last gifts to get. This one for Lexi, and she needed to find something for Carter. What do you get the man that is your best friend, who you are also in love with, but he has no idea how you feel?

"Lexi, can you come here please?" Harper called down the hall. When Lexi came running into the room Harper smiled. "You know how you and mommy are going to go shopping today?" Lexi nodded excitedly. "Carter wants to take you shopping tomorrow." Lexi squealed in delight.

Clara came a few minutes later to watch the boys so Harper could take Lexi to the store. The little girl had wanted to pick out things for her uncles and Carter. Harper was surprised at the gifts Lexi had picked out. She knew the men had mentioned needing each item at least once since they had known them during the last few months. Harper was still undecided on what to get Carter, when her eyes caught on a display case as they were leaving the store. Harper walked closer to take a look and her breath caught.

"Those are pretty." Lexi said in awe.

"They sure are." Harper said as she looked over the stunning rings Lexi was looking at.

Harper had been drawn to the case for a different reason. Next to the rings were watches. Carter's watch had broken last week. She pointed to one as the sales lady walked up. Glancing down, she saw Lexi still entranced with the rings.

"This one here can have an engraving put on the back if you would like." The sales lady said in a bored tone.

Harper took the watch from the lady to get a better look. The thick leather band had wolves etched into it. She knew it was perfect. "I'll take it." Harper said with a smile. The sales lady asked about the engraving on the back, and Harper told her what she wanted. When an assistant took the watch to be engraved, Harper humored Lexi by looking at the rings.

"Which is your favorite, mommy?" Lexi asked.

"Hmm. That one is pretty." Harper pointed at a simple band with a single diamond, but then a ring several spots over caught her eye. It had a diamond in the center with sapphires going down the sides as if they were leaves on the vines that were etched into the band. "That one is amazing." Harper said and Lexi enthusiastically agreed.

"It really is stunning. We had a man come in a few days ago that purchased one similar to that one. Would you like me to pull it out so you can see it better?" the sales lady asked with a smile.

"No thank you, we are just looking while waiting for the watch." Harper told the lady.

Twenty minutes later they were heading back to the house and Lexi was singing along with the Christmas songs on the radio. Harper was relieved to only have one more thing she needed to get, but that would have to wait for tomorrow. Harper pulled into her driveway and turned back to Lexi. The girl was passed out. Harper carried her daughter up the porch and into the house. Clara helped bring in the bags while Harper laid Lexi in her bed.

"How did it go?" Clara asked with a smile. "Is your Christmas shopping all done?"

"I have that lady coming over tomorrow, but other than that, I think I am finally done." Harper picked up Bo and pressed a kiss to his cheek. "How were my boys?"

"They were angels." Clara laughed. "Have you decided on what you are going to do?"

Harper sighed. "Not yet. Carter will have Lexi all day tomorrow, so we will not be leaving until the next day anyway."

"Carter is taking Lexi?" Clara raised her brow.

"That way she doesn't see when Mrs. Harvey stops by." Harper shrugged. "It makes keeping it a secret that much easier."

Clara agreed with a chuckle. "How is Lexi doing at night?"

"She isn't having them every single night anymore. She will go a few days without them, and then the nightmares come back for several days." Harper glanced down the hall. "I think after Christmas I'm going to get her in to see someone."

Clara and Harper talked a little more before Clara left. Harper spent the next hour wrapping presents and sticking them under the tree. Lexi and the twins woke up not long after, and they spent a quiet evening watching

Christmas movies until Lexi's nightly phone call with Carter. Once Lexi and the twins were in bed, Harper took a shower before climbing in her own bed. She had a few big decisions to make before the end of tomorrow.

The next morning, Harper woke early and curled her hair, put on some makeup, and got dressed. Now that the twins were sleeping better, she was able to put more effort into her appearance.

She was cleaning up breakfast when a knock came at the door. "Lexi, grab your shoes and coat!" Harper called down the hall as she wiped her soapy hands on a towel and pulled open the front door.

Carter took her in from head to toe before he cleared his throat. "Morning." he said as he stepped inside.

Harper closed the door and smiled. "Good morning. How were the roads?"

"They were fine." Carter's eyes took in her hair and face again. "You look amazing, Harper. Any special occasion?"

"Just getting back to a more normal routine now that the twins are sleeping better." Harper moved to walk past him, but Carter's arm slid around her waist. Harper fought to keep her heart from beating out of her chest as she stared up into Carter's eyes. "Can I help you, Cowboy?" She asked.

"I sure hope so." He whispered as his head started to dip down towards hers.

"Mommy, I can't find my other boot!" Lexi yelled from her room and the spell around them was broken.

"I'll be right there, sweetheart." Harper called back. Carter turned his head to look down the hallway and Harper took the opportunity to rise on her toes to press a quick kiss to Carter's cheek. His hold on her loosened and Harper stepped away. She didn't look back as she made her way to Lexi's room.

Harper easily found the boot, then helped Lexi finish getting dressed. When they entered the living room, Carter was holding both Bo and Colt. He pressed a kiss to each of their heads before laying them back down on their playmats. "Ready to go, Princess?" he asked as he lifted Lexi into his arms.

Harper followed them out to Carter's truck. A gust of wind blew, and she wrapped her arms around herself to keep warm. "You should go inside where it's warm." Carter said, turning to her with a smile after he finished buckling Lexi into a car seat.

"I will." Harper said. "I just…" Harper looked back at the cab door that he had just closed.

"We will be fine, Dove." He studied her for a moment. "What's really on your mind?"

Harper shivered and Carter wrapped his arms around her, sharing his warmth. She pressed closer to him. "I have to make a decision, well two, before the end of tonight. And I don't know what to do." Carter pulled back so he could see her face again.

He cupped her cheek. "If you haven't figured it out by the time we get back, we can talk about it. With the two of us, I'm sure we can work it out." He leaned down and pressed a light kiss to her cheek. "Plus, you are stronger than you give yourself credit for. I don't doubt you will know what to do."

He gave her a smile before climbing into the truck and Harper made her way to the porch. Before going back inside, Harper turned to see Carter wave as they drove away. She slowly closed the door behind her as she looked around the living room, her gaze settling on Bo and Colt. She was all the family her kids had. Carter, the guys, and Clara were all like family, but she was their only blood relative. Taking a deep breath, Harper reached for her phone and made the call she had been debating about for a full week.

After her call, Harper felt so much lighter. She was anxious and worried about driving all that way by herself, but she knew this was the right decision. She played with her sons before fixing them bottles. She put them down for their naps in their crib and turned on the baby monitor. Harper sat on the couch and reached for her laptop. She scrolled through the information the counselor had sent her. She had prayed about this for weeks, yet she was still unsure if she had done the right thing.

A knock on the front door pulled her from her thoughts and she stood to answer it. Mrs. Harvey stood on the porch with a big smile on her face. "It's good to see you again, Harper. Do you want me to bring them in or do you want to come out to the truck?"

"I can help you bring them inside." Harper returned the woman's smile. Her earlier excitement returned in full. She pulled on her boots and coat before following Mrs. Harvey out to her truck. The older woman opened the back door and reached in. When she turned around, she had two puppies in her arms. Harper's smile grew as she was given both puppies to take inside.

There were four puppies, all males. They ran around the living room and kitchen area exploring their new environment. "They aren't purebreds." Mrs. Harvey said as she took a seat on the couch. "Our Australian Shepherd and our neighbor's lab got together by accident."

"That's fine. I wasn't necessarily looking for a purebred. Can you tell me about their parent's personalities and what you have observed in each puppy?" Harper asked as she started playing with two of the puppies that were close by.

The more she heard about the mother dog, the more she fell in love with the idea of one of the puppies for Lexi. They talked for an hour about the individual puppies before the twins woke up. Harper went and got the boys from the back room, eager to see how the puppies reacted to the babies.

One of the pups followed her to the bedroom and back. He was the only blue merle of the group, with one blue eye and one brown. He was confident and playful. He was curious about the babies but wasn't rough. Harper loved that his coat wasn't as long as the others. As the afternoon wore on, the puppies grew tired and the one Harper had been leaning towards, curled up on Lexi's blanket on the couch and fell asleep. She was sold.

"They will be eight weeks on Christmas Eve." Mrs. Harvey said with a knowing smile.

They discussed a time for Harper to come out to the Harvey's ranch to pick up the puppy. Harper helped load them back into the kennel on the back seat of Mrs. Harvey's truck. She thanked the woman and headed back inside, more excited than ever.

This puppy would not only be a companion, but he would function as an emotional support dog for Lexi to help with her nightmares. A notification came in as Harper was starting dinner. Lexi had asked for chicken nuggets, but Harper was making steak and potatoes for herself. She pulled out her phone and opened the email. She skimmed through it and froze when she saw the word: Accepted. She didn't know what she wanted to do. Laugh? Cry? Do a happy dance?

"Mommy!" Lexi's voice came at the same moment the front door burst open.

Harper spun around quickly with her heart hammering in her chest. Lexi came running up to her and gave her a hug. "Did you have a good time?" Harper asked, recovering from the email and Lexi's sudden arrival.

"I love Carter! He got me ice cream." Lexi said excitedly. "You were right, ice cream is so much better in winter."

Harper laughed and kissed her daughter. "Why don't you take your coat off and get ready for dinner. Then you can tell me all about your day." Lexi ran off down the hall leaving Harper and Carter in the kitchen. "Are you staying for dinner?" Harper asked as she turned to Carter.

"For the record, the ice cream was right after she ate lunch and a very small amount." Carter said as he crossed the room. "And dinner sounds great."

He stopped a few feet away and shrugged out of his coat, hanging it over a dining room chair. Harper closed the distance and threw her arms around his neck. She needed to feel his steady comfort right now. She wasn't sure she was capable of starting school at this time in her life. She didn't even know why she had filled out the application.

"Hey, is everything okay?" He whispered, pulling her closer.

She sighed and rested her head on his chest. "Just a little overwhelmed." He tightened his arms around her, and Harper closed her eyes. They stood like that until Lexi came running down the hall.

As Carter helped set the table, Harper finished cooking. She listened with a smile as Lexi told her everything Carter had taken her to do. They laughed when Lexi told Harper about Carter slipping on the ice and falling on his back. Carter just smiled and rolled his eyes.

Lexi started to crash after all the excitement of the day and Carter carried her to her room. When he came back out, Harper was feeding Bo a bottle while sitting on the couch. Without saying a word, Carter cleaned up the kitchen and made a bottle for Colt. He sat on the couch next to her and swapped Bo for his brother so he could burp Bo while Harper fed Colt.

"Thank you for helping." Harper said as she leaned her head on his shoulder. "And for taking Lexi. I think she is going to love him."

"Who is him?" Carter asked, laying Bo in his bassinet and turning to look at her.

Harper looked down the hall before looking back at Carter. She couldn't help the grin that spread on her face. She lowered her voice to a whisper. "Lexi's Christmas present." Carter blinked in confusion, which only made Harper smile more. "He has the prettiest eyes." Carter's expression hardened. "Are you okay?"

"Who is he? I think the guys and I should meet him before you bring him around the kids." Carter said stiffly.

Colt finished eating and Harper took a few minutes to burp him before answering Carter's question. The longer the silence, the more tense he became. She finally laid Colt in his bassinet and turned to Carter with the most innocent look she could muster. "Are you upset with me, Cowboy?" She asked.

Carter glared at her. "That innocent look isn't going to work on me, Dove. Who is he?"

"Now you are starting to sound jealous. Afraid your role as Lexi's favorite is going to be taken from you?" Harper teased. Carter's glare didn't soften, so Harper grabbed his face and with her thumbs, pressed the corners of his mouth up into a smile. "That's better. Even though it is missing the dimple."

Carter grabbed her around the waist and pulled her closer. Careful of the bruises she still had, he started to tickle her. Harper squealed as she tried to get away, but he was too strong. "Okay, okay." Harper wheezed out. He stopped tickling her and she sagged against him, still giggling. "I got Lexi a puppy. A little Aussie-lab mix, and he is the cutest. The owner brought several of them today so I could see them."

Carter laughed and relaxed behind her. His arms stayed around her as they sat in silence for several minutes. "Why were you so overwhelmed earlier?"

"Way to kill the mood." Harper muttered and sat up. "A few weeks ago, I did something I'm not sure I'm ready for." She sighed. "I reapplied to college. I just got the acceptance email."

"Harper, that's great." Carter said excitedly. "What degree are you looking at?"

"I have nine-week-old twins and a four-year-old, Carter. I don't know if I can go back to college right now. Money isn't an issue, but time is. How on earth am I supposed to be a mom and student?" She turned to look at him. He was watching her closely.

"Dove, you can do whatever you set your mind to. You don't have to be enrolled full-time. You can start by taking a class or two and see how it goes." he said softly as he tucked her hair behind her ear. "I'm guessing you are wanting to do it online, so you don't have to find a sitter?"

Harper nodded. "If I were to do it, I would go online, but Carter, seriously I don't know if I can. It just seems too...overwhelming."

Carter pulled her back to him, and she curled into his side. Harper took several slow breaths to calm herself from her anxious thoughts. She reminded herself that she had prayed about it, and it had felt right. Maybe her upcoming visit with her father was stressing her out. "There's something else." She whispered as she stood and began to pace. "I'm not asking permission." She glanced over at him. "I'm just letting you know so that you don't freak out tomorrow."

"Why would I freak out tomorrow?" Carter asked, standing as well. His tension was back.

"The kids and I are leaving for Denver in the morning." She stopped her pacing and wrapped her arms protectively around herself. Carter's expression became worried. "I have been in contact with my dad since we got back with Bo. He wanted us to spend Christmas with him, but I told him that would be impossible. There was no way I was going to be spending Christmas away from home this year. As a compromise, we are going down to spend a day with him."

Carter watched her for several minutes, her already anxious feelings about this trip hitched up another notch. What was she thinking? She couldn't do this. Turning her back on Carter, she placed her hands on the island and hung her head. Was it too late to cancel her trip? She already had the hotel and her father had sounded so excited on the phone.

Carter's arms slid around her slowly and she turned and leaned into him. "I think it is good that you are trying to repair your relationship with your father, Harper." He whispered. "I know this can't be easy for you. It is not easy seeing you having to face that man. I don't have the nicest feelings towards him, but I will support you any way you need me too."

Harper tightened her arms around Carter's torso. He was her rock. How was she going to face her father without having Carter to lean on? But she couldn't ask him to come with her, no matter how much she wanted to. She could still text him and call whenever she needed to. Lexi, Bo, and Colt deserved to know their grandfather.

"What are your travel plans?" Carter asked, pulling back enough to see her face.

"We will leave early tomorrow morning and stay at a hotel. The next day, we will spend most of it with my dad and head home the following morning." Harper could see the questions in his eyes, and she pressed on. "I can send you the hotel information and let you know when I leave and arrive at our hotel."

"I would appreciate that, Dove." That dimpled smile appeared, and Harper smiled back at him. "If you are planning on leaving early, I should go so you can get to bed." Harper nodded hesitantly. She didn't want him to go, but knew he needed to. He still had an hour drive back to the ranch. It was getting so much harder to say goodbye to him. Harper slipped her coat and boots on and followed Carter out to his truck. "You know you don't have to walk me to my truck every time I leave." Carter smiled teasingly.

Harper shrugged. "I know." she said in a soft voice as she stared at the ground.

The teasing in Carter's tone disappeared as he looked at her. "Everything will be okay, Harper. And you can call or text me anytime. You don't have to stay the full day with your dad if it becomes too much."

She nodded but kept her eyes down. He hooked his finger under her chin and forced her to look at him. He pressed his lips to hers as he shifted his hand to the back of her head while his other hand snaked around her waist. Her arms found their way around his neck and pulled him closer. He responded by deepening the kiss. By the time they pulled apart, they were both out of breath. Carter rested his forehead against hers for a moment before pressing a quick kiss to her lips. "Goodnight, Dove. Let me know when you head out."

Harper nodded as she stepped back. "Goodnight, Cowboy." He hesitated before climbing into his truck. Harper watched from the porch in a daze as he drove away. Had that really just happened? She could still feel his lips on hers. Harper shook her head and went back inside. She needed to have a talk with Carter once she got back from Denver.

# Chapter 19

Harper let out a sigh of relief when Lexi finally fell asleep. The car ride had been brutal. The twins did not like being in the car seats, and Lexi was angry that her Carter wasn't with them. She had sent Carter a text when they got into their hotel room, but she hadn't checked for a reply because she was busy getting all three kids down for a nap.

Beth was planning on bringing pizza for dinner, so that they could catch up on everything that had happened over the last several weeks. Beth also mentioned that she had been contacted by Henry's lawyer to discuss his life insurance and will. Harper had no idea he had a will. Harper was sitting on the uncomfortable couch with her computer going over the new student paperwork when a light knock sounded at her door.

Harper set her laptop off to the side before moving to the door. She looked through the peephole and gasped. She quickly unlocked the door and opened it. Carter stood there looking disheveled and tired. "Carter? What are you doing here?" She asked in a whisper. She looked back at her sleeping kids before grabbing his arm and pulling him into the room, closing the door quietly. "What's going on?"

"Harper, I need to know what I need to do in order for you to give me a chance." Carter said keeping his voice quiet so he wouldn't wake the kids. "Please, I can't just be your friend. I haven't been able to since you gave me a bloody nose." He paused and looked at Harper, but she was stunned into silence. "One of the hardest moments of my life was watching the girl I loved being loaded into the back of a car as she screamed for me to save her, but unable to do anything. I was crushed when I asked Henry if I could seek you out after we were released from active duty, only for him to tell me you were married with a daughter. I thought I had been getting over you after I bought the ranch, only for you to come crashing back into my life. But I was wrong. I've never gotten over you."

Harper opened her mouth to say something, but nothing came out and Carter ran a hand through his hair. "It has been torture seeing you go through everything with Luther. When he shot you, I thought my world would come crashing down. I can't even begin to express the anger I feel for the man that somehow captured your heart but has also broken it. I know you can't just turn your feelings off whenever you feel like it, but please, all I am asking for is a chance to earn your love." Carter's eyes were filled with determination and hope and pleading.

A knock at the door snapped Harper out of her shock. Carter put his hands in the front pockets of his jeans and looked down at the floor. Harper moved back to the door and let Bethany in. She stopped only a step through the door when she saw Carter. "Am I interrupting?" Beth asked, looking between the two of them.

"I…We…" Harper tried to speak but she couldn't quite find words.

"I'll watch the kids while you two finish whatever this is." Beth said, gesturing to Carter and then back to Harper.

Harper thanked Beth in a quiet whisper before grabbing her wallet and phone and stepping out into the hallway. Carter followed her out. "I am assuming you have a room here." Harper managed to get out. When Carter nodded, she gestured for him to lead the way. He looked like he was going to say something, but clamped his mouth shut and walked towards the elevators.

They rode the elevator up two floors before Carter walked to the far end of the hall. Her shocked mind was slowly starting to function again by the time he unlocked the door and stepped back for Harper to enter first. She walked in and began pacing the small space. The door clicked closed but she didn't look up. She could feel Carter's eyes on her as she tried to process what he had just said.

"Harper." Carter started to say, but she held up her hand to stop him.

He was in love with her? From the time they were kids? All this time they were in love with each other, but too afraid to say anything. Harper rubbed her forehead. All the things Devon had been saying or hinting at finally made sense. The questions about her being in love with a soldier, and if she would ever move on. Was he trying to figure out if Carter even had a shot with her?

"Let me get this straight." Harper said slowly, irritation coloring her voice. "You have been in love with me since I punched you in the face, ignored me for years, and protected me and my kids, all while hiding the fact that you are still in love with me?" Harper turned to face him.

The pain and guilt in Carter's eyes nearly undid her. "I thought it was some childhood crush that would fade with time. I thought that if there was distance, the feelings would go away, but you wouldn't leave me. Then after basic, all the guys were getting tattoos. Henry and I had strayed a bit from the church during that time. We rolled dice to see what category the tattoo had to be in and where we had to get it. Henry had to do something that gave him purpose on his back. He chose the American flag and an eagle." Carter ran a hand through his hair. "I had to get one of something I loved on my chest. Henry convinced me to put it over my heart. He said it was fitting. I got a tattoo of a brown wolf with blue eyes. The guys were confused, but I think Henry figured it out."

Harper could only stare at him. She had no idea that Henry had strayed from the church. "Harper, I know that you are still in love with your soldier. And I know I may just be setting myself up to get hurt, but please give me a chance."

"You want to know who your competition is?" Harper snapped at him. She stomped up to him and turned him so that he faced the mirror on the wall. "Do you even realize how many chances I have given you?" Harper threw her hands up as she paced away from him. "I felt so betrayed when you didn't stop dad from putting me in that car. And when you didn't come get me when mom's boyfriends tried to sneak into my room. I was crushed when you didn't come with Henry to graduation. You are the reason for that stupid list." Harper turned and glared at him.

She couldn't stop all the hurt she had felt over the years from coming out. "You were my rock, Carter. I needed you and you weren't there." She took a deep breath. "I thought I could protect myself. I thought we could just be friends, so that Lexi could still have you in her life."

"Harper?" Carter said quietly as he took a step towards her.

"I'm so mad at you, Carter." Harper could feel tears rolling down her cheeks. "I'm mad and I'm scared."

Carter closed the distance between them and hugged her. The dam on her emotions broke and she started to cry. Carter held her tight until her tears turned to sniffles. He pulled back and used his thumbs to wipe her tears. "I'm sorry I wasn't there for you when you needed me, Dove. It killed me to watch the girl I had always imagined marrying, drive away. Your dad saw my bike and backpack at the side of the house. He threatened to charge me with kidnapping if he ever found out I took you away." He pressed a kiss to her forehead.

"Why didn't you tell me?" Harper whispered.

"Even though I realized you had my heart that day in the bathroom, Henry said he could tell I liked you even before that. I guess punching three guys who stared at you too long, and then getting into a fist fight with your brother after he teased you until you cried was a giveaway." Carter smiled and his dimple appeared. "In case you haven't figured it out yet, Harper Nicole Anderson, I am hopelessly in love with you."

Harper's breath caught at the sincerity in his eyes. Was this really happening? Harper slowly ran her hands up Carter's chest and around his neck. His gaze stayed firmly on hers as he waited to see what she would do. "Carter, I don't know if this is a good idea. I have the kids to think about. What if they don't like you?" Harper barely got the words out before he kissed her.

Carter pulled back. "Those kids love me." He smiled. "The only thing I don't know is if their mother does." Harper rose on her toes and pressed her lips to Carter's. He pulled back with a smile. "Does she?" He asked and Harper tried to kiss him again, but he stayed just out of reach. "I'm not kissing you again until you answer me."

"What was the question again?" Harper asked as she tried to step away.

His arms kept her in place. "Do you love me, Harper?" There was a hint of uncertainty in his eyes. Harper looked over at the clock and a crazy idea formed in her head.

"Do you have your keys?" Harper asked as she pushed off Carter's chest and headed for the door.

"Yes, but what…"

"Hurry, we don't have much time." Harper nearly jogged to the elevators.

Inside the elevator, Carter pulled her to him. "What is going on, Dove? You have that look in your eyes that usually means I am going to have to step in to save you." Harper tried to kiss him, but he once again didn't let her. "You still haven't answered me."

The doors opened to the lobby and Harper stepped out of Carter's arms. She walked out into the parking lot as she pulled her phone out of her pocket and sent a message to Beth letting her know they were going to be a while longer. "Where are you parked?" Harper asked.

Carter grabbed her hand and led her to the far side of the parking lot. He didn't unlock the truck when they got there. Instead, he pushed Harper up against the side of it. "Harper, you are torturing me. Please, just answer my question."

Harper smiled. "I have answered, you just haven't been listening." Carter growled and Harper pressed her lips to his while he was distracted. He kissed her back, but when she ended the kiss, Carter looked frustrated. "I do love you, Cowboy."

Carter reclaimed her lips and she laughed. "You are such a handful, you know that?" Carter said as he dug in his pocket. He kissed her again and she felt him slip something on her hand.

She pulled back and looked down. "What's this?" Harper stared down at the ring on her finger. It was similar to the one she had seen at the store. She laughed as her eyes rose to meet his. "You were the guy?" At his confused look, she continued. "When I went shopping with Lexi, she wanted to look at all the pretty rings on display. The sales lady mentioned a man had come in and got a ring similar to one we were looking at."

Carter smiled as he pressed a kiss to her forehead before he knelt down on one knee. "Harper Anderson, I have loved you all my life and I have fallen in love with each one of your kids. You four are my world. Please say you will marry me?"

Harper laughed. "Sorry, Cowboy. You don't have a say in the matter." Carter stood back up and laughed. "Unlock the truck so we aren't late."

"No say, hmm? And where may I ask, are we going?" Carter opened her door for her, but stopped her from climbing in.

"We are going to the courthouse." Harper pressed a kiss to Carter's cheek.

"You were going to ask me to marry you?" Carter laughed.

Harper smirked at him. "No, I'm telling you, not asking." Carter laughed harder.

"Yes ma'am." Carter grinned as he closed her door and climbed into the driver's seat.

He held her hand all the way to the courthouse and as they waited in line. He had asked if she was sure multiple times, but Harper would only smile and kiss him. She was positive. There was no way she was going to let Carter change his mind. She loved him and he loved her. Lexi adored him and had even wanted her to marry him. There was no reason to wait. Harper was surprised at how fast the whole process was. Within an hour of arriving at the courthouse, Harper and Carter were married.

It was all surreal. It felt too much like a dream. Harper didn't even notice that Carter had taken them back to his hotel room until he opened the door with his key. "We have a few things to discuss before we go back to your room." He said pulling her in after him.

As soon as the door was closed, his lips were on hers. Harper laughed. "This isn't discussing things." She pointed out.

"We need to figure out when we are going to tell people that you dragged me to the courthouse and married me." Carter pressed a kiss to her cheek. "Are we telling your dad?" He kissed her neck by her ear. "When are you moving back to the ranch?" Another kiss along her neck. "Are we sharing a room tonight?"

Harper pushed Carter back a little so she could see his face. "Not until Christmas. No to my dad. After Christmas. And not tonight." At his scowl, Harper laughed. "Lexi and the twins are in my room. No privacy."

Carter looked around with a smile. "They aren't here now." He said as he scooped her up into his arms and dropped her on the bed causing her to laugh.

\* \* \*

Harper held tightly to Carter's hand as they knocked on her hotel room. Beth answered it with a raised brow. "Four hours Harper, really?" Beth crossed her arms over her chest.

"Sorry, Beth. Carter and I had things we needed to discuss." Harper said quietly looking over at Carter who winked at her.

"Carter? As in…" Beth trailed off as she took a closer look at Carter. "You never said how incredibly hot your Carter was." Beth raised her brows at Harper with a smirk.

"Carter!" Lexi ran over and Carter scooped her up into his arms. "Mommy said you weren't coming."

"That's because mommy didn't know I was coming." Carter kissed Lexi's cheek.

Lexi looked over at Harper with a big smile, but her smile turned into a frown. "What's that?" She pointed at Harper's neck.

Carter laughed. "We can talk about that in a minute, okay Princess? Now, did you leave me and your mom any pizza?" Lexi wiggled down and ran across the room. Carter stepped closer to Harper. "We might need to tell Lexi tonight?" He kissed her cheek then followed Lexi across the room to the table in the corner.

Harper watched him walk away confused. "Is that a hickey?" Beth asked in a harsh whisper.

She quickly stepped to the mirror and looked at her neck. "Carter!" She cried. "You did that on purpose." She scolded, but he only shrugged with a proud smile. She tried to glare at him, but she couldn't stop the smile that formed.

"Spill." Beth hissed.

Harper gave Beth the watered-down version of her conversation with Carter and how they went to the courthouse and got married. Beth looked at her in shock before she burst out laughing. She said her goodbyes shortly after and Harper claimed a piece of pizza before sitting on the bed next to Lexi. Carter sat on the other bed as he fed Bo with Colt kicking next to him.

"Carter rented a movie." Lexi told her as she jumped on the bed. "He said we had to wait until you said we could watch it."

"Why don't you go get ready for bed and brush your teeth first." Harper smiled and watched as Lexi ran to her suitcase. Once she was in the bathroom, Harper moved over to sit by Carter. "I can't believe you gave me a hickey."

Carter leaned over and kissed her. "You weren't exactly complaining, Dove."

"And how am I supposed to explain it to Lexi?" Harper asked quietly.

"Hmm." Carter's eyes twinkled. "We could tell her that her daddy loves her mommy, and he kissed her."

The bathroom door opened. "I'm ready." Lexi announced.

Harper took Bo from Carter so he could get the movie going. He tucked Lexi under the covers before helping Harper get the twins ready for bed and laying them in the portable crib. He climbed onto the bed next to Harper as she snuggled Lexi. He leaned in close to her ear to keep Lexi from overhearing. "I think we need to tell Lexi."

Harper turned her head in Carter's direction. "Why's that?" She whispered back.

"We really didn't get the opportunity to discuss things earlier."

"Whose fault is that, Cowboy?" Harper smirked at him.

"Yours. You were too tempting." Carter kissed the corner of her mouth. "I think we should tell Lexi and we can wait until Christmas to tell everyone else. We will move you back home after Christmas, like you said. But I want to stay here tonight with my family."

Harper couldn't resist the pull and she kissed Carter. She knew she should end it, but she didn't. She loved this man and couldn't believe they were married. She finally ended the kiss and snuggled against him while keeping an arm around Lexi.

Near the end of the movie, Harper told Carter to go get his stuff from his room, and they would tell Lexi together before they put her to bed. The movie ended and Carter left. Harper was gathering her clothes so she could take a shower while Lexi sat in the middle of the bed.

"Is Carter going to be my daddy?" Lexi asked without preamble. Harper stopped looking for her pajamas and turned to her daughter. "He was kissing you and you were smiling. Do you love him?" Harper opened her mouth to say something to stall until Carter got back, but Lexi continued. "Hannah said her mom gets marks like that from her dad. She called it a love bite. Did Carter give you a love bite?"

"Lexi, hold on just a second, okay? Why don't we wait for Carter to get back, and the three of us can talk." Harper grabbed her phone and sent a quick message.

**Harper:** Get your bag and get back here, ASAP!!!

**Carter:** On my way back now. Everything okay?

**Harper:** Just hurry.

Harper watched as Lexi began to bounce up and down as she continued with her rapid-fire questions. Are they moving back to the ranch? Can she have her own horse? Will she go to school with Hannah? Harper quickly opened the door when a knock came. Lexi was just asking about having a baby sister next, as Carter stepped into the room.

"You told her?" He asked.

"No. She apparently heard about love bites from Hannah, because Clara had one. Then she has been asking question after question since you left." Harper explained as she looked over at Lexi, who was oblivious that Carter had returned.

Carter stepped around Harper. "Alright, Lexi. I know you have many questions, but I need you to listen, okay?" Lexi sat back down and gave Carter her full attention. He put his arm around Harper. "I love your mom, Lexi. I came here to ask her to marry me. Calm down, Princess. Let me finish." Carter chuckled when Lexi started bouncing again. "You were taking a nap when I stopped by."

"Did she say, yes? Are you going to say, yes?" Lexi couldn't control her obvious excitement.

"Lexi, Carter and I got married while Beth was watching you." Harper said and Lexi stopped bouncing. She stared at them with wide eyes.

"So, you are my daddy now?" Lexi asked.

"If you want me to be." Carter said as Lexi threw her arms around both Harper and Carter's necks. Harper was trying to keep her quiet so she wouldn't wake the twins, but then Lexi pulled back and dropped back on the bed with a panicked look. "What is it, Princess?"

"I asked Santa for you to be my daddy. If I get my Christmas wish now, does that mean I don't get any presents on Christmas?"

Harper laughed. "No, baby girl. You will get plenty of presents on Christmas."

"It is getting pretty late. I think it is time for you to go to sleep." Carter picked Lexi up and tucked her under the blankets. "We have a big day tomorrow."

"Goodnight, daddy."

"Goodnight, Princess. I love you." Carter kissed Lexi's head before moving to Harper's side. "Time for you to get in bed too, Love."

"I need a shower first." Harper turned back to her bag and started pulling everything out of it.

"What are you looking for?" Carter asked curiously.

Harper let out a huff of frustration. "I think I forgot to pack my pajamas."

Carter kissed her cheek. "I got you." He knelt down and unzipped his bag. He pulled a shirt from it and handed it to Harper as he stood.

Harper kissed him one more time before heading for the bathroom. She took a quick shower and pulled Carter's shirt on before French braiding her hair. She suddenly felt nervous standing there in only Carter's shirt and her underwear. Luckily, the shirt was long enough to reach mid-thigh.

Taking a deep breath, she opened the door. The room was dark with just enough light for her to make her way to the bed easily. She crawled under the covers and Carter immediately pulled her close, pressing a kiss to her shoulder. "Goodnight, Dove." He whispered.

Harper rolled over and snuggled close to him. "Goodnight, Cowboy." She whispered as Carter kissed her forehead.

# Chapter 20

Carter woke up with a smile. Harper was cuddled up to him with her head on his chest. He pressed a kiss to her forehead, and she snuggled closer. He was so glad she had suggested that they get married immediately. There was no place he would rather be at the moment, than lying in bed holding his wife.

Bo and Colt had gotten up several times during the night, and to his surprise, Lexi had slept through everything. He didn't know how Harper ever got any sleep having to do this by herself. Lucky for her, all three kids were still asleep, so she could rest a little more. He glanced at his wrist, but inwardly groaned when he saw it was bare. He really needed to replace his watch.

He looked over at the alarm clock and saw that it was nearly four-thirty. His normal wakeup time. Knowing he wouldn't be able to go back to sleep, Carter carefully got up, grabbed his bag, and went into the bathroom. He was just wrapping a towel around his waist after his shower when the door opened, and Harper stepped in. Seeing him standing there her face turned red and she tried to step back out of the room, but he grabbed her arm.

"Good morning, Dove." He smiled at her.

Harper's eyes were glued to his chest. "Morning." She breathed out.

"Harper, are you nervous?" he asked as he tugged her a little closer. Her eyes snapped up to his and he could see the uncertainty in them. "What's wrong?" he asked.

She shook her head and stepped closer to him. He wrapped his arms around her and waited. Something was bothering her, and she needed a moment to gather her thoughts. He hoped she wasn't regretting yesterday. "I'm nervous about today. I don't know what my dad expects from me. I don't know what I expect from him."

Carter lifted Harper and set her on the counter next to the sink. He rested his hands on her thighs as he looked her straight in the eye. "Don't stress, sweetheart. We will take it a minute at a time. The first step is just having a simple conversation with him."

Harper took a deep breath. "I don't know why I thought I could do this without you." She whispered.

Carter leaned in and gave her a quick kiss. "I changed my mind on the first step." He murmured against her lips, causing her to giggle as he dragged her closer to him.

*     *     *

Harper dressed and brushed her hair. She gasped when she saw a new hickey on her neck next to the one from yesterday. She was going to have a serious talk with him when he got back from getting breakfast.

Lexi and the twins were still asleep when he got back. He placed doughnuts and orange juice on the table before laying down on the bed. Harper climbed onto the bed next to him and he pulled her close.

"You really need to stop giving me hickeys." Harper said softly.

"You have another one? Let me see." Carter turned her head to the side and studied her neck for a few moments before kissing the spots. Harper tilted her head to give him more access. "I will stop giving you hickeys the day you start protesting instead of doing that when I kiss you."

"That's not fair." Harper smacked him and tried to move away.

Carter chuckled as he pulled her back to him. "I'll behave for now. Just try to lay down and enjoy a little more rest." Harper sighed and laid her head on his shoulder.

She must have dozed off because the next thing she was aware of was Lexi's giggle. She opened her eyes to see Lexi staring at her and Carter. Carter was holding her tightly to him with his face buried in her hair and a hand cradling her head. Harper smiled over at her daughter and carefully extricated herself from Carter's arms. She put her finger to her lips to tell Lexi to keep quiet as they moved over to the table. Harper handed Lexi a doughnut and glass of orange juice before helping herself to one. They finished eating and Harper was able to feed and change both Bo and Colt while Carter slept.

It was getting close to the time they needed to leave. Lexi volunteered to wake Carter, and Harper watched with a smile as she climbed onto the bed. But before Lexi could jump on him, Carter grabbed her and tickled her. Lexi squealed and laughed until Carter kissed her cheek and let her go. He stood and sat next to Harper on the couch. "You know. I find I don't like to wake up without you beside me." He muttered to her as he took a bite of a doughnut.

"We have only been married for one night and you are already so attached." Harper teased. "Has anyone ever told you that you are a cuddler?"

"Considering I have never slept with anyone else, I would say no." Carter smirked at her. "However, Henry and a few guys on missions said I kicked and moved a lot in my sleep."

"You weren't kicking mommy." Lexi supplied. "You hugged her tight like this." She tried to imitate him, causing Harper to laugh. "And you kept complaining when mommy tried to move away."

"Alright Lexi, go brush your teeth and make sure your clothes are back in your bag. It's time to go." Harper told her daughter.

Harper carried Colt's car seat and held Lexi's hand while Carter carried Bo's carrier and the diaper bag as they headed for her truck. Carter took the keys from her, insisting that he was driving.

Her father's house was thirty minutes away, giving Harper plenty of time to stress about what was to come. Carter had taken hold of her hand soon after starting the truck and she held onto him tightly. His thumb stroked her knuckles and eventually she began to relax.

They pulled into the driveway of a decent-sized house that looked just like all the others on the block. Carter helped her out before unloading the kids. Lexi became shy and was hiding behind Harper as Carter knocked on the front door. They only had to wait a few minutes before her father opened it. He took them in with a smile as they stood on his front porch. His eyes hardened when his gaze landed on Carter. Her father didn't say anything as he gestured them inside and led the way to a living room at the back of the house.

Lexi had settled herself between Harper and Carter on the couch. Harper glanced at her daughter and then at her father. "Lexi, sweetheart, this is my father, your grandpa." Lexi gripped onto Carter's arm when he sat back with Bo in his arms. Harper unbuckled Colt from his seat and put him to her shoulder. "This is Colt, Lexi, and Bo."

"They all look just like you and Henry." Her father commented with a smile. The hardness she had seen in his eyes when he looked at Carter was gone as he studied his grandchildren. "If you would like, I have some of your mom's and uncle's old toys in that basket. I pulled them out of the garage for you." Harper was curious and handed Colt to Carter.

"Let's see what your grandfather has." Harper grabbed Lexi's hand and sat on the floor with her. She started pulling toys from the box. She smiled at the army action figure Henry had given her. "Your uncle gave me this so I would know that he wanted to be a soldier." Harper handed it to Lexi who took it with interest. Near the bottom, Harper froze. She slowly pulled out a black Friesian horse figure that was large enough for a barbie to ride on.

"If I remember right, that was your most treasured possession." Her father said quietly. "I can't even remember where you got it from, but you took that thing everywhere."

"I was upset about the mustangs being stuck in the horse trailer and I had let them out. You were so mad. Some of the locals were able to round them up and get me off one of the horses. You grounded me for two weeks from going to Carter's ranch." Harper smiled at the memory.

"I gave you that horse the night after the stampede." Carter spoke up from the couch.

"That was the night I caught you sleeping on the floor holding her hand while she slept in her bed." Her father's tone hardened as he glared at Carter. "I don't know why it even surprised me to see you here with my daughter. You were always with her."

"Here, Lexi, why don't you play with Mozart." Harper handed the horse to Lexi. "I need to talk with your grandfather and Carter outside for a few minutes."

She laid out blankets on the floor and put the twins on them. She walked to the sliding door and waited for both men to walk out before closing it again. She stood where she could still see inside, but not be easily overheard. She looked between Carter and her father several times before her father uncrossed his arms and pointed at Carter.

"Ever since you were kids, Carter has been smitten with you. Sure, he and Henry were friends, but even when Henry was gone, Carter stuck around for you. The night he spent in your room was the last straw." Her father fumed. "When your mother decided to go her own way, I insisted on you going with her. I knew that if you stayed, it was likely you would end up pregnant and married to him before you graduated. You would be stuck in that small town regretting your decisions."

Harper's mouth fell open as she stared at her father. "Carter is not you and I am not my mother. Just because you made mistakes and mom went crazy doesn't mean I would have. I was strong in the church, until I went with mom. I wanted a forever family and was determined to not become my mom even back then. When we left, she got into drugs and alcohol and all sorts of crap. She even forced me to try some. To earn her a little extra she even tried to convince me to..." Harper clenched her hands and glared at her father. "At least if I had stayed, I would have had Henry and Carter to keep me going to church. My faith meant everything to me. I even started going back to church on my own. And in case you were wondering, I kept my precious flower intact until I was married." Harper turned her back on her father and paced away, barely feeling the cold winter air.

She was furious. She had to live with her mother all that time because her father was worried she would end up with Carter. "You're right, sir. I did sleep in your daughter's room when I shouldn't have. I was ten and foolish enough to think that sleeping on the floor was okay. Harper had been upset and even then, I couldn't stand to see her that way. I would do anything to make her feel better. I'm sorry I crossed that line." Carter said and Harper turned to look at him. "You were also right that I would have married your daughter a lot sooner if she had stayed in town."

"Married sooner?" Her father's angry face lost its reddish color as he looked between the two of them. "You're married?"

"As of yesterday." Harper said as she caught Carter's eye and he winked. "Look dad, I didn't come here to fight. You said you wanted a relationship with your grandkids. I don't want to deny them their grandfather, but if you have a problem with Carter, hash it out now and move on or we are leaving." Harper peeked back inside and saw Lexi showing the horse to Bo and Colt. She looked back at her father and Carter.

"I would like to say I'm sorry for punching you after graduation. I had waited until I was eighteen so that I could take my anger out on you, and for you not to get in trouble for hitting a minor." Carter said with a guilty look.

"I never did find out why you punched me before Henry dragged you away." Her father rubbed his jaw as if he could still feel the punch.

Carter chuckled. "You sent away the girl I loved. I had looked for her but couldn't find her. Henry didn't even know her location." Carter shrugged.

"You looked for me?" Harper asked, surprised.

"Up until Henry convinced me to sign up for the military and I was unable to continue the search. Then Henry got a graduation invitation." Carter gave Harper a small smile.

Harper shook her head in disbelief. Carter hadn't told her he had looked for her. She shivered in the cold and Carter took a few steps over to her. He wrapped his arms around her and moved to the door. "Go inside with the kids before you catch a cold. Your father and I will work things out."

Harper turned around and gave Carter a stern look. "Your fists will not come in contact with any other person."

Carter smiled and pressed a kiss to her forehead. "Yes ma'am."

Harper stepped back inside but sat where she could see Carter and her father talking. There were a few points where things looked a bit heated, but no one punched anyone. Carter gave her a smile as he came back inside. She was holding Colt while sitting on the couch next to where Bo played on the floor. Carter crossed to Bo and picked him up. Bo immediately started to scream. Carter's eyes went wide in surprise. Bo's cries only increased in volume. Harper tsked as she stood and took Bo from Carter.

"Your hands are freezing, Cowboy." She said with a light laugh. Bo's crying caused Colt to start up too. "Please, go make bottles while I try to calm down the boys." Carter leaned down and kissed her before grabbing the diaper bag as he headed for the kitchen.

Harper watched Carter for a few minutes as he stood at the sink. She finally pulled her gaze from him to find her father watching her. "You love him." It wasn't a question, but Harper still nodded. "I'm sorry, Harper. I shouldn't have forced you to go with your mother." She could see the sadness and pleading in his eyes.

"Let's just start from here." she said over the cries of the babies.

Her father gave her a small smile then switched his attention to the twins. "Have you tried singing to them? You always loved music. At times that was the only thing that would calm you down as a baby."

Carter came back over, picked up a blanket and wrapped it around Bo before lifting the still crying infant from her arms. He handed one of the bottles over to her before offering the one he kept to Bo. A moment later, silence filled the room as the twins ate. Lexi walked up to her grandfather slowly. "Did you sing to mommy like she sings to us?"

Harper listened as her father told Lexi all about her as a child. They had lunch and put the twins down for their naps. Lexi had climbed up into her grandfather's lap as he read her a book. Harper and Carter sat on the couch and watched them from across the room. Sighing, she settled more comfortably against Carter. He pressed a kiss to her head before he pulled out his phone. Carter read the group chat message and chuckled.

**Devon:** Any update?

**Jeff:** Seriously man you were like a caged animal.

**Devon:** I thought he wasn't going to last the night before charging back over to Harper's.

**Carter:** I made it to Denver.

**Tank:** Got that from the GPS.

Harper laughed before taking his phone. He didn't mind. He read as more chats came in.

**Jeff:** If I don't get answers from you, I'll text Athena.

**Carter:** Found her last night.

**Devon:** And? Did you man up or chicken out?

He tightened his arms around Harper, and she looked up at him with a mischievous smile. He couldn't help but give her a quick kiss.

**Carter:** I told her.

**Tank:** When is the wedding?

**Carter:** She was so angry.

Carter laughed. "You were pretty angry. I was fully expecting another bloody nose." Harper smiled before laying her head on his shoulder.

**Jeff:** No way she was mad. I know for a fact she likes you.

**Carter:** She got a babysitter and marched me to a more private location, so she could yell at me without Lexi hearing.

**Devon:** Is she still planning on bringing the kids over for Christmas?

**Carter:** Unknown.

**Tank:** Do whatever you need to and fix this.

**Carter:** Working on it.

Harper handed him back his phone. "I think you just gave them a heart attack and made them hate me." Carter told her.

"I'm sorry. Did you want to go stay at the ranch for a few days while we are at the rental?" Harper asked with a raised brow. She could see the wheels working behind his eyes. "Now they will assume you are still working on making me forgive you. They won't question you being away longer." Carter shook his head as he smiled.

Harper couldn't believe how fast the day had flown by. Before she knew it, they were loading the kids into the truck. Carter started the vehicle before coming back around to her side. He shook hands with her father. Harper tentatively stepped up to her dad and gave him a hug. Things between them were still rough, but she felt like today was a good start. When she pulled back there were tears in his eyes. She invited him to come up for New Years and he agreed with a smile.

Back at the hotel, the kids fell asleep quickly after dinner. Harper laid with her head on Carter's shoulder while he ran his hand through her hair. "Remind me again why it took us so long to get to this point." Harper whispered, turning her face up to look at him.

"Because I was a coward and too afraid of scaring you away." Carter pressed a kiss to her lips. "You should sleep before our boys decide to wake up again."

"Our boys?" Harper asked with a smile.

"I have been involved in their lives almost from the time that they were born. They are my sons, and I will fight anyone who says otherwise." Carter pulled her closer and kissed her breathless. "Goodnight, Harper. I love you."

"I love you too, Carter." Harper whispered as she closed her eyes and enjoyed the feel of Carter holding her.

# Chapter 21

Harper smiled as she watched Carter play with Lexi in the kids' zone at the fast-food restaurant where they were having lunch. Being married to Carter had so far been way easier than their relationship as "friends". There was no guessing. No fighting to keep her feelings buried. And he never had to leave her side. The confusion and tension between them were gone and she loved it. Her phone rang and she looked down at it to see who was calling. Jeff's name popped up on the screen.

"Hello." she said, biting into a fry.

"Hey, Athena. You haven't been answering my texts." Jeff scolded her. "I was beginning to worry."

"I have had a lot going on the past two days." Harper pointed out. He knew she had been stressed about this trip and meeting up with her dad.

"Is Carter with you?"

"Not at the moment. Why?" Harper tried to keep the smile out of her voice as her eyes wandered back to the kid zone and Carter.

"He went to Denver to talk with you." Devon's voice came on the line.

"Am I on speaker phone?" When she heard Tank say hi, she laughed. "Is this some kind of intervention or something?"

"We are just worried. Carter mentioned yesterday that you were mad at him." Devon hedged.

Harper sighed. "Of course I am mad. Disappointed, frustrated, confused." They were all quiet, so she continued. "Don't worry, I'm still planning on bringing the kids over for Christmas. No matter what is going on between me and Carter, Lexi needs you guys." Harper smiled down at her ring. "Can I ask you guys for a favor though?"

"Anything." Tank said quickly.

"Can you guys go to my house and take all the presents back to the ranch? They are all wrapped and either under the tree or in my closet. I also have an address I need one of you to go to on Christmas Eve. I'll let Mrs.

Harvey know I'm sending you." Carter and Lexi started heading back to their table.

"What's at Mrs. Harvey's?" Jeff asked.

"Lexi's gift. But she is coming back so I am not going to say any more about that." Carter lifted his brow in question as he sat next to her. "And I understand you guys are concerned about Carter and me, but you don't need to be stepping in. I'm a big girl and can make up my mind on things without my three older brothers thinking they need to protect me from everything." Carter leaned over and started kissing her neck. She bit her lip to keep from laughing.

"Okay, Athena. We get it. And we will bring the presents back to the ranch. Are you planning on coming over on Christmas or Christmas Eve?" Jeff asked, sounding disappointed.

"I think we will be over late on Christmas Eve, so Lexi can open her presents there in the morning." Harper looked over at Carter, silently asking his thoughts. He gave her a nod of agreement before turning to his half-eaten food. Harper finished her call and turned to Carter. "You weren't helping, Cowboy." Carter smirked and took another bite of his food.

Harper placed her hand on his thigh and took a bite of her burger. Two could play his game. Out of the corner of her eye she saw Carter's movements slow. She inched her hand higher, and he turned to her. She gave a gentle squeeze while keeping her facial features even. Carter grabbed her hand and raised it to his lips. "You, Dove, are playing with fire." He murmured close to her ear, and she smiled at him.

The rest of the drive went smoothly. When they walked into the rental, Harper immediately noticed all the presents were gone. The guys didn't waste any time in collecting them. Tomorrow was Christmas Eve, and Lexi would be so excited to spend the night at the ranch. She frequently asked when they were going back.

The kids were exhausted, and Harper was glad when they didn't fight going to bed early. To be truthful, Harper was tired too. The twins were asleep in their room and Carter was reading Lexi her story, so she got in the shower.

Harper was rinsing the conditioner from her hair when she felt Carter's hands on her waist. She opened her eyes and saw him gazing at her with such love and affection, Harper nearly melted. "You still have bruises." His voice was tense as he ran a hand over the bruising along her collarbone.

She rose on her toes and kissed him. "Bruises take time to heal, Carter." Her eyes dropped to his chest. She hadn't really seen his tattoo the other day. The brown of the fur was nearly the same shade as her hair. A smile lifted the corner of her mouth as she traced her finger over the wolf. "You know, I never figured you were the type to do something as wild as get a tattoo. You were always the one that kept my wildness in check."

"For a time, I stopped caring about the consequences of my actions. Then I was nearly killed on our first mission, which was a wakeup call. I vowed I would go back to church and renew my faith in God." He kissed her forehead. "I never went on a church mission, but Henry and I worked hard, and we were able to go through the temple for the first time two years ago."

Harper had been able to go to the temple with the youth once, before her mom found out about it and moved them away. She had always wanted to go back. She wanted a forever family. Her eyes lifted to Carter's. She wondered what his views were on the matter.

"I know we just got married, and this is all so new, but what are your thoughts on going to the temple to be sealed?" Carter asked hesitantly.

Tears stung Harper's eyes. Her tears mixed with the water from the shower as she pulled Carter down to her. He gently kissed her before pulling back. "I would love nothing more." She whispered and Carter smiled, his dimple making an appearance.

Carter woke the next morning with Harper in his arms. He would never get tired of it. He ran his hand down her side, and she shifted. Carter smiled. He hadn't realized how ticklish she was. Her hand rested on his chest, and he couldn't help tightening his arms around her. He still could not believe she was his. He had dreamed about this for most of his life and now that it had happened, he couldn't be happier. Correction, the only thing that would make him happier is adopting Lexi, Bo, and Colt.

"Carter?" Harper's sleepy voice mumbled as she snuggled closer to him.

"Yes, Baby?" Carter pressed a kiss to her head.

"I love you." She breathed out.

Carter chuckled. "I love you too, Dove." As much as Carter would love to stay in bed all day, they had kids that would be up soon. "Sweetheart, we should probably get dressed before Lexi comes in." Harper huffed, pulling the blanket more over her. She did not want to get up yet. She heard Carter's quiet chuckle. He rolled over, pinning her beneath him causing her to squeak in surprise before kissing her.

*     *     *

Harper stood in the kitchen making eggs when Lexi came running down the hall. "Mommy! All the presents are gone!" She exclaimed. Worry filled her little voice.

"I had your uncles come and take them to the ranch so we can have Christmas with them." Harper smiled over her shoulder at Lexi. "We will go over tonight before Santa comes." Lexi cheered before running back down the hall.

Carter came into the kitchen laughing. "Lexi seems excited to be going back to the ranch." He walked over and kissed her. "Good morning, my love."

Harper smiled against his lips. "You do realize you are going to have to behave yourself while we are at the ranch."

"That's why I'm indulging now." Carter kissed her again. "Plus, I needed to give you a heads up." He took a step back with a wicked grin. "You have another one." He touched his neck and Harper threw the hot pad at him. He caught it as he chuckled.

"You need to stop, Cowboy." Harper felt her cheeks heat.

Carter moved back to her side, placing the hot pad back on the counter. "I told you, Love. I will as soon as you start complaining while I'm giving them to you." Harper playfully smacked his chest, and he caught her wrist. "What is on the agenda for today?" he asked as he pressed kisses along her neck.

"What are the guys planning on for Christmas dinner?" Harper asked as Carter released her so she could stir the eggs. He wrapped his arms around her as he stood behind her. She leaned back against him as she continued to cook.

"Usually, we just cook a steak or burgers. Whatever we find in the fridge. This is our first Christmas since we've been out." Carter shrugged. "What would you like to have?"

Harper turned off the stove and turned around, putting her arms around Carter's neck. "We are not having steak or burgers. We can run to the store and get ham, potatoes, stuff to make rolls, and fruit salad."

"That sounds delicious. When do you want to go to the store and when are you wanting to get to the ranch?"

"Daddy? Can you help me find my socks?" Lexi yelled from down the hall. "And Bo and Colt are stinky."

Harper laughed as she kissed Carter. "Have fun, Sweetheart. Breakfast will be ready when you get done." Carter sighed, but his smile remained as he headed out to help Lexi and change the twins.

After breakfast they packed their bags for their stay at the ranch. They talked to Lexi about keeping Carter and Harper's marriage a secret for the time being. Harper had her doubts that the little girl would be able to keep the secret. She was way too excited about Carter being her dad.

They went to the store to get the groceries that Harper was going to need for Christmas dinner. The trip was quick, and the roads were clear. They made good time, and Harper smiled when the ranch came into view. A sense of homecoming washed over her, and she sighed. This was home.

The truck was just coming to a stop when the front door opened, and Jeff stepped out onto the porch with a big smile. Tank and Devon were running out of the barn. Harper unbuckled as Carter put the car into park. Her door was pulled open, and she was dragged out by Jeff before being crushed into a fierce hug that had her laughing. "If I didn't know any better, I would have thought you missed me."

"You have no idea." Tank said as he pulled her from Jeff and gave her a hug. "Meals aren't the same."

"It is a good thing I came early then. I also brought stuff for Christmas dinner." Harper said as she hugged Devon. "Why don't you guys help get everything inside."

"Lexi fell asleep." Carter said as he stepped around the hood of the truck. "Do you want me to take her upstairs?"

"Yes, please. Thank you." Harper barely glanced in his direction as she reached inside the truck and grabbed the diaper bag and Colt's car seat.

Jeff and Tank reached into the bed of the truck and started grabbing bags. Devon grabbed Bo's car seat and waited for her to reach him. "After everything I heard was going on, I'm surprised to see you and Carter showing up together."

"He refused to let me drive home by myself with the kids. Especially after he heard how rough it was on the drive down." Harper shrugged and put the baby down in the living room and looked around. There was a fire going in the fireplace and a large Christmas tree with white lights in the corner. There were tons of presents under the tree already. "I think you might have gone overboard on spoiling Lexi and the twins." She laughed.

Carter came down the stairs and both guys went back out to unload the truck. She took the time to take both babies out of their car seats. As soon as everything was in, the twins were quickly claimed by their uncles, and Harper made her way into the kitchen to put things away. Her phone buzzed and she pulled it out as she stepped into the pantry.

**Carter:** I was lectured.

**Harper:** What did you do now?

**Carter:** For not fixing things between us. When are we going to tell them?

**Harper:** Let's tell them when someone notices the ring. And for the record, you are in the doghouse.

**Carter:** They are observant guys, shouldn't be long. And what did I do?

**Harper:** I had to use so much makeup on my neck this morning, Cowboy.

Harper put the contents of the grocery bag on the shelf and turned to get another one. She gasped when Carter stepped into the pantry with a few grocery bags. "Do these go in here?" he asked with a grin. He stepped closer and she smiled. His eyes dropped to her neck. "Makeup? Hmm. I think I liked it better without." His voice was low so it wouldn't carry.

"You would." Harper pressed her lips to his and Carter pushed her gently against the shelves. "Now go see if there are any more pantry items that need to be put away, please." He kissed her one more time before leaving her to put the items on the shelves.

"What have you been feeding the twins?" Devon asked from the kitchen. "They have grown since I saw them last."

Harper walked out of the pantry to find Carter making bottles, with Devon leaning up against the counter. She smiled and told Devon all about what they had been up to over the last few weeks. Carter took the bottles to Jeff and Tank. Harper and Devon joined the others in the living room, and she sat in a chair.

She pulled out her phone to look at recipes for the next day, but she could feel Carter's eyes on her. She glanced at him, and he gave a pointed look at the empty seat beside him. She smiled as she returned her eyes to her phone.

Lexi came down the stairs rubbing her eyes. She walked over to Harper and crawled up into her lap. Harper rocked Lexi as she hummed quietly to her. The past several days had been rough on Lexi with the long road trip and then coming here. She didn't do well with change and hadn't had time to settle back into a normal routine. When Lexi's routine was disrupted too much, she tended to get more nightmares than usual.

"I like that you are singing more. It makes me feel safe." Lexi whispered as she snuggled closer to Harper.

Harper kissed her daughter's head. "When we get the house to ourselves, we can have a singing party while we bake cookies." She whispered. Lexi perked up with a smile.

"When do we kick them out?" Lexi asked excitedly. Cooking together was the only thing that Luther had allowed them to do without coming in and yelling at them.

"You just woke up, and you already want to get rid of us?" Jeff asked in mock horror. Carter caught Harper's eye. He was watching Lexi with concern. He had never seen her when she was in this state. This was how Lexi had acted the whole time they had been with Luther. Quiet, meek, and curling in on herself. Maybe the long trip and then meeting her grandfather had pushed her too far.

"Why don't you go upstairs and get Mozart so he can join us." Harper suggested and Lexi hunched her shoulders as she made her way slowly back up the stairs.

"Is everything okay with Lexi?" Devon asked as he stared at the empty stairs.

Harper took a deep breath. "This is how Lexi was until we got here. Luther had sucked the life out of her. I think the trip to Denver and meeting a strange man, was a little much for her. She needs some time to readjust. Cooking is one of the activities that has always been routine for her. She needs to get back to what is familiar."

"Why do we need to leave in order for you to cook with Lexi?" Tank asked.

"Because I promised her a singing party, and I am not singing with you guys in the house." Harper said.

"You were literally just singing to her in front of us." Jeff pointed out.

"Singing soft lullabies is one thing. Singing at the top of one's lungs while cooking and dancing in the kitchen is another." Harper folded her arms over her chest.

"We have a Christmas Eve tradition to go shooting." Carter stood and put Bo in the bassinet. "We can go now and give you and Lexi some time."

Harper sent him a grateful look as Lexi came back down the stairs. When she saw all the guys looking at her, she ran to Harper with tears in her eyes. Harper hugged her daughter close. "Oh sweetheart. What's the matter?"

"I can't find him, mommy. I can't find Mozart." Lexi began crying.

Carter walked over and crouched down, so he was level with Lexi. "I think I saw him in the truck, Princess. Come on, let's go see if he is there." Lexi wrapped her arms around Carter's neck as she continued to sniffle. It took some coaxing, but Harper and Carter were able to get Lexi's coat on her.

Harper rubbed a hand over her face. She was worried Lexi was falling back into her old routine. One of fear and nightmares. She went back to the rocking chair and sat down rubbing her temples. A hand settled on her shoulder, and she looked up to see Tank standing over her. He gave her a small smile before walking towards the door. Jeff and Devon both gave her a look of concern before they, too, went outside. The door opened back up and Carter came in holding Lexi. She clutched the horse in her hands while resting her head on Carter's shoulder.

Carter put Lexi into Harper's lap and crouched down next to the chair. "Harper, Lexi said she had a bad dream."

Harper wrapped her arms around her daughter and hugged her close. "She gets them frequently." Harper whispered and Carter's arms went around both of them.

He kissed Lexi's cheek. "Are you okay now, Princess?" Lexi didn't say anything but gave a small nod. "I love you, Lexi. I'm going to go with your uncles for a little bit so you and your mom can have some girl time, okay?" He brushed the hair off of her face and kissed her forehead. He gave Harper a quick kiss before standing.

"I love you, daddy." Lexi whispered.

Harper held Lexi until she heard gunshots in the distance. "Should we bake cookies or cupcakes?" She asked. "And what music should we listen to?"

Lexi sat up with a smile. She chose both cupcakes and cookies and she wanted a mix of music. Harper gladly agreed. She had forgotten how fearful Lexi had been.

Lexi was finally starting to shake the fear that had clung to her by the time their fourth batch of cookies were cooking. 'There She Is' by The Tuten Brothers, came on and Lexi squealed as she ran up to Harper. Harper turned up the speaker, picked Lexi up and danced while they waited for the cookies to finish baking. Out of the corner of her eye, she saw that the guys had returned and were watching them with smiles on their faces. Carter stepped up and lifted Lexi from Harper. He started dancing with her, causing the little girl to giggle. Tank stepped up and offered his hand to Harper and she laughed as she put her hand in his and he spun her.

When the song ended, Carter set Lexi down. "Would you ladies like to come out for a little shooting?" Harper was going to point out that they were in the middle of baking, and the twins couldn't go out, but Carter continued before she could. "Jeff volunteered to take out whatever you have in the oven, and to watch the boys for a little while."

"I want to shoot mommy's gun." Lexi ran from the kitchen.

"She seems in better spirits." Devon commented with a smile.

"Cooking and music have always been an escape for us." Harper said as she moved to the oven and pulled out the cookies that had just finished.

"I did mention that I am available, right?" Devon teased.

"No way is my Athena going to marry you. I am dead set on her marrying me." Jeff crossed his arms over his chest and playfully glared at Devon. Harper laughed and shook her head. "You really don't realize how incredibly hot you are, especially dancing in the kitchen with Lexi."

"You don't even know everything I have to offer." Harper smiled over at Jeff.

"Do tell, little sister." Jeff said curiously.

"Luther had far more money than I had thought. In the divorce, all I wanted was half of what was in the bank. Luther was livid and the judge couldn't believe I didn't' fight for anything else. I just wanted out and figured fifty grand would help me and the kids get settled somewhere. Once everything was finalized, I was given a check for just over five million."

Jeff whistled. "That is a good chunk of change. Are you sure you don't want to marry me?"

"Are you sure you don't want to know what else I have?" Harper raised her brow in question.

"There's more?" Tank asked.

"Bethany just informed me that Henry's will had a stipulation in it that I wasn't allowed to know about until now. I guess you three went in with my brother to purchase the ranch and his portion of it has been going into an account in his name."

"He said he met with a lawyer through video chat a few weeks before he was killed." Carter said as he moved closer to them. "He said he found out something that happened back at home that he needed to take care of."

"I talked with Henry's lawyer last week. Someone had sent Henry all the domestic reports from the police. I guess my father came across them and sent them to Henry. Henry was livid. He wanted to find a way to press charges but was told he wouldn't be able to. He wanted to take care of me, get me out of there. He changed his will so that once I divorced Luther, everything went to me."

"You have five million, a share in the ranch, and whatever investments Henry was into?" Devon asked. He shook his head. "Forget Jeff, marry me."

"I have already told you that I am unavailable. Now if you will excuse me, I need to stop Lexi from loading my gun." Harper squeezed between the men, giving Carter a wink as she passed him. "Lexi, don't touch my gun!" Harper called as she rushed up the stairs.

Harper got to the room in time to see Lexi digging through her duffle bag. She grabbed the bag and set it on the bed. Harper had practicing shooting the gun a few times over the years with Lexi when Luther was gone. She had taught Lexi basic firearm safety and how to turn off the safety. She had felt it important just in case Luther was going to hurt her.

Harper had started shooting every day for the past couple of weeks and Lexi loved to watch. Pulling out the ear protection she bought for Lexi, she passed it to her.

When both Lexi and Harper had their boots and coats on, Harper tucked her handgun into her waistband before they made their way back downstairs. Devon, Tank and Carter were waiting for them when they stepped out onto the porch. Lexi bounced with excitement as they walked to the North field. "So, what are we shooting?" Harper asked.

"Targets." Devon said with a laugh.

"I was referring to the type of guns." Harper rolled her eyes.

They made it to where several targets were set out and ready to go. Two rifles and a shotgun were set out on the table. Tank helped Lexi get her ear protectors on and set her on his shoulders, so she could see better. Harper watched as Carter and Devon took shots with the rifles.

It had been a while since she had shot a rifle. She had been fifteen. She hadn't been too bad of a shot. Her boyfriend in high school had let her shoot when he saw her interest in firearms. According to him, she was a natural. Henry had told her the same thing after graduation when he had taken her shooting at the range for the first time with the handgun he bought her.

"Harper, do you want a turn?" Devon asked, turning to her.

Harper slowly stepped up to the table taking off her thicker coat. She had layered on a warm thin jacket to make shooting easier, but she wanted the thicker coat for when she was just standing there. She examined the firearms on the table for a few moments. Harper picked up the one Devon had used and tested the feel of it before deciding to use the table to help keep her steady. She bent down, resting her elbows on the table and looking through the scope.

She smiled when she heard Carter groan softly behind her. She let out her breath and pulled the trigger. Her shot went high. She reloaded the gun and took aim. This time she hit near the center of the target. She shot four more rounds before standing back up. She had a nice cluster. Harper turned around and took her headphones off.

"Marry me." Devon said with a straight face.

"Sorry, not interested." Harper laughed.

"Can I shoot?" Lexi asked.

"No." The men chorused. Harper's irritation flared. Lexi had been firing a gun since she was three. Harper of course helped her. She felt like proper firearm safety was important for a child, especially in a home with multiple guns.

"Let's have a competition." Harper suggested. "We all shoot with .9mm. The person with the most points after five rounds wins."

"What's the prize?" Tank asked suspiciously.

Harper shrugged. "What do you want as a prize?"

"I think the winner gets to marry you." Devon smirked.

"And if I win, Lexi gets to shoot." Harper crossed her arms. She saw Carter's jaw clench. She knew she was going to have to make it up to him later. She knew these guys were retired military, but she had been able to outshoot Henry. She was positive she would win this.

Tank set Lexi down on the ground and helped Devon reset the targets. Carter stood next to her with a stoney expression. "Lexi is only four. And you are my wife."

Harper looked over at Carter. "Are you doubting your own abilities?" she asked with a raised brow. Carter only scowled at her.

Devon and Tank returned, and Harper knelt to make sure Lexi's ear protection was still on correctly. Tank and Devon fired first, then collected their targets. Carter and Harper stepped up to the mark.

Carter sent her another glare before taking his five shots. He stepped back and Harper pulled her gun from her waistband. She checked over everything before taking her stance and aiming. Rapid fire, she let out five shots. She confidently walked up and collected her and Carter's targets. Harper laid hers next to the guys and smiled triumphantly. It had been close. Carter nearly beat her, but she had won. All five of her shots were in the center ring.

"How did you...?" Tank asked in disbelief.

"Henry bought me the gun as a graduation/birthday present. He spent an hour showing me how it worked. I have shot it a few times since." Harper reloaded the clip before she grabbed Lexi's hand and led her out to the field with a fresh target. Together they put it up and walked back to the firing line. "Before you can shoot, tell me the parts of the gun." Harper nodded and listened as Lexi pointed to each part, saying its name. "And what do you do when you pick up a gun?"

"Never touch the trigger. Check the safety." Lexi said seriously. "It should always be locked."

Harper drilled her daughter on safety measures about what you do when you have a gun and how to properly shoot. After she had Lexi check her handgun to make sure the safety was on, she got in her shooting stance. Harper knelt on the ground behind Lexi and helped her hold the gun.

They aimed, flipped the safety off, and when she felt Lexi let out her breath and her finger tighten on the trigger, Harper helped pull the trigger the rest of the way. They finished off the clip. Lexi reengaged the safety before Harper stood back up. The little girl ran to her target and pulled it down. The shots were everywhere but Harper was just trying to help Lexi with basic safety for now.

Lexi went running back to the guys with a huge grin on her face. "Did you see me?" she asked excitedly.

Carter scooped her up and kissed her cheek. "You were amazing, Princess. I'm impressed with how much you already know."

"Mommy said we needed to know how to protect ourselves from him." Lexi squirmed to get down. "Now that we are safe, we do it for fun. Mommy said one day I can have my own gun."

"When did you start teaching Lexi about firearms?" Carter asked, curiosity in his voice.

"I started teaching her firearm safety when she was two. How to shoot, she was three." Harper said quietly as memories of Luther flooded back into her mind. He had become so violent at times. There were times he would knock her out, leaving Lexi unprotected and she had been desperate to keep Lexi safe. Lexi knew to hide in the closet whenever possible, because that was where Harper kept her gun.

"Harper?" Carter said softly as he touched her arm. She blinked several times and took several deep breaths. She hadn't realized she was breathing hard, and by the tone in Carter's voice, it wasn't the first time he had called her name. "Are you okay?" Worry was written all over his face.

She cleared her throat and blinked a few more times. "I'm fine." She glanced around and forced a smile for Lexi. "Shall we go in and see if Jeff left us any cookies to decorate?"

Lexi cheered and ran off back towards the house. Harper didn't look at any of the guys as she followed after Lexi. Once inside, she pulled her coat off and slipped out of her boots. She asked Jeff to keep an eye on Lexi while she put her gun away.

Harper locked the door to the room and put the gun back in its case. She placed it on the top shelf in the closet. Her hands were shaking as more memories crashed into her.

Luther was pinning her against the wall as he squeezed her throat with one hand and punched her with his other. Her only thoughts were to get Lexi to a safe spot. Hands touched her face and she jerked away. Looking up, Carter was kneeling in front of her. She had no idea when she had ended up on the floor. Carter's panicked expression finally registered in her brain. Luther wasn't there. She and Lexi were safe. Carter reached for her, and she willingly moved onto his lap. He held her tight until her shaking stopped.

"What happened, Sweetheart?" he asked softly as he rubbed her back.

Harper snuggled closer to him and swallowed hard. "I don't know. I was fine and then the memories." She whispered. "Luther and waking up. Finding Lexi crying in the closet holding the gun because she was terrified. She thought he had killed me, and he was going to find her." Tears leaked onto Harper's cheeks.

Carter's arms tightened around her, and he kissed her head. "I think we should get you and Lexi into counseling. You both have experienced more than anyone ever should."

Harper nodded. She had thought the same thing. "I think I'm ready to go back downstairs." Harper whispered as she sat up.

Wiping her tears, Carter studied her. "Are you sure? We can stay up here a little longer if you need to. Jeff said you were pale and not yourself. They would understand." Harper nodded and Carter helped her stand. "Harper, do you get panic attacks often?" he asked, his arm still around her back.

"Sometimes. It usually happens after the kids are in bed and I'm alone. I think the quiet of the house triggers me sometimes." Harper let out a slow breath. "But I'm okay now. I promise." She gave Carter her best smile and he kissed her softly.

They made their way back downstairs and caught the tail end of Lexi telling Jeff about her being able to shoot. She didn't miss the frequent glances in her and Lexi's directions the guys were shooting at them as the evening wore on. Dinner was simple and Devon offered to clean up the kitchen after.

Harper was cuddling with Lexi on the rocking chair. They both needed the contact after Lexi's nightmare and Harper's panic attack. Carter held Colt while Bo sat in Tank's arms. Devon and Jeff were lounging around the room as they all listened to Carter as he read the Christmas story from the Book of Mormon. When he was done, they knelt in a circle and prayed.

Peace filled Harper and a calm settled over her. She tucked Lexi into a cot on the floor in her room and put the twins to bed in the crib that was still there. When she was done, she sent Carter and the guys a message saying she was going to go to bed, too. She received four quick replies, telling her goodnight.

She pulled on one of Carter's T-shirts and climbed under the covers. Harper was dozing when she felt someone kiss her cheek and slide into bed behind her. She smiled as she rolled over.

"You are supposed to be asleep, Dove." Carter whispered in her ear.

"And I thought you were sleeping in the other room." Harper whispered back as she laid her head on his shoulder.

"Not after today's events." He gave her a kiss. "Goodnight, Harper. I love you."

"Love you too, Cowboy."

# Chapter 22

Carter woke to Harper singing softly. It was still dark outside. He was lying on his back, but Harper was on her side facing away from him. He scooted close to her back and peered over her shoulder. She was cradling Lexi who had silent tears rolling down her face.

He sat up and lifted Lexi over Harper, causing the little girl to protest being taken from her mom. Lexi settled against him once he started to whisper to her. He laid her down, so she was between him and Harper as he cradled her close. Harper's head rested against his as she ran her fingers through Lexi's hair. With his free arm, Carter draped it over both Lexi and Harper.

Carter pressed his lips to Harper's forehead, and she placed her hand on his jaw. Lexi fell asleep not long after he started holding her, and Harper not long after Lexi.

Carter laid awake for hours as he held his girls and prayed that the nightmares would not come back. When the twins woke up, he quickly got them bottles, so they would not wake Harper and Lexi. By the time he climbed back into bed, the sun was starting to lighten the sky. Lexi rolled and wrapped her arms around his neck. Carter smiled and closed his eyes. He was glad that Lexi was sleeping soundly.

"Carter. It is time to get up." Harper's voice was soft and her hand on his face sent warmth coursing through him. He slowly opened his eyes and took in his beautiful wife. She smiled down at him. "You and Lexi need to get up." Carter pulled his eyes from Harper as his sluggish brain slowly recalled the events of the night before. He looked down to see Lexi was still cradled in his arms sleeping soundly.

"Let me and my baby girl sleep a little longer. She had a rough night." Carter closed his eyes. He was exhausted. "You should be laying down beside me sleeping as well."

"You do remember it is Christmas, right? Lexi has three overly excited uncles out feeding the horses and starting breakfast." Harper pressed her lips to his. "I mean, if you aren't wanting to get a shower in before the day starts, that's okay." Carter was instantly awake.

He smoothed back Lexi's hair and kissed her forehead. "Hey, Princess. Are you ready to see what Santa brought you?" Lexi stirred slowly and then she was wide awake.

"It's Christmas!" Lexi yelled as she jumped out of bed.

"You need to get dressed first." Harper said as she set Lexi's bag on the bed.

Carter got up and stretched. He grabbed his things and headed for the bathroom, but stopped when he noticed Harper wasn't following. "I thought you said something about a shower." he said, pulling her into his arms.

Harper smiled up at him with a twinkle in her eye. "I already had mine. I was referring to yours."

Carter narrowed his eyes. "You little tease." He growled in her ear. He started backing towards the bathroom, dragging her with him.

"Carter, let go." Her eyes danced with amusement. "Maybe you should take a cold shower." She laughed before kissing him and breaking away. "Bo and Colt are already downstairs with Devon, but I need to get back down there. Lexi can wait for you before coming down." Harper called over her shoulder. Her smile was radiant this morning.

Carter shook his head and jumped in a quick, five-minute shower. Lexi was already bouncing up and down near the door by the time he was done. The wonderment and excitement that filled Lexi's face when she walked into the living room and saw the Christmas tree and presents, was perfect. He was glad Harper had waited for him to be able to see this instead of taking Lexi down while he showered.

Lexi let go of his hand and ran to the stocking with her name on it. She started pulling the items out of it and squealed in delight. Harper stood in the kitchen doorway holding the twins, smiling as she watched Lexi. She was beautiful and she was his. All he wanted to do was pull her into his arms and kiss her senseless. How had none of the guys noticed the diamond ring on her hand yet? He glanced down and saw that the baby blankets were covering her hands. He wasn't sure, but he suspected that it was the same most of the day yesterday, too.

"Did we miss it?" Jeff asked as he and Tank walked inside, shrugging off their coats.

"Uncle Jeff! Look what I got." Lexi held up a pack of Chapstick in the shape of various candies.

The adults made their way to chairs around the room. To his relief, Harper was sitting next to him on the couch. The day before had been torture with her sitting across the room. He took Colt from her, and she gave him a large smile.

Tank volunteered to pass out the gifts. The twins got several toys and lots of clothes. Lexi got all sorts of toys and clothes and craft supplies. Harper had been right; the girl was getting spoiled. She even had her own pair of cowgirl boots and hat.

Harper was surprised to have things under the tree for her, which surprised Carter. She was nearly as excited as Lexi over the things she received. They were nearing the end of the presents and Lexi had Jeff and Devon helping her open one of her new toys.

"Heads up." Tank tossed him a smaller box and Carter caught it. He turned it over, but all it had on it was his name with no signature of who it was from. The wrapping was also different from all the other presents. He glanced around the room, but everyone was occupied. Slowly he unwrapped the paper and lifted the lid. It was a watch with a thick leather band. He took it out to get a better look. Wolves were etched in the band. He ran his thumb over them. He loved it.

"What's that?" Devon asked from across the room.

"A watch." Carter said as he continued to look at the incredible details on the band.

"Who gave it to you?" Tank asked as he moved closer to get a better look.

"I'm not sure." He glanced around the room again. Jeff, Devon, and Tank were watching him. Harper had gotten up and was in the kitchen talking with Lexi as she made a bottle. He passed the watch to Tank so he could see it.

"Who's Griffin?" Tank asked, confused. Carter snapped his eyes back to Tank. "There is an inscription on the back of the watch."

The watch was passed around as Carter watched. Griffin? Did he get someone else's gift by mistake? The watch was handed back to him and he turned it over. *My Griffin* was engraved on the back. Carter's heart skipped a beat. He looked up and his eyes locked with Harper's. She was watching him closely. Lexi asked her something and she looked away.

He put the watch on as he hid a smile. After he started calling her Dove, Harper started calling Henry, Cap, and him, Griffin. Cap because Henry was never without his baseball cap and Griffin was the symbol of a protector.

A protector like a wolf at the back of the pack. Harper's tattoo. Carter glanced back at her. He was going to ask Harper about it the next chance he got.

"I think there is one more gift." Harper said and Tank pulled an envelope from the tree.

"It says it's for you, Lexi." Tank gave an overly dramatic puzzled look at the letter before handing it to the little girl.

Lexi took it to her mom who helped her open it. Jeff asked what it was, and Lexi told him it was pictures. "This one looks like a barn." She said with her brow pinched together in confusion.

"Maybe your gift is in the barn." Harper suggested.

Lexi ran to the door, but Carter jumped up and caught her. "Coat and shoes first." He said with a laugh. Lexi ran upstairs and returned only a minute later with her boots on. Carter helped get her coat on, then grabbed her hand so she couldn't run out the door. "Is everyone coming, or is it just us?"

"I'll watch the twins." Devon offered and Harper thanked him.

She slipped her coat on and slid into Carter's extra boots. Tank opened the door, and Carter was pulled out onto the porch. Lexi let go of his hand saying he was walking too slow and latched onto Tank and Jeff. In no time at all, Jeff, Tank, and Lexi disappeared into the barn, leaving Harper and Carter alone. When they reached the point they were no longer visible from the house or barn, Carter pulled Harper into his arms. He kissed her until she melted against him, and they were both out of breath.

"Thank you for the watch, Love." He whispered as he rested his forehead against hers. He chuckled. "I had your ring engraved, too."

Harper pulled back in surprise. She looked at the ring before slowly pulling it off and looked inside. *My Dove* was etched into the band. She smiled up at him and he couldn't help himself. He kissed her again.

"I realized something a minute ago." Carter grinned at her.

"What is that?" Harper asked suspiciously.

"The wolf at the back of the pack, the one with the dog tags, you said was your protector." Harper gave a hesitant nod. "I'm your protector. I'm the wolf." Carter watched Harper's face turn red. "I knew it." He laughed before pressing his lips to hers.

"What does the three mean?" Lexi's voice brought him back to the present. With a smirk, he let Harper go. He couldn't believe it hadn't pieced it together earlier. They walked side by side into the barn. "Mommy. What does this mean?" Lexi ran over to them.

Harper crouched down so she could look at it with Lexi. "That almost looks like a door with a three on it." Harper said in a puzzled voice.

"Horse stalls have doors and there are lots of those in here." Lexi looked down the row of stalls. She gasped. "That one has a bow on it!" Lexi yelled as she ran down the row, stopping in front of it. "Can I open it?" Lexi looked back at Harper with hopeful eyes. Harper laughed and told her to go ahead.

Lexi pulled open the door with Tank's help, and out ran a blue merle puppy. It jumped all over the place and Lexi screamed in delight. The little girl sat on the floor and the puppy ran up to her, licking her face and wagging his tail. Carter smiled as he watched. Harper leaned against him, and he wrapped an arm around her.

Harper prayed this puppy would help Lexi with her bouts of anxiety and fear. She was so glad Lexi and the puppy seemed to be getting along. "What are you going to name him?" Harper asked Lexi.

Lexi looked up at her with the biggest smile. "I'll call him…Flynn." Lexi giggled as she hugged the puppy close.

Tank and Jeff went back inside after a few minutes, but Harper wanted Lexi to have as much time with Flynn as possible. With Lexi occupied with Flynn, Harper turned to face Carter. "You seem awfully proud of yourself." She whispered.

"I can't believe it took me so long to connect the dots." Carter smiled. "But there is something I don't understand."

"What is that?" Harper asked.

"The dog tags. How did you know I would go into the military?"

"You and Henry were inseparable and talked about being soldiers ever since I could remember. Was it ever a question you would end up joining?" Harper shrugged.

Lexi and Flynn ran up and down the length of the stalls. "I wasn't sure I would. I was more concerned with finding something I lost." Carter gave Harper a kiss. "Then Henry reminded me that you would be furious if I didn't do something with my life."

"He was right. I would have been angry if you threw away your life." Harper smiled. "Plus, I'm liking this military bearing you have going on. You were kind of scrawny and awkward when we were kids."

Carter laughed before kissing her again. They stood there watching Lexi toss toys for Flynn. He brought them back to her with his tail wagging a mile a minute. When Lexi shivered, Harper knew it was time to get her inside. Lexi pouted the whole way back to the house. But as soon as she had her coat off, she ran to Devon and started telling him all about Flynn. Harper smiled as she laid on the couch. The day had been good so far. She closed her eyes, promising herself it would only be for a minute.

*   *   *

Carter looked over at the couch for the millionth time. Harper had rolled over, so her back was facing the room. He wanted to pick her up and carry her to bed. Her panic attack yesterday and long night with Lexi had worn her out. He could see in her eyes how tired she was.

He was sitting in the rocking chair with Bo, feeding him a bottle. Devon and the guys were in the kitchen starting the ham and potatoes for dinner. They had agreed to allow Harper time to rest. Lexi came over to him and climbed up on his lap. He repositioned Bo to accommodate Lexi.

"How are you doing, Princess?" he asked softly.

She leaned her head on his shoulder. "Daddy, I'm tired." she said softly. Kissing her forehead, he set the chair rocking gently.

A song his mother had sung to him when he was sick came back to him. He closed his eyes and sang softly close to Lexi's ear. Less than five minutes later he felt Lexi's weight grow heavy against him. Bo finished his bottle and Carter dropped it on the floor. He would pick it up later. He sighed and closed his eyes.

"Want me to take the baby?" Devon asked quietly.

Carter cracked his eyes open. "Thanks. I think Lexi had a rough night." He glanced in Harper's direction.

"Harper seemed tired today." Devon carefully lifted Bo. "What happened yesterday? She suddenly just froze and it looked like she saw a ghost."

"She said she gets panic attacks periodically. Talking about Lexi and the gun triggered one. And Lexi has nightmares about…him." Carter rubbed a hand over his face. He needed to figure out what he could do to help them through what Luther had done to them.

Devon patted his shoulder. "It's going to be okay, Carter. Luther is gone and we can figure out a way to help them. How are things going on the home front?"

Carter smiled. "She didn't push me away when I tried to comfort her." Carter was tired of not being able to hold his wife whenever he felt like it, but he had promised not to say anything until the guys noticed the ring. They better notice it tonight or he was going to lose his mind.

"Well, that's a start." Devon shook his head. "You will work it out. She makes you better, gives you purpose. You have been just going through the motions since Henry died. He was the only one who was able to keep you from wandering. Since Harper came, you've been less...lost." Carter nodded. He knew he had been living life a day at a time. Harper was his guiding star. Devon gave Carter one last look before carrying Bo upstairs while Carter continued to rock Lexi.

\*         \*         \*

Harper stretched as she turned around and looked about the living room. Carter was asleep in the rocking chair holding Lexi. Harper sat up and rubbed her eyes. Voices from the kitchen drew her attention and she moved in their direction. Jeff, Devon, and Tank were at various spots at the counter preparing dinner.

"You should have woken me up." Harper scolded as she moved to the sink to wash her hands.

"Yeah right. You looked tired and yesterday you looked like the devil himself was after you." Jeff glanced over at her.

"He was after me." Harper sighed. They were bound to know at some point if they didn't already. "I sometimes have flashbacks, panic attacks. Explaining why I had been teaching Lexi about firearms triggered one, I guess."

She paused, biting her lip. Clara said talking about it might help. Deciding to give it a try, Harper continued. "I was trying to leave to go to Henry's funeral. He didn't like me leaving." Harper filled the sink with soap and water so she could start doing dishes.

She told them of that day, Luther grabbing her and hitting her. What she had awakened to and finding Lexi. The fear and the desperation of that day. Seeing Lexi clenching the gun and the bruising on her own face and body. Harper then told them about finding out she was pregnant six weeks later. Finding Beth by chance and living the next nine months with Luther's increased abuse. "He thought I had cheated on him and that the baby was someone else's. I seriously think he was trying to force a miscarriage, because I refused to get an abortion." Harper said quietly.

Tank moved to her side and put an arm around her. "If he was still alive, I'd kill him." Tank growled.

"You can say that again." Carter's tense and angry voice came from the doorway and Harper turned around to see him leaning against the wall with his arms crossed. Harper looked behind him, afraid Lexi had overheard. Carter followed her gaze then looked back at her. "Lexi is still asleep. I laid her down on the couch." His voice had softened slightly when he looked at Lexi. He turned his attention back to those in the kitchen and his face turned hard again. He clenched his fists as he began to pace.

"Carter, calm down." Harper said as she took a step towards him.

He whirled on her, fury burning in his eyes. "Calm down? Your husband beat you into unconsciousness and raped you. Then tried to force a miscarriage by continuing to beat you." Carter's jaw clenched. "He raped you, Harper. And you are telling me to calm down?"

"I am well aware of the fact that I was raped, Carter, not once but twice." Harper snapped. "He couldn't stand the fact that I couldn't handle his touch and that I wanted out. At the apartment, he admitted to drugging me before I found out I was pregnant with Lexi. Then Lexi came and I was stuck. I understand how horrible of a person Luther was. If anyone has the right to be angry, it's me." The kitchen was quiet, and Harper took a deep breath. "Watch the kids, I'm going out." Harper stormed past Carter, ignoring his attempt to grab her arm and snatched her coat before stepping into the cold winter air.

She walked to the barn as she pulled on her coat. She headed for Raider's kennel. She let him out, slipped through the back of the barn and headed for the cemetery. She needed her brother. When she got there, she knelt in the snow and stared at his headstone. She needed advice, but Henry was no longer able to give it to her. Harper pulled out her phone and scrolled through her contacts before finding the one she wanted. She closed her eyes as she listened to it ring.

"Harper? Merry Christmas."

"Daddy?" Harper whispered around the lump of emotion in her throat.

"Hey, what's going on? Isn't Carter with you?" Her father's cheerful voice changed to worry.

"I lost my temper, dad. I yelled at him and then I ran away." Tears slipped down her cheeks.

"What did you guys argue about?" He asked.

"He found out that Luther raped me, twice." Harper winced when she heard something slam down. "Carter was so mad. I told him to calm down and he snapped at me. I yelled back. I have been afraid for so long. Luther did so many things to me. I'm not used to people being there for me, dad. And I'm scared."

"Sweetheart, you have every right to be scared. You were in a very abusive relationship that has no doubt left scars. Talk with Carter, honey. He loves you and the two of you together can get through this rough patch." She heard him take a deep breath. "Have you thought about talking with someone about what you went through?"

"Yes, and Carter also suggested it." She wiped at the tears off her cheeks. "What if he doesn't want to talk with me? What if I ruined everything?"

She heard her father chuckle. "He waited four years to punch me for sending you away. I don't think that boy would give up on you so easily." He paused for a second before continuing. "It's going to be a long road dealing with Luther's effects on you and that little girl, but you are strong enough to do it. Now, it's Christmas, honey. Take a moment. Pray. And then spend the rest of the day enjoying your family." He hesitated. "I love you, Harper."

"I love you too, daddy. And thank you." Harper took a deep breath. "Merry Christmas."

She hung up the line and finished wiping the tears away. She felt better after talking with her dad. Doing as he suggested, Harper bowed her head and prayed. She prayed for help in dealing with her memories and that Lexi would escape the nightmares. She prayed she would know what to say to Carter. When she was done, she sat quietly for a while. Her phone buzzed and she pulled it out to look at it.

**Carter:** I am sorry, Dove. Please come home.

**Harper:** Not yet. I need to talk with you. I'm with Cap.

Harper stroked Raider's side as she waited. She didn't need to wait long. Carter came jogging into the clearing and she stood. He didn't stop until she was in his arms. He held her tight as if he were afraid she would disappear.

"I am so sorry, Harper. I shouldn't have lost my temper or snapped at you." Carter said quietly.

"I'm sorry for yelling at you too. I'm still trying to process everything Luther did. I'm a mess and I'm sorry." Harper clung to Carter as she struggled not to cry. "I'm sorry." She whispered.

Carter leaned back so he could see her face. "There is nothing for you to be sorry about. You, my love, are not a mess. You are a warrior. My warrior. And we will get through this together." He pressed his lips to hers in a gentle kiss. "I will do my best to control my anger. I just...I just...I don't like the idea or the fact that he hurt you and Lexi."

Harper smiled as she kissed him. "I love you too, Cowboy." She wrapped her arms around his neck and held him close. "I called my dad. He reminded me that it is Christmas and that I need to enjoy my family."

"Wise words." Carter rubbed the tip of his nose against hers. "Lexi and the boys just woke up and dinner's almost ready. My question though is, do I get to hold my wife after dinner while we watch our kids play with their new toys?" He recaptured her lips.

Harper pulled him closer, and he deepened the kiss. When they finally pulled apart, she smiled up at him. "Did the guys say something about the ring?" Carter groaned and tilted his head back. "I will do my best to get them to notice it." Harper grabbed Carter's face and gently forced him to look at her. "I want them to figure it out on their own. They have been meddling in our relationship from the beginning, and I want to have a little fun with them."

Carter pressed a kiss to the corner of her mouth. "You always did like to mess with people. I will play along, Sweetheart. But if they don't notice tonight, I'm not holding back tomorrow."

Harper laughed and agreed. The past few days had been rough for her as well. She missed Carter. Which was silly considering he was right there. She missed his comforting arms and his kisses and attention. They walked back hand in hand, until they got back to the house.

Inside, Carter helped Harper remove her coat before they entered the kitchen. Raider settled on the floor under the table. Lexi seemed back to her happy carefree self. Harper smiled at the sight of Tank playing dress up with the little girl. He had on a crown and several necklaces.

Jeff spotted her first and started clearing the toys from the table. Dinner started and conversation centered around Lexi's exciting Christmas and what they should do for New Year's. There seemed to be an unspoken agreement, and no one mentioned Harper's outburst, panic attacks, or Lexi's nightmares. True to her word, Harper made a conscious effort to keep her ring where everyone could see it. Dinner ended and Carter sent her a look that had her biting her lip to keep from laughing. He was not happy with his friends at the moment.

They watched a family movie with Lexi before the kids' bedtime. Harper tucked Lexi into her and Carter's bed to hopefully keep the bad dreams away. When she returned downstairs, the only seat available was next to Carter. She sat with a sigh, and he handed her a mug of hot chocolate. They were talking about the ranch when Tank's gaze passed over her, snapped back and locked on her. Harper swallowed the last bit of her drink and set the mug on the coffee table with her left hand. The diamond caught the firelight as she sat back.

"What the…" Jeff said as he grabbed her hand, nearly pulling her off the couch. "What is this?" he asked without taking his eyes off her ring.

"A ring." Harper slowly pulled her hand from his and settled back on the couch, making sure to keep a straight face.

"When did you get it?" Devon looked between her and Carter as his brows pulled together in confusion.

Tank let out a bark of laughter. "Who gave it to you? And when is the wedding?"

"I got it a few days ago. And there is no need for a wedding. I am content with my current relationship." Harper smirked at Devon.

"I'm not." Carter growled. Harper let out a squeak as Carter pulled her into his lap. "Now, I'm content." Harper laughed and snuggled against him.

"I'm confused." Jeff said slowly.

Devon shook his head. "That makes two of us."

"You are all idiots." Carter countered, sending his friends a glare.

"Be nice." Harper scolded with a smile.

"I thought you were mad at Carter?" Tank asked.

Carter chuckled. "She was. You should have seen the way she was pacing the room as she yelled at me." Carter nuzzled her neck. "Then she dragged me to the truck and demanded I drive. She practically kidnapped me."

"That's not exactly how it went." Harper rolled her eyes. "I was mad at Carter. The dummy kept the fact he was in love with me for years a secret. Do you have any idea how frustrating it is being in love with someone who you think could never love you, but turned out to be in love with you the whole time? Yeah, I was mad. So, I decided to make sure he wouldn't leave me again." Carter tightened his hold around her before pressing a kiss to her cheek.

"Okay. When is the wedding? Does Lexi know you two are engaged?" Devon asked with a smile.

"Oh, we're not engaged." Harper said with a straight face. Jeff, Devon, and Tank were so confused. A smile started to tug at her lips as the silence in the room stretched.

Carter smiled at her before turning to look at his friends. "Guys, I want you to meet my wife, Harper Nicole Michaels."

Tank was the first to react. He started laughing which caused everyone to start laughing. The rest of the night the guys asked questions about what had happened in Denver and what Harper and Carter planned for the future. A scream from upstairs caused all conversation to stop.

"Daddy!" Lexi screamed.

Harper slid off Carter's lap and he ran upstairs. "I think we are going to call it a night." Harper said, worried that Lexi had another nightmare. The guys said their goodnights and Harper quickly went to her room. She slipped into the room. "How is she?" Harper whispered anxiously.

Carter was sitting on the bed holding Lexi. His face was pinched with tension. Harper climbed onto the bed and sat next to him. He looked at her with sadness. "She fell back asleep. She kept saying he stabbed you."

Harper lifted her sleeping daughter off of Carter and tucked her back into her own bed before rejoining Carter. "Carter." Harper said slowly. "I love you and I don't mean to keep things from you. I honestly can't remember everything that happened. Five years is a long time, and I can't remember everything off the top of my head." Carter took a deep slow breath. "Lexi was almost three when he stabbed me in the leg. I received several stitches."

"Come here, Love." He whispered as he pulled her close as he laid down, pulling the covers over the both of them. "We can talk about this later. Right now, I just need to hold you." Harper willingly snuggled closer to him. She closed her eyes and sighed. How did she ever feel safe enough to fall asleep without him?

# Chapter 23

Harper had been making progress with her counseling sessions. Carter even attended some with her. They both felt it was important for Carter to know all that she had been through. Lexi was doing better as well. Flynn and the counseling were helping with Lexi's anxiety. Her nightmares were coming less frequently as well. It was amazing the progress three months can make in coping with nearly five years of abuse.

Even with all of Harper's progress, she felt close to an attack as she paced the living room. Clara was coming over so that Hannah and Lexi could play, and so that Harper could get a break. She had been taking a few classes online and everyone thought her stress was coming from that.

In truth, her classes were nothing compared to this. She had been fighting with herself for weeks, but she just needed to know at this point. She just didn't want anyone around when she did. Lucky for her, today all the guys were off on the ranch and wouldn't be back until dinner, which gave her a few more hours to herself.

A knock on the front door startled her and she jumped. Clara and Hannah walked in a moment later and Harper sighed in relief. "Thank you for coming and watching the kids."

"No problem. You have been stressed for the past several weeks with school and all. You deserve a little alone time to relax." Clara gave Harper a quick hug before shoving her out the door. "Don't worry, I have everything under control here. You go and have fun."

Harper forced a smile and headed for the barn. Raider barked. He went everywhere with her when she was alone. She opened the kennel and gave the Doberman an affectionate pat on the head. She saddled Mozart quickly and was riding through the south field with Raider at her side in no time.

As she rode, she couldn't help checking her pocket multiple times to make sure they were still there. It took an hour, but she made it to the orchard at the edge of the property. Dismounting, Harper tied Mozart to a low hanging branch. She walked for a while before she stopped and looked around for a place to sit.

Her hands were shaking, and she thought her heart was beating out of her chest. She just needed to get it over and done with. Knowledge was power. Taking several deep breaths, Harper finally pulled them out of her pocket.

She looked down at her hands slowly and stared at the tests. All five of them said the same thing. Tears blurred her vision as she shoved them back into her pocket. What was she going to do now? She had been adamant about waiting until the twins were older. Carter wholeheartedly agreed with her. They were still new to the whole marriage thing, she had just started online classes, and the twins were only five months old. They had been so careful since Christmas when Harper realized they weren't on anything.

Harper ran a shaking hand through her hair. She couldn't believe this was happening. She was so scared. She didn't think she would be able to handle another baby right now. And Carter, what would he do?

Flashbacks of her telling Luther she was pregnant with Lexi slammed into her. Luther yelling at her, accusing her of cheating. He had demanded she get an abortion. In her heart, she knew that Carter would never act the same way that Luther did, but her brain kept bringing up Luther's reactions. Carter would never hurt her physically, but would he be angry enough to leave? Would he abandon her?

Fear, so strong it choked her, made it hard to breathe. She fell to her knees as Raider whined nearby. Harper pulled out her phone and sent a message to Carter telling him she was at the orchard and needed him. She didn't know how long she waited as she sobbed into her hands.

"Sweetheart, what happened?" Carter called as he dismounted and ran towards her. Harper was in full blown panic mode, and she scooted away from Carter as he reached for her. Confusion and worry filled Carter's expression. "Dove?" He softened his voice and spoke slowly. "Harper, talk to me."

Harper wanted to lean on Carter, but at the same time she was terrified of what he was going to do. She resisted the urge to pull away when he reached for her hand. The feel of his hand on hers was comforting and familiar. She continued to cry. Carter scooted closer to her slowly until his shoulder touched hers. She turned and buried her face in his chest. Carter wrapped his arms around her as he whispered soothing words in her ear.

"I'm sorry." She sobbed. "I'm so sorry."

Carter rocked back and forth as he held her. He had never seen her so upset. She had pulled away as if she were afraid of him. She was shaking and continued to say how sorry she was. He had no idea what she was sorry for, but her fear was palpable. Carter cupped the back of her head and continued to hold her tight. Slowly her sobs stopped, and she began to hiccup. He continued to hold her, prepared to wait as long as it took until she was ready to talk.

Harper clung to Carter's shirt even after she had stopped crying. She tilted her face to look up at him. "I'm sorry, Carter." She whispered. "I didn't know. I didn't want to know. I'm so sorry."

Carter's brows pulled together in confusion as he brushed her hair out of her eyes. "Why do you keep apologizing? Tell me what happened, Dove." He spoke softly, but Harper could still hear his worry and confusion.

Tears filled her eyes again and she found it hard to swallow. She tried to pull away from him, but Carter wouldn't let her go. "I didn't mean to. We were so careful. I don't know what happened." Harper took a shuddering breath. "I'm so scared." She breathed out.

"What are you talking about, Harper? Why are you scared?" Carter was so confused. What had happened?

"Carter, I..." Harper tried to tell him, but the words stuck in her throat as tears spilled onto her cheeks again. She shook her head and reached a shaking hand into her coat pocket. She withdrew one of the tests and handed it to Carter.

He took it slowly and turned it over to look at it. Harper squeezed her eyes shut and waited for the yelling or for him to push her away before storming off. She felt the breath leave his lungs as he tensed. Her shaking increased as she continued to wait for his reaction.

"Harper?" Carter whispered and she flinched. "Sweetheart, look at me." Harper slowly opened her eyes. Carter was studying her face, and she was sure he could see how terrified she was. "Is this...Does this mean...?" Carter glanced back down at the test in his hand before looking back into her eyes.

"I'm so sorry." Harper's chin trembled and Carter's expression softened. He pressed his lips to hers.

Carter pulled back and rested his forehead against hers. "Before you get any crazy ideas, Harper, I am not mad." Harper blinked in surprise. "We may not have planned for this baby." He slid his hand over her stomach with a small smile. "But we are going to be okay. Lexi is going to be beyond excited for another brother or sister."

Harper shook her head. "I don't know if I can do this. We were wanting to wait until the boys were older. I have been so sick, Carter, and I'm terrified."

Carter wiped Harper's tears away. "If I need to hire an extra man or two to cover me on the ranch, I will. Harper, you and our kids, including this one, are my priority." He said rubbing his thumb on her stomach. "Every appointment, every ultrasound, every step of the way, I will be by your side." He pressed a kiss to her forehead.

"But…"

"We can't change the past, Dove. Yes, we said we wanted to wait for Bo and Colt to be a little older. And yes, it would have made our lives easier to wait a bit longer. But Sweetheart, nothing that is worth it in life is ever easy. We will get through this together and when this baby comes, we will love and cherish her just like we do Lexi, Bo, and Colt." Harper leaned against Carter, feeling completely exhausted. His arms tightened around her. They sat quietly for several minutes with Carter rubbing her stomach. "Honestly, I'm nervous, too. With Lexi and the boys, I knew what to do because I had younger cousins growing up. I don't know what I'm doing when it comes to pregnancy and birth."

Harper laughed lightly. "If it makes you feel any better, I don't really know what to do either. The last two times, I had to hide my pregnancies and was never seen by a doctor until the day of the birth. It will be the first time for both of us." Carter kissed her temple, and she closed her eyes.

"How far along are you?" Carter asked.

Harper pulled out her phone and typed in some information. "Around twelve weeks, I think." She turned to look at him. "When I started to feel sick, I thought it was just stress with starting school. Then I started noticing other things and I got worried. I tried to ignore it, but when I couldn't button my jeans, I got scared. I finally picked up some tests when I got groceries yesterday and asked Clara if she could babysit."

"How do you want to proceed, my love?" Carter nuzzled her neck. "Do you want to tell everyone immediately or wait?"

"I am still trying to process the fact that we are having a baby. I don't think I am ready to tell anyone yet." Harper took a deep breath and closed her eyes.

Carter kissed her again as he hugged her close. "A baby. Our baby." He chuckled. "I'm starting to like the sound of that." The rest of her anxiety faded as she sat in Carter's arms and listened to his heartbeat. This hadn't even been a possible outcome in her mind an hour ago. "Harper, if you are ready, I think we should head back."

Harper glanced down at her phone. She had been gone for three hours. "Can I ride back with you?" she asked, making no effort to get up.

"Of course, Sweetheart." Carter helped her to her feet. He lifted her onto Ranger before untying Mozart and tying his reins to the saddle. Carter swung up behind Harper. She leaned back against him, and he tightened his hold on her. He could tell she was completely emotionally and physically exhausted.

The ride back to the ranch was long, but peaceful. Harper had fallen asleep halfway back. They got to the barn and Carter sent a text to the guys asking for help in the barn. He only had to wait five minutes before Tank and Jeff walked in.

"What happened?" Jeff asked as he rushed over.

"Help me get Harper down without waking her." Carter said, ignoring Jeff's question. Tank reached up, and with some effort, managed to keep Harper asleep. Carter took her back into his arms before heading back to the house. "Get the doors." He said quietly and Jeff rushed ahead and opened the doors.

"Carter?" Harper mumbled.

"I'm here, Love. Just go back to sleep." Carter whispered in her ear as he climbed the stairs and entered their room. He laid her in their bed and pulled the blanket over her. Pressing a kiss to her head, he told her he would be right back before he went downstairs. He knew the guys were going to have questions.

"What happened?" Jeff asked again as he crossed his arms over his chest.

"Harper had another panic attack." He explained, noticing Clara and Devon stepping out of the kitchen. "It was a bad one and she is exhausted. She sent me a text letting me know where she was, and that she needed me, before it fully hit. She should be fine in the morning." Jeff let out a tense breath while Tank nodded his head. They had witnessed a few of Harper's attacks over the last several months and knew they tired her out. "I'm going to go lay with her for a while, she doesn't want to be alone."

"I'll take care of the horses." Tank offered as he moved to the door.

"We will take care of the kids." Devon said with a nod. "Go take care of Harper."

Carter thanked them and headed back upstairs. He understood her reaction. Luther had become incredibly abusive when she had told him she was pregnant. She was no doubt terrified something like that would happen again. He changed into clean clothes before climbing into bed behind Harper. Carter vowed to make sure Harper knew that he was there for her and this baby.

He put his arms around her and marveled at the small bump of her stomach. Harper had been wearing sweatshirts and yoga pants or sweats lately. He hadn't thought anything of it. She usually slept facing him, so he hadn't noticed any big difference. But now that he knew she was pregnant and with his hand resting on her stomach, the baby bump was obvious. He smiled as he pressed a kiss to Harper's shoulder. She sighed and rolled towards him. He pulled her closer, placing a soft kiss on her forehead.

He knew this wasn't going to be easy. Harper was scared of what this baby meant for them. For him, this baby was just the beginning of their story, and he couldn't wait to see what else life had in store for them.

\* \* \*

Two weeks later, Carter was holding her hand as they exited the temple. Harper smiled up at her husband and he grinned down at her. Lexi held Tank's hand as she twirled in her white dress. Jeff and Devon were carrying Bo and Colt. As soon as they were out of the way of the main entrance, Carter pulled her to him and kissed her. She smiled against his lips.

Listening to the sealer as he spoke to them about the covenants they were making and the blessings they would receive had been just what Harper had needed to overcome her anxiety about this pregnancy. In its place, was excitement. She knew that everything was going to be okay.

"How does it feel knowing you're stuck with all five of us for eternity?" Harper asked Carter when he ended the kiss.

He glanced over her shoulder before returning his eyes to hers. His dimple deepened as his smile widened. "You do realize they can hear you, right?" Carter said quietly.

Harper shrugged. "It doesn't really matter. It is not like they are going to have to listen to a crying newborn all night this time now that the other house is almost finished." Carter laughed at the exclamations of surprise from those around them.

Harper continued to amaze him. She had been struggling the past several weeks, but as soon as they got to the temple, she seemed like a weight had been lifted off of her.

She smiled up at him with her sparkling blue eyes and radiant smile. Her beautiful cream dress didn't fully hide her slightly rounded belly. He slid his hand from her back until it rested on her baby bump. "How did I get so lucky to have you as my partner in crime?" He kissed her softly.

"Partner in crime? She commits the crimes, and you have to bail her out. Unfortunately, it's too late to change your mind." Jeff laughed.

"You're just mad because I can out ride you and you lost the race yesterday." Harper turned in Carter's arms as she smiled at Jeff.

"Sweetheart, I think we might need to tone down your antics until after the baby comes." Carter kissed her cheek.

"Saving me again, Cowboy?" Harper looked over her shoulder at him.

"Always, Love." Carter turned Harper back to face him. "You are mine to protect now and through the eternities." He kissed her as the guys started to laugh and cheer. Carter pulled back and she looked into his amazing brown eyes. Eternity with Carter? That was a future she was looking forward to.

THE END

## The Hunter Guardian Series

The Hunted Guardian
The Stone's Keeper
The Stone's Secret

## Other books by this author:

Left Broken
Embracing Dove

## When Worlds Collide Series

Prey of the Corrupted Alpha
When Worlds Collide

## Paranormal Books

Enforcer's Mark

## Upcoming Books

Hoodwinked
Two Sides of the Same Coin

www.ingramcontent.com/pod-product-compliance
Lightning Source LLC
LaVergne TN
LVHW012016060526
838201LV00061B/4329